James Locker The Duality of Fate

Martin Lundqvist

Published by Martin Lundqvist, 2018.

JAMES LOCKER THE DUALITY OF FATE

First edition. July 20, 2018.

Copyright © 2018 Martin Lundqvist.

ISBN: 978-0-6487245-3-7

Written by Martin Lundqvist.

Also by Martin Lundqvist

Divine Space Gods
Divine Space Gods: Abraham's Follies
Divine Space Gods II: Revolution for Dummies

Sabina Saves the Future
Sabina's Quest to Open the Portal in the Sun Pyramid
Sabina's Expedition to Stop the Apocalypse
Sabina Saves the Future: Full Trilogy

The Divine Zetan Trilogy
The Divine Dissimulation
The Divine Dissimulation (Shortened Edition)
The Divine Sedition
The Divine Finalisation

Standalone
Matt's Amazing Week
James Locker The Duality of Fate
The Portal in the Pyramid
Money Laundering in the Laundromat
James Locker: The Duality of Fate (Second Edition)

Sabina's Pursuit of The Holy Grail
Pyramidportalen
Matts Fantastiska Vecka
Divine Space Gods Trilogy

Watch for more at martinlundqvist.com.

Chapter 1 Prologue

C rime Inspector James Locker was lying awake in his bed, sweating profusely. He had stopped taking his anti-depressants, which was necessary to feel anything at all and live a healthy life. James Locker was thinking about her, and he still could not comprehend what had happened that fateful day seven months ago. James and Emily Luong had been in a massive fight. Why had they fought? His memory was so blurry so that he, in retrospect, could not understand it. She had left with $ 20,000 of their savings and a day later he had received a text message stating that she despised him and that she never wanted to see him again. Of course, he could have filed a police report with the stolen property department as she had stolen his money. But he never did as money was not an issue for him, and his primary concern was to understand what had happened so he could avoid it happening again. James had loved Emily too much to report her to his colleagues and have her deported. He thought about calling her, but he did not.

Ironically, James' career had improved a lot during the seven months that had passed. He had been able to solve some high-profile cases through his intelligence and dedication to his work. Walking in an emotional desert was apparently a good thing when it came to solving murder cases, and James had been promoted to the rank of police inspector a few months earlier and seemed to be in line to further promotions if the legendary Crime Detective Michael Fuller was to resign. That wasn't likely to happen anytime soon, as Michael Fuller was nine years away from retirement, and Michael was a man who was living for his work. In this way, James had become very similar to Michael in the last year.

James Locker's nightstand clock showed 3 AM, and it was five hours to go before he and his colleagues and best friends Thomas Anderson and Adam Smith were bound to head to the airport for a month of travelling in Asia. Adam and Thomas had persuaded him to join them for a crazy month of travels, adventures, boozing, and banging.

Adam Smith had put it like this: *"Hey look, James, I know it's been tough for you with this Emily thing, but it's time to man up and meet some other girls. Let's go to Asia, and hook you up with at least ten girls to build your self-esteem again".* James smiled realising that his friends would probably pay some local talent to pretend to be genuinely interested in him and then sleep with him to build up his self-esteem.

James decided to play along with his friends' plan, as he believed that it could work better than psychologist sessions he had attended. If his friends, however, did not intend to pull this off, he would not visit prostitutes on his own. Not because he had any strong moral objections to paid sexual services, but merely because he was not very turned on by the concept. James Locker took a shower, made himself some breakfast and enjoyed it in front of the TV while waiting for his friends. Despite his insomnia, he felt relaxed knowing that he would probably fall asleep on the plane and thus have more energy than his friends once they reached the destination. The date was the 17th of July 2013.

Chapter 2 A Past Case Summarised

As three broken, but happy heroes James Locker, Adam Smith and Thomas Anderson came back to the police station a month later. To their great relief, the impressive Michael Fuller had solved another challenging, high-profile case while drinking whiskey in his bathtub. This would give them at least a few quiet days to recover before the heat started again. The police policy was rewarding the staff for solving a case quickly and correctly as this encouraged staff to work a lot of overtime in the critical first days of a murder case. Since the police department lacked the funds to give performance bonuses, the staff members were rewarded with the cases being divided equally between the different murder investigation teams. Since Michael Fuller was an incredibly dedicated detective, this usually meant they would have to work very hard for the first few days until the solution just magically popped into Michael Fuller's head, often while he was drinking whiskey in his bathtub. It was an internal joke in the department that if they gave Michael Fuller a bathtub and a whiskey bar in his office, he would never need to go home, and the rest of the staff would never need to go to work. This joke was of course not entirely accurate as it sometimes happened that James Locker solved a case or two. What was true was that Michael Fuller was an exceptional talent and that more than 90 per cent of the cases assigned to his team ended up with a conviction.

Michael Fuller greeted the talented trio:

- Good day mates, great to see you all. Due to my brilliant brain, I solved another tricky case last Friday so this won't be the busiest return to work week for you. Let's go to the lunch room and have a chat about your holiday and my latest case!

They went into the lunch room, and each had a cookie. James Locker started the talking:

- Hey, Michael, I can't get how you solved that last case so fast. From the media reporting, the case was very bizarre.

Thomas Anderson interrupted the conversation:

- Sorry guys for not following the news while enjoying my life 8000 kilometres away, what was the case?

Michael Fuller

- It was the Father Walker case; a senior Anglican priest was killed and found horribly mutilated.

Adam Smith

- Yeah, we get those cases sometimes, what was the full story?

Michael Fuller

- We found the priest tied to the altar. His genitals were first corroded away by boiling sulphuric acid, and then half his face was burnt away using a blow torch. After that, the numbers 666 were tattooed on his forehead, and finally, a sharpened crucifix was driven straight through his heart.

Thomas Anderson

- That's psychotic, how did you solve it? Was it an escaped patient from a mental institution?

Michael Fuller

- No, it wasn't an escaped patient. You see this act took a lot of planning; firstly, the perpetrator would have to sedate the priest to get him tied up on the altar. Secondly getting all this equipment mentioned would be difficult for a person chased by the government and thirdly I got a feeling this case was very personal against this specific man and not just aimed at any priest.

James Locker

- Yeah, I agree with all these claims, but I don't understand how you could get Agnes Montecristo so quickly. I mean, they had not met in seven years.

Michael Fuller

- Because I am better than you are mate. I am more experienced, and I have a wealth of knowledge. You see, I am not only lying alone in my bathtub listening to classical music and drinking excellent Scotch. The bath and whiskey help my thinking, but to have a method of reflection a man also needs input from the outside.

- So, I read a lot, and I have probably read most of the literature related to my job as a crime detective.

James Locker

- I see. What source of ancient wisdom did you apply this time?

Michael Fuller

- I found the solution in the third amendment to the Anglican religious law written by the Archbishop Humphrey Godspeed during the witch hunts in 1734...

- In this book, I found out that the murder resembled an execution method for a very particular horrible crime.

Adam Smith

- So, the priest was a child molester? That seems like an old story these days.

Michael Fuller

- Not exactly, the punishment was for a man who raped his sister and the outcome was a 'demonic child', IE a child suffering from incest-related diseases

James Locker

- So, you found his sister then?

Michael Fuller:

- Yes, but it was not easy since no sister existed in father Walkers family history. But I realised one thing, that the perpetrator must be a woman in father Walkers past. I asked the church administrator for the names of formerly devout churchgoers who suddenly stopped going. That how Agnes Montecristo's name came up. After checking the registry, she indeed had a daughter born approximately nine months after she stopped going to church. These events took place, seven years ago.

Adam Smith:

- So how did you proceed?

Michael Fuller

- I just confronted her with what I knew, and as I expected, she broke down immediately. But don't worry even if she changes her mind, we have a lot of evidence against her now! If you are interested, you can read about in the report when it's time for her trial.

James Locker:

- I am sure I will, but until then I just have one question, why did she act the way she did?

Michael Fuller:

- Well. She was very religious, and abortion was out of the question. So, to protect her unborn baby from the truth, she left and kept the secret to herself. She did well; she moved to the USA and set up a religious bookshop, which was flourishing. All of this changed a year ago when her daughter got sick, and the hospital deemed that it was due to incest-related diseases. The social services took custody of her child, and this shattered her life. She decided to go back to Australia and get revenge on the man who ruined her life.

Thomas Anderson:

- A truly tragic and scary story

Adam Smith:

- Indeed, but let's now focus on something genuinely uplifting instead: Let us tell you the great story of our wonderful month in Asia!

Chapter 3 An Awesome Month in Asia.

S ince the group was not very busy, they went out to buy some coffee at the local coffee shop and then brought it back to Michael's office to chat about their holiday. Unfortunately, Adam managed to turn on the microphone to the intercom which led to the rest of the Central Sydney Murder Investigation Department hearing their conversation.

Thomas Anderson:

- Woo, how strange this coffee tastes? I can't remember when I last had a non-alcoholic drink, apart from water that is.

Michael Fuller

- So, you did not drink coffee at all in Asia? The caffeine withdrawal must have been killing you?

Thomas Anderson:

- We drank heaps of coffees boss, just that all the coffees were of the Irish variety

- The problem with drinking Irish coffee in Thailand, however, is that you must get it mixed with the local Thai Whiskey which has a rancid taste. But since they charge an arm and a leg for real Scotch, we just had to suck it up and drink it anyway. The effect is the same, and after a few drinks your tastebuds numb off, and it all tastes the same.

Michael Fuller:

- Yeah, so say the aboriginal goon drinkers as well. But I am a well-paid man with sophisticated taste, so I only drink whiskeys that come at around $100 a litre.

Adam Smith:

- Oh anyway, the lousy whiskey had an impressive effect on James who managed to outperform even the highly set hunting goals we had in mind for him. For the first time since Emily came into his life, he was the pickup artist we all know he can be.

Michael Fuller:

- Hunting goals? Let me get this straight. You guys set up a goal for how many women James should have sex with?

Adam Smith:

- That is correct sir. You see, according to Neil Strauss in the Game, the best way to get over an ex-girlfriend is to hook up with ten random women. Since we have been listening to James whine about Emily for seven months, we thought it was time to get him laid to end the whining once and for all! And how he did it twelve women in a month! The Master Hunter is back.

Michael Fuller:

- So, you guys bought prostitutes in Asia, and now you brag about it? How lame is that?

James Locker:

- To be fair Adams story is not accurate. I did date the same woman for most of my time in Asia, but sadly I did not feel that she was what I am looking for. I had sex with two other women, but that is far from the man-whore Adam describes me as.

Adam Smith:

- I stand corrected. To be fair since I did not put a spy cam in James' hotel room; I don't know what he did with the women he brought there. He did, however, bring twelve women to his room during our holiday.

- But he is right about the women not being prostitutes. His cover story about going to a third world country to find true love, also known as buying a wife, worked out just fine. Since he is only 32, have a fit body and a hot face he was a lot more attractive than the competitors who were generally over 45, fat and ugly. I must say...

Adam Smith was interrupted when the newest addition to the team Samantha Robinson entered the room. She was 22 years old and fresh from the academy. Samantha was around 170 cm tall weighing around 60 kilos. She had the perfect mix of strength and physique as well as femineity. Samantha was a beautiful policewoman and would probably have won "the hottest policewoman of the year" competition if the Sydney police department promoted such a contest, which they did not. She smiled at Adam Smith with a very sarcastic smile.
Samantha Robinson:

- Great to have you back guys, and it's even greater that you are sharing the best of your stories via the intercom.

Adam Smith panicked and turned off the intercom, and the other guys did not feel at ease either.
Samantha Robinson:

- Don't worry guys Adams voice is the only one that I could hear, probably due to him sitting closest to the microphone.

The other guys looked relieved while Adam Smith looked like he was getting close to a panic attack.
Samantha Robinson

- Oh, and don't worry about me reporting you to HR. I don't mind you sharing your 'hunting stories', although you should do so at the pub during after-work drinks and not over the intercom

- Oh, and Adam I bet you a hundred bucks that the BITCH is angry with you right now.

The BITCH was the commonly used nickname of Barry Itch, the head of The Central Sydney Murder Investigation Department. He had received his nickname because the E-mail addresses in the CSMI department was in the format initial+lastname@CSMI.gov.au which led to the E-mail Address of Barry was bitch@CSMI.gov.au

Barry was a very tedious and annoying person who through his strive for political correctness and antidiscrimination policies was the de-facto dictator of the department as he had a rigid interpretation of anti-discrimination policies where most things could be offensive to someone. Barry Itch was very easily offended, so most of the time anyone in the department felt offended it was Barry Itch who was behind the report. He was thoroughly disliked, and there were two disparate theories in place as for why he acted the way he did.

- Michael Fuller and James locker thought he acted the way he did to overcompensate for how he acted when off duty. From this point of view, they believed that he was living in a sadomasochistic relationship with his wife, and thus acted overly politically correct to cover this up as he lived in shame of his real behaviour. Since both Michael Fuller and James Locker disliked people who they believed were beating up their wives, they disliked Barry Itch thoroughly

- Adam and Thomas, on the other hand, saw Barry Itch as whinger who was dominated by his wife Wanda Itch also known as the Witch. They both felt that Barry Itch was making their lives difficult and his focus on promoting *"values" instead* of results had cost them both well-deserved promotions and pay raises. They were both stuck on their entry-level salary even though they had six and four years of work experience in their field. They hated his guts.

Adam Smith swallowed the frustration over his mistake, sighed and spoke:

- Well, I guess I better go to his office and apologise before the fucker has time to sharpen his knives. See you later.

Adam Smith left the room, and Thomas Anderson who had a long-time crush on Samantha Robinson felt compelled to say something.
Thomas Anderson

- Hey, Samantha, just so that you know, I don't share Adams values and I don't like the way he speaks about women.

Samantha Robinson

- Why is that? You are his best friend, and you hang out with him all the time. You can't honestly think, that I believe that you don't share values.

Thomas Anderson:

- Well yes, but there is more to me than that, please have dinner with me sometime so I can show you my better sides.

Samantha Robinson:

- Well sadly Thomas this is the saddest attempt ever for two reasons:

1. If you are doing this because you are afraid of me reporting you to HR, you are wasting your time and money. I have no intention whatsoever to report you in for any of that antidiscrimination bullshit. I have a full understanding that you are discussing your *"conquests"* with your friends. I do that as well.

2. If you are doing it because you have a crush on me, you should not hit on me by pretending to be someone else. I like MEN and WOMEN, but I don't want an insecure boy who is lying to get into my pants. I am sick of women, so if you can prove to be a MAN to me; you may take me out to dinner and maybe get lucky. Oh, and I kind of like Adam so don't pretend to be different from him. Unlike Adam, you are also good looking.

Thomas Anderson was left speechless by Samantha Robinson's words. She studied him for a while and then shook her head and left the room. After a while, Thomas Anderson found his words.

Thomas Anderson:

- Oh my god, she is so hot, I think I am in love.

Michael Fuller

- Well Mate, don't sweat yourself. Playtime is over, time to get back to work!

Chapter 4 Michael Fuller Gets Busted

Michael Fuller was working on the report for the Montecristo case. The whole concept of report writing bored him a lot. The police report before a murder trial could easily span over a total of 1500 pages, and in a lot of the cases, the report writing for the court took more time and resources than apprehending the perpetrator. Luckily for Michael Fuller, Barry Itch had implemented a procedure where ghost-writer wrote most of the police reports, which gave more time for Michael Fuller to do what he enjoyed doing and was good at; solving murder cases and apprehending criminals. Having said this, it still took a lot of effort to make a report since he had to review the works of the ghost-writers and come with necessary input to make the police report consistent with the actual case. Anyway, Michael Fuller was happy that Barry Itch had implemented the system with ghost-writers as it at least gave him some more freedom.

While reviewing the report, Michael Fuller started daydreaming about his coming holiday. In a few weeks, he would be on a plane to The British Isles where he would attend the *"Castles and Whiskeys"* tour. The tour consisted of three weeks in Great Britain and Ireland, and during this time Michael would stay at fourteen different castles and enjoy the local's specialties when it came to whiskey. It would be amazing to see some of the places where they made his favourite brands, and he could not wait to taste them in their natural environment. The only thing that made him sad was that he had to go on this tour alone. All his friends were either busy with their families or in the cases where their children had reached adulthood; they usually had a wife who did not approve of them spending all their annual leave going to Great Britain for a whiskey tour.

When thinking about this, he felt sad that he was not close to his 21-year-old daughter Rebecca from a failed marriage. He had asked her if she wanted to join him at his expense, but she had responded that whiskeys and castles were not her things. The problem with this, of course, was not that she did not like whiskey, but rather the distance between them. She had accused him of being distant to her and focusing too much on his work during her childhood, an accusation he could agree on, but what to do about it now? *"Oh well, she is graduating from police academy next year, so maybe she will understand by then,"* he thought to himself. He was interrupted in his daydreaming by a phone call from Barry Itch telling him to come by his office immediately *"Oh well, no point in beating around the bush"* he thought and headed over.

Michael Fuller entered Barry Itch's impeccably clean and orderly office, which to Michael Fuller signalled that apart from being tedious and annoying Barry Itch also had a slight hint of OCD in his personality.

Barry Itch

- Welcome Michael, please have a seat

Michael Fuller

- Thank you, Barry. Is this about the intercom incident earlier today? Because I agree with you that Adams' behaviour earlier today was inappropriate.

Barry Itch

- Great to have your support on this Michael, although I find surprising that you agree with me and still did not interrupt him. Nevertheless, this incident will only affect Adam's career prospects, and it seems likely that he will not receive any pay rise this year either.

- I surely hope he will enjoy unpaid participation in five days long Workplace Equality seminars held by my wife Wanda Itch on Saturdays.

Barry Itch smiled grimly while Michael Fuller sat in silence.
Barry Itch continued talking:

- No, the reason I called you over is the Lopez case, I hope you recall it?

Michael Fuller

- Yes, of course, it was only six weeks ago, and it got massive media coverage. How would I forget, I am not THAT old! From an investigation point of view, it's dead though with the alleged killer being dead. I am sure you remember that we handed it over to the Organized Crime department since the high command believed there was nothing more we could do from our end.

Barry Itch:

- Yes, that case was a real disgrace for the entire police department with two airport police officers sent to the Intensive Care Unit with severe injuries and the hired gunman Angelo Ramirez shot at the airport. Sad for the city's reputation

Michael Fuller:

- I seriously don't follow you. We got a picture of the killer face from a hidden CCTV camera that showed us the whole chain of events. Of course, we matched the description with our database of suspected hitmen. Anything else would be negligence of duty. Furthermore, once we identified him, we found out that he just had passed the passport checkpoint at the airport and we had to have the airport police arrest him as we could not get there in time ourselves, all done by the book.

Barry Itch:

- You are missing the serious point of this. The CCTV feed shows a suitcase on a desk at the time of the murder. We can see that Angelo Ramirez was not taking the bag while leaving. A bit after the killing, the CCTV feed ends, and in your report, there is no suitcase mentioned.

Michael Fuller

- Because there was none! I don't know what happened in the period between the murder and the time we got there. I have not thought much about it as the case was handed over to the Organized Crime department.

Barry Itch

- Well, here is the problem. The Organized Crime department has received an anonymous tip about you having illegal drugs that you stole from the crime scene.

Michael Fuller

- That's preposterous, why would I steal the drugs?

Barry Itch

- Because of the street value of at least $100,000.

- Look; we can do this in two ways. Either I contact the internal investigations, while you remain detained in a holding cell. Or you can just stay in my office, while two men from a private security company I am cooperating with searches your house. You see, I don't want the reputation of this department sullied down by your supposedly criminal activities. If you do agree to have your home searched by the company Sydney True Blue Security Inc., please sign this indemnification form, and all their findings will be between you and me.

Michael Fuller:

- Well, I don't want my life turned upside down by internal investigation guys, please let me sign the contract and here are my house keys.

Barry Itch

- Great. Just sit tight, and we'll search your house in no time.

At 8 PM after three hours of tense waiting in Barry Itch's office, two men in suits came in.
Greg Bloom:

- Sir, we found this bag containing 3.5 kilos of cocaine in Michael's basement. It's full of Michael's fingerprints and some DNA which we believe is his. We have taken pictures of where we found it. How do we proceed?

Barry Itch:

- That's a great question. Michael, how do we proceed?

Michael Fuller got pale from fear and shock

- You set me up, that is not my cocaine; I have never seen it before!

Barry Itch:

- Well, that's your version of course. But the facts remain. The bag disappeared from YOUR crime scene, it was found in YOUR house, and it's full of YOUR fingerprints.

- But rest assured, I have no interest in ruining the reputation of this department, and its most famous co-worker, so here is the deal. I overlook this event, and in return, you sign your immediate resignation stating health reasons. That way you can live a retiree's life while the reputation of this department stands firm. Do you agree?

Michael Fuller realised that he had been set up. But by whom, and why would Barry Itch set him up? He quickly decided that he did not want to take his chances with a long-term prison term at stake to keep his job.

Michael Fuller:

- I accept and sign my resignation immediately, how do we proceed?

Barry Itch:

- Well, you hand over your gun and police ID. After that, you go to my toilet, open the bag and flush down the cocaine; I want nothing to do with it!

Michael Fuller did as Barry instructed.
Barry Itch shook his hand and said:

- Sorry things ended this way; you were the best detective we have ever had. I hope you find something positive to do with your life.

Michael Fuller said nothing and left the station.

Chapter 5 James Has a Twisted Dream.

J ames Locker woke up in the middle of the night. The nightstand clock showed 3.00 am. How long had he been asleep? From what he remembered he came home around 6 pm and crashed instantaneously. It felt like he had been asleep for an eternity and that the sleep had been deep and dreamless until the last five minutes before he woke up. He had dreamt about her for the first time in over a month. Emily Luong had looked so different in this dream compared to his previous. In those old dreams, she always looked beautiful like a paradise long gone, in this dream; however, the essential features were the same, but the magic was gone, and the loving smile had twisted into an empty shell. Was that fear he had seen in her blank gaze or was it something else, was it the gaze of a person that was dead inside or even physically dead? He had to get the picture out of his head somehow.

James sat up on the bed. Even though it was an August night, and his room was cold he was sweating enormously. His hands were shaking roughly, and his vision was blurred. He had seen these symptoms in a lot of people the symptoms of alcohol withdrawal. *"Well I guess that's what a month of heavy drinking do to you,"* he thought. As James did not intend to end up as an alcoholic, so he would just have to live with the physical symptoms until they disappeared.

He thought about what his friends had said about getting rid of the memory of a loved one by hooking up with random women. In his case, it seemed this process had not removed the memory but rather twisted it to a worse one. He considered the option of what was the worst:

- Have a very positive memory that nothing in your everyday life can compare with so your daily life becomes dull and pointless
- Have a very negative memory that comes back and haunt you in your nightmares.

"*Oh well they are both curses*" James concluded. Now all he needed was to stabilise his emotional life and get rid of his anxiety. He took one of the anti-depressants for the first time in six weeks, and he soon fell asleep to a dreamless unemotional sleep.

Chapter 6 James Gets Promoted

Barry Itch was contemplating his options on how to proceed. Since Michael Fuller resigned, the team needed a new detective. Looking at the length of service and chain of command the natural officer to promote would be John Dean, who had always been close to Michael Fuller and had a lot of experience as he had served in the team for 15 years. But Barry Itch had some objections to promoting John Dean since he considered it likely that John Dean had been an accomplice or at least known something about the cocaine scandal involving Michael Fuller. Secondly, he did not feel that John Dean was a natural leader at all. It's one thing being the right-hand man of a genius who solves most of the cases singlehandedly and an entirely different thing being the one in charge presuming responsibility. Third and finally he had never liked John Dean on a personal level.

Another option would be to promote someone from another team to lead this team. Barry did not enjoy this idea either as there had been no-one who had stood out positively in the other groups. In the best of worlds, he would get an outstanding detective to transfer from another metropolitan area, Brisbane had a few good ones, for instance, so the CSMI got in some new blood and some fresh ideas. This plan would take some time, however.

Barry Itch looked at James Locker's file. James Locker had had an unusual and bizarre development. James Locker had suffered from severe depression for the last seven months medicated with heavy antidepressants. Strangely enough, James Locker had an outstanding track record for this period, out-performing even Michael Fuller. Barry Itch finally found the solution: He would offer James Locker a three-month amendment to his contract where he was serving as a provisional detective for the team. If he turned out to be a great detective, he could always be offered the position permanently after-wards, and if not, the official version would be that James Locker was only intended for the temporary position and it was always Barry's intent to get the replacement from another metropolitan area.

Barry called James to come over to his office, and a few minutes later James entered the office

James Locker:

- Good day sir. What gives me this great pleasure?

Barry Itch:

- It's about Michael; he suffered from some severe liver problems yesterday and will probably be away for at least six months. I told him that the most sensible thing to do would be to resign considering his age which makes him eligible for sick leave pension if we look at his liver condition as a work-related issue.

James Locker:

- Oh my god, this is a tremendous loss for the team, Michael is the best detective Sydney has ever seen.

Barry Itch:

- Yes, and that's why I called you here, but first I need to know. How is your depression going?

James Locker:

- Oh, it has improved a lot, I make it through most nights without my antidepressants, and I have not experienced any daytime issues for over two months.

Barry Itch:

- That is great to hear. Well, I have some good news for you. I have reviewed all the police inspectors at the CSMI, and you are the one with the best results over the last six months. You even superseded Michael Fuller's outstanding performance

James Locker:

- I am delighted to hear you say that sir.

Barry Itch:

- And I am happy to see such advancements among my subordinates. And that's why I called you over. I plan to hire an outstanding detective from another metropolitan area to take command of the team. But since it will take time to find and recruit the right candidate the team will need a provisional detective for three months, and that's where you come into the picture. Would you be interested in this opportunity?

James Locker:

- Well, sir. I must say this came as a surprise and I have not considered the option until now. But of course, it's a great opportunity, so I accept your offer.

Barry Itch:

- Great, please sign this contract then. Your first task will be to lead the team meeting that I am setting up this afternoon. Godspeed Detective.

James Locker:

- Thank you, sir, see you this afternoon.

Chapter 7 James, Adam & Thomas Having Lunch at the Pizza Place

Later that day James had lunch with Adam Smith & Thomas Anderson at a pizza place close to the police station.
Adam Smith:

- So, James, we get an E-mail from the BITCH about a team meeting this afternoon, and you seem so happy, so you offer both of us pizza at this expensive pizza place. Can these two be related? Are you guys getting married?

Thomas Anderson:

- Well Adam, you if someone, would know that gay marriage, is not allowed in Australia yet.

Adam Smith:

- Don't worry Thomas; I am not going to marry you anyway. And I am sure there is some country where gay marriage is legal if you ever find the man in your life.

James Locker:

- Guys, I do hope you realise that it's this kind of talk that gets your "values" rating at rock bottom every performance review? You would make a lot more money if you could cut it out.

Thomas Anderson:

- I am sure we'll be alright if Adam stops tampering with intercom. But tell me James, what's the occasion?

James Locker:

- Oh, it's great news, you'll find out at the team meeting in a couple of hours.

Adam Smith

- Okay, sounds good

James Locker:

- Hey, guys, you are my best friends, are you not curious?

Adam Smith:

- *"Hey James, this talk makes me so curious, I am dying to know before everyone else."*

James Locker:

- Less sarcasm, please! Oh anyway, the great news is that Michaels' liver finally shut down after all the whiskey in his bathtub, so he had to resign immediately. I will be the one sitting in his office and cashing in his fat paycheck for the next three months. Agent Smith, you might start calling me detective Locker!

Thomas Anderson:

- Cheers to that detective!

James Locker:

- Wait a sec, Mr Anderson, are you not drinking coke? Why are you saying cheers with non-alcoholic beverages? That's bad luck I reckon!

Thomas Anderson:

- Well I guess about 80 per cent of my drink is coke so let's say I am. I don't know about you, but my alcohol withdrawal has been horrible, so I have decided to cut it down step by step instead of going cold turkey. I am still 30 years younger than Michael, so my liver should make it for a while longer.

James Locker:

- Yeah, my alcohol withdrawal is rough as well, but I prefer riding it out. Oh well, let's head back to the station.

Chapter 8 James Lockers Inauguration Speech

At 4 pm the team was gathering in the meeting room of CSMI. The room was dull and boring. If one were focusing on an unusual angle, that person could see a glimpse of the sun and the harbour. From every other corner, however, the only thing visible was the grey concrete fundament of the highway. The entire team had gathered including Barry Itch who was the director of CSMI. The group in full consisted of James Locker provisional Head Detective for CSMI team 1, John Dean police inspector, Adam Smith, Police assistant, Thomas Anderson, Police Assistant, and Samantha Robinson Police Assistant. It also consisted of the following four other police representatives named Johnson, Baker, Chung, and Lee. All in all, there were nine team members in the room.

Barry Itch opened the meeting.

> - Dear Fellow officers. The reason you are here today is the sudden and sad resignation of Michael Fuller who had to resign immediately yesterday due to health issues. Michael was one of the greatest detectives of all times in the CSMI, and he will be hard to fully replace. It's my long-term ambition to hire a prominent detective from another Metropolitan area as I believe that this team needs fresh ideas being led by Michael for the last fifteen years. For the next three months, however, you will be led by James Locker who is appointed provisional detective effective immediately. James, it is your turn to speak.

James Locker went to the podium and overlooked the team he was supposed to lead. To James, it seemed like most of the colleagues were favourable towards him although many of them seemed shocked that they had lost the man who was their patriarch for all these years. From John Dean, however, James received another signal, the signal of a cold, hateful gaze. James Locker cleared his throat and started his short speech.

James Locker:

- Dear team members. Due to health issues, Michael Fuller has re-signed from his position. Losing Michael leave us in a troubled position as we didn't have time to make a handover of his duties. Furthermore, we have lost access to one of the sharpest minds that this department has ever seen. However, I implore you to see the opportunities ahead. I have identified a severe flaw in Michael's leadership that it is my ambition to remedy.

- Michael had a lot of faith in his ability which is usually a good thing. From my point of view, however, he sometimes took it too far and refused to seek the counsel of his colleagues. By doing this, Michael has inhibited some of you from reaching your full poten-tial. I intend to be a lot more open while seeking counsel from all of you and hopefully this will empower and stimulate you to grow as police officers.

- So, to summarise we have lost our strongest team member, but hopefully, a new, more open approach to teamwork will make us stronger and even better than before.

The team members were applauding, and they addressed a series of mi-nor issues before Barry Itch finalised the meeting, and everyone could go home.

Chapter 9 Thomas and Adam Discuss the Events at the Gym

S ince neither Thomas Anderson nor Adam Smith liked the prospects of becoming alcoholics, they turned down their usual Tuesday night pastime, bowling and drinking to do physical exercise in the gym instead and they pushed themselves through a hellish hour of boxing. Afterwards, they chilled out in the Sauna drinking various recovery drinks, and they started discussing the latest events.

Thomas Anderson:

- Such a strange day, I wonder what happened with Michael, no-one finishes like that bang boom because of health reasons.

Adam Smith

- I hear you mate. I reckon that the BITCH is covering something up. But what, and should we be bothered? I say we should not.

Thomas Anderson:

- Don't you get curious then?

Adam Smith:

- Yes, I am curious, but we have done enough of corrupt things during our years in the team. We should not put our noses in other peoples' businesses. And anyway, are you going to miss Michael? I am not going to miss him!

Thomas Anderson:

- Well he was condescending, and I was not close to a raise or promotion during the entire time I was working under him, so I guess you are right.

Adam Smith:

- Of course, I am right, and now James leads the team. This could be perfect for us. A lot better than if John Dean had got the promotion for sure.

Thomas Anderson:

- True that! There is, however, a few things that freak me out when it comes to James.

Adam Smith:

- Oh really? I think he is awesome most of the time. Except when he is whining about some shit. He is paying a psychologist to listen to that whining, isn't he? Why does he have to "share" it with me?

Thomas Anderson:

- Well, I did not mean that at all, but one thing freaked me out yesterday.

Adam Smith:

- What is that?

Thomas Anderson:

- Well you know when he denied your story about all the chicks he banged in Thailand and instead told Michael the story about how he dated the same girl for most of the holiday?

Adam Smith:

- Yeah, that was lame, but who cares if he can't stand up for being a man-whore? After all, he is he a career-oriented and telling your superior inappropriate details regarding your sex life doesn't pay off.

Thomas Anderson:

- Well, it might be unverified cold reading techniques, but what I read from James was that he was retelling from memory and not lying.

Adam Smith:

- I am not following you...

Thomas Anderson:

- Well if my theory is correct; James believes that he dated the same girl for a month in Thailand.

Chapter 10 Michael Fuller Seeks an Ally on the Inside

M ichael Fuller was sitting on his couch listening to classical music on high volume. The music was composed by a famous French composer and to honour him, Michael was drinking brandy instead of Scotch. He emptied the glass, sighed and summarised the facts to himself.

Michael couldn't make sense of what had happened to him. Someone tipped Barry Itch off regarding drugs placed at his house. The same person had probably planted the drugs there as well. But how had they gotten Michael Fuller's fingerprints on the bag? And if the cocaine indeed was from the Lopez case, why had his enemies waited until now? And what would be the motive? Michael Fuller wrote down a list of people who would potentially want to set him up. Since Michael Fuller had put a lot of lowlifes behind bars, the last decades the list became extensive, for this story, however, the following names stood out on the list

Barry Itch:

Speaking for it was that Barry Itch had the means to do it. His suspicious looking thugs from that security firm could easily have placed the cocaine in his house and then claim to have found it there to get leverage against him

Speaking against it was that Barry Itch had absolutely nothing to gain from setting him up. Also that he had thrown out the cocaine in the toilet. Why would anyone corrupt with ties to the organised crime syndicates throw away 3.5 kilos of cocaine to have someone resign? There were cheaper and easier ways to achieve this.

John Dean

Speaking for it; John had the means and the motive to do it. He was at the Lopez crime scene before Michael, and he also visited Michael's house a lot of times. The last time he visited was only a few weeks ago. His motive was that he was the likely successor to crime detective position of the team

Speaking against it; John had been his friend for ages and didn't seem corrupt at all. Besides only a total psychopath would frame his friend for a crime that could give several years in prison just to get a promotion.

James Locker:

Speaking for it; he and Michael had had their disagreements in the past. James was very ambitious, and Michael felt that he could be ruthless at times.

Speaking against it; James was not involved in the Mauricio Lopez case. Furthermore, James was not the natural successor to Michael in the team so there would be no distinct advantage for James to get rid of him.

Antonio DiMaestro: Owned the warehouse where Mauricio Lopez was killed. Since it was uncommon that people working for legitimate businesses got shot at work during the middle of the night, Michael Fuller suspected that Antonio DiMaestro's business was a front for cocaine smuggling. Both the murder victim and his assassin where Colombians which strengthened the cocaine smuggling theory.

Michael had been deeply unsatisfied with this Mauricio Lopez investigation and had made enquiries about the case even after it was transferred to the organised crime department. Michael kept thinking about Antonio Di-Maestro, who had both the means and the motive to get rid of him. After all, it was easier for a mobster to sacrifice some cocaine to frame a crime detective, than hiring a hitman to kill him and create a lot of unwanted attention.

Michael Fuller realised that he needed an ally in the police force to further investigate Antonio DiMaestro. Michael Fuller decided to take his chances and called John Dean.

Michael Fuller:

- Hi, John. It's Michael we need to talk.

John Dean

- Hi, Michael. Are you drunk? You should not be drinking with your liver condition.

Michael Fuller:

- I can assure you that my liver health, is the least of my concerns. I am calling to see if you can refresh my memory on Antonio Di-Maestro and if possible, send me some information about him.

John Dean

- Well mate, I am not sure. I am not allowed to hand out information on ongoing cases to former team members. Besides, I don't have much since the case was transferred to the Organized Crime department.

Michael Fuller:

- I know that, but please meet up with tonight so that I can tell you my case. There is something rotten in this mess, and I want to investigate it thoroughly.

John Dean:

- Well, I am not sure I am following you, but I can hear you out for sure. I am busy tonight what about tomorrow night?

Michael Fuller:

- Great see you at the sports bar in your neighbourhood tomorrow night. Oh, another thing can you at least give me the address to DiMaestro Mansion? I can't remember it right now.

John Dean

- Well, I strongly advise you against confronting him yourself, but I can't prevent you. The address is The DiMaestro Mansion, The Esplanade, Mosman, 2088, NSW.

Michael Fuller:

- Thank you, John, see you tomorrow!

Drunk and against better judgment Michael Fuller opened a can of energy drink to refresh. He took his car keys and went to his vehicle. *"Now let's see what this bastard has to say for himself"* he muttered before entering his car for the 45 minutes' drive to Mosman. He checked his watch; it was Tuesday the 20th of August 2013 and the time was 09.15 PM.

Chapter 11 An Unpleasant Phone Call

M iranda DiMaestro finished the phone call and tried shaking of the discomfort it had caused her. It was 10PM when a rude drunken person calling on the intercom, claiming to be a police detective requesting to talk with Antonio DiMaestro. Miranda had told him that Antonio DiMaestro had been away for five weeks conducting business with his import-export company. The person had spit out some curses over the intercom, and she had seen no option but to contact the home security company. The security guards arrived ten minutes later just to make sure that the drunken man who had offended Miranda wasn't lingering in the neighbourhood.

Once the guards left, Miranda felt relieved and happy knowing that she would finally see Antonio DiMaestro tonight. She had offered to meet him at the airport, but he had declined the offer stating he had to take care of business first, and it would be a great pleasure for him to come home to enjoy her to the full extent of her beauty.

Miranda watched herself in the mirror and smiled as she indeed was beautiful. Unfortunately, her beauty had not given her the happiness she wanted from life yet. Working as a barmaid in Bogota she had not lived a very glamorous life, and she never felt safe in her home city. Miranda had been excited when Antonio DiMaestro first started courting her, and she was over the moon when he married her on her 20th birthday, two years earlier. She had felt thrilled at first in Sydney living in his mansion, but after a while, her unhappiness had returned. When they first met, Miranda had believed Antonio when he said he was a legitimate businessman doing exports/imports with Australia. After all, the market for canned kangaroo meat was booming in Colombia, and the reason he was hiring Colombians on working visas in Sydney was that many customers preferred conducting business with people from their own culture. Since there was a large group of South Americans in Sydney, it made sense to have a construction company by South Americans for South Americans. But after a while, the façade fell apart. Miranda was no dimwit, and she realised that a legitimate businessman did not store hundreds of thousands of dollars cash at his home. Furthermore, all the secrecy seemed utterly unnecessary for the kind of business he was supposedly doing.

There were also other factors about their relationship that made Miranda unhappy, but Antonio being 18 years older than her was not one of them. On the contrary, she found it very attractive that he had experienced so much more than her and had so many stories to tell and so much to teach her. No, what bothered her was his lack of presence both when he was physically missing due to long *"business trips"* but also the lack of presence she felt when he was with her. It seemed to her that he had lost most of his interest in her once they got married and that he nowadays merely saw her as a possession to use as he pleased. Although there were days when he proved her wrong, these days were too few to change her general impression.

The worst part about Antonio was his jealous and controlling nature. Miranda had felt very relieved when he told her that he wanted to bring her to Australia to be his housewife the Mosman Mansion. After all, being a beautiful woman working in a bar in Bogota was not easy with all the overconfident and arrogant cokeheads hanging around. But after a while in Australia, Miranda had started to feel frustrated just passing the time, not carrying her own weight and always being dependent on her husband's money. Keeping her off the work market was Antonio's way of keeping track of her, but Miranda had not rebelled against his attitude. It was not fear that had made her not bringing it up but rather a feeling of a debt of gratitude towards him. After all, he had improved her life a lot compared to how it had been before and the last thing she wanted, was to let him down. She received a text from Antonio DiMaestro *"I will be home in an hour, words can't describe how much I have missed you these last five weeks, you are my Venus, my only love, my everything kisses Antonio"* Miranda smiled to herself. Tonight would be a night to enjoy and she could worry about the future later.

Miranda prepared the romantic surprise that she had made for her husband. The time was reaching midnight.

Chapter 12 From the Killers Perspective

The Killer was sitting in a car watching Miranda via a laptop. Fortunately, the DiMaestro Mansion was full of security cameras, that he had hacked so he could follow every step she made. The person who installed the cameras did an outstanding job in keeping them hidden from someone who was in the room but also did a very sloppy job when it came to protecting them from computer hackers via the Internet. The consequence of this was that it would be easy to get in and out of the house unnoticed.

The Killer wondered who had called on the intercom. Whoever it was, the call had upset Miranda enough to have the premises searched by security guards. *"A good thing I did not decide to strike earlier,"* he thought to himself. The Killer had not managed to access the intercom as it contrary to the security cameras was a secure system.

Now the Killer faced a dilemma. Was he going to watch Miranda in her sexy lingerie and enjoy himself or would he finish her off right now? Most of all he wanted to fuck her. Oh, he damned himself over how much he wanted to fuck her. He brought himself together knowing that if he did, he would leave his DNA all over the place which would be a nightmare in the long run.

The Killer thought about the killing part, and it didn't appeal to him. He was not an animal like his enemy, and he did not appreciate the concept of killing at all. But he had a critical mission, which would ultimately bring him freedom and full control of his own life. As a murder weapon, The Killer had picked what he thought would be the most comfortable weapon to kill with a .22 calibre revolver equipped with a silencer. On the bright side, he would have no problem with the recoil and casings spreading around the crime scene, although he would have to shoot several shots to ensure the kill as a .22 calibre gun with a silencer would have a little punching power. The Killer felt uncomfortable: although he technically had killed before, this felt like the first time, and he wondered how losing his murder virginity would feel.

The Killer's wristwatch showed a quarter past midnight. If he struck now, the timing would be perfect, and his message would be sent the way he planned. If he did not move now, he would fall behind schedule as he had to wait until tomorrow night, which meant both an increased risk of detection and the risk of more delays. He was not THAT eager to watch Miranda in her lingerie anymore.

The Killer prepared to strike. First, he sent a text message to Miranda DiMaestro with the words *"I have lost my keys, can you please open the back door so that I can sneak in. I am looking forward to playing some sexy hide & seek"* then he studied her via the security camera when she opened the backdoor. It was time to proceed; the killer disabled all the security systems in the building via his computer. Then he grabbed his gun and jumped over the wall to the DiMaestro Mansion from the back-alley direction. He knew where Miranda was hiding. He walked into the master bedroom which was heavily scented with roses and cinnamon. He met her gaze which was filled with horror. *"I am sorry,"* he said, raised his gun, and shot her, one shot to the head and five to the chest. Miranda DiMaestro fell off the bed, dead within seconds.

The Killer went back to his car and checked his watch. The time was 1230. He was right on schedule. He logged into the mansions security system and activated the intruder alert. He started his car and drove away from the crime scene.

Chapter 13 A 3AM Phone Call

James Locker woke up with a twitch as his phone rang in the middle of the night. He watched his nightstand clock which showed the time 3.00 am. He reached for his phone and somehow managed to press the respond button. It was John Dean on the other line.

John Dean:

- Good Morning sunshine, time for your first assignment as a detective.

James Locker:

- What the fuck? Why can't criminals work in the day? It would be a lot better for my rhythm! And how come the local police called you before they called me?

John Dean:

- Well, they haven't updated their staff listing, so they called me when they could not reach Michael Fuller. Ironic that they called the right person by mistake!

James Locker:

- Yeah, I could tell by your reaction at the staff meeting that you were disgruntled, but don't let that shit affect your work.

John Dean

- Just saying, detective! The crime scene is at the DiMaestro mansion at the Esplanade in Mosman. Come as quickly as possible; I will assemble the team.

James Locker took a shower and made himself a strong coffee. He felt nauseous from sleep deprivation. Today was going to be a long day as he steered his car towards Mosman.

Chapter 14 At the Murder Scene

James Locker arrived at the crime scene at 4.30AM. He was late, as he should be at a crime scene within an hour after receiving the call. But he had felt very nauseous when taking his shower, so he had decided to stick his fingers in his throat and throw up. After throwing up, he had felt a bit better, but James had still decided to drive slowly to avoid an accident despite the roads being empty in the middle of the night.

The entire team was there, and Adam Smith greeted James.

Adam Smith:

- Good morning James you are late, and you don't look very well, did you get stuck with your thing in a glory hole on Oxford Street?

James Locker

- Still working hard to keep your "values" rating at a minimum I hear. To be honest, it's the alcohol withdrawal that's killing me.

Adam Smith

- That's a shame; you should have joined Thomas and me for the gym last night, an excellent way to sweat out some of the bad stuff.

James Locker

- I guess so, you never called me last night. Where is John Dean? He was the one who got me here.

Adam Smith

- John is in the master bedroom, where the murder took place, you should meet him there.

James Locker entered the mansion. Although he was no Ace on the property market, he estimated that a house like this would be sold for at least $5 million and probably a lot more. *"Oh, even the rich people kill each other"* James muttered before proceeding down the hall. Suddenly, he stopped and stared at a painting. James had never been to this house before, and yet the art seemed so familiar, almost like he had seen the lady it depicted before. She was staring into his soul and whispering to him, but he could not understand what she said since she spoke a foreign tongue. Thomas Anderson approached him James and spoke:

- What's the matter boss you look like you're a seeing a ghost?

James Locker:

- Almost! That painting looks so familiar. I am sure I have seen it before.

Thomas Anderson:

- Oh, I did not know you were a big fan of art?! Well, you might have, provided it's stolen and a famous piece. Do you remember the lecture Barry gave to two months ago about the new app we would use to identify stolen art quickly?

James Locker:

- Vaguely, but I did not pay very much attention.

Thomas Anderson:

- Well, I remember the lecture quite well. They were showing some famous pieces of missing art and how to use the app. This could be the right time to put this application into action.

The stolen art cell phone app was the latest step by Interpol to quickly identify stolen high-value art. The app used face recognition software used by anti-terrorist agencies for ages and applied this technique on paintings. Thomas took a high definition picture of the artwork and uploaded it onto the Interpol database. A few minutes later he got a match, for a piece stolen from an Australian collector a few years earlier.

Thomas Anderson

- Great, I am sure the stolen property team will be overjoyed, and this could help us as well, now go and see John, I am sure he is eager to see you.

James walked down the hall and entered the master bedroom where John Dean and two members of the forensics department were looking for traces. John turned around, looked at James with a crooked smile and spoke:

- Oh, look who is here. Princess Aurora finally woke up from her beauty sleep.

James Locker did not like the arrogant tone of John Dean who no doubt was still upset about not getting the promotion. He decided to bite back in a similar tone.

James Locker

- I arrived a while ago, and I have already discovered that this mansion contains stolen art. Considering how much longer you have been here, why is the killer not apprehended?

John Dean:

- Okay, let's calm down and focus on work, shall we?

James Locker

- Since you are my subordinate, I would appreciate that you acted that way.

John turned red from anger, and he struggled for a while to keep his composure before continuing speaking.

- We have not captured the killer yet; the killer did not stay here and wait for the police. However, from what we know this far, we can make some assumptions.

James Locker:

- Hit me!

John Dean:

- Well firstly, there was no sign of forced entry into the building. So, whoever the killer was, the murdered woman Miranda DiMaestro let him in willingly or he had access to keys and alarm codes. Secondly, the bedroom is decorated with roses, an ice bucket with a champagne bottle and live candles, so she was expecting a romantic encounter. Thirdly, the way she died implies a hitman and not a crime of passion.

James Locker:

- Well, that's a great start. Let's gather the team for a briefing. I am starving so let's meet up at the coffee shop just down the road.

The team gathered, and they headed for the cafeteria just down the road. The time was 5.30 am, and it would still take some time before the sun would rise and spread some warmth this crisp August night.

Chapter 15 Team Briefing at the Coffee Shop

T he team gathered at the posh but still friendly and welcoming Mosman cafe. Even though they were alone when they arrived, the group asked for the conference room for their meeting. The entire team was present, and James Locker started the talking

James Locker

- Okay, so this is what we know.

- Miranda DiMaestro, Colombian National and the wife of the businessman Antonio DiMaestro is found dead in their Mosman mansion. From the way she was killed, it looks like we are dealing with a professional killer. It appears she was waiting for someone for a romantic encounter. There are no signs of a break-in, so we assume the killer was let in by Miranda or had the keys and access codes to the building. In the mansion, we found stolen art and the stolen goods department will be called in to assess if there are any other stolen objects in the house. Any suggestions on what would be our first step?

Adam Smith:

- Well, finding her husband Antonio DiMaestro should be our first step. Fortunately, due to the stolen art, we have increased authority and can request to have him arrested on sight.

James Locker:

- Very well that's your task

John Dean:

- Speaking with the security company would be a priority. After all, it was a security guard who found her after someone set off the alarm.

James Locker:

- I leave that to you, John.

Thomas Anderson

- I will look through her computer and phone to see if there are any clues why anyone would want her dead.

James Locker:

- Great! Well to the rest of you I implore you to knock doors in the neighbourhood to see if anything interesting comes up. I will return to the office and coordinate our efforts. Please update me continuously with your findings. Please meet up at the CSMI building at 3 pm for our daily staff meeting. We should have received a report from the forensics team by then, so we'll take it from there.

The team split up, and James headed straight to his office. He would need to take a nap if he was to make it through the day. James turned down the blinds and locked the door. He was to brief the BITCH at 11AM, lead the team-meeting a 3PM and a hold a press conference at 5 PM. *"I hope no one calls me before my nap is over,"* he thought before he closed his eyes and fell asleep to a light sleep full of vivid warm dreams.

Chapter 16 John Dean Faces Troubling Circumstances

J ohn Dean's task for the day was to contact Mosman Scrooge Security (MSS), the security company responsible for the safety of the DiMaestro Mansion. He called the company and reached the voicemail referring him to an emergency number. He called that number and was referred to a third number and was told that helping police investigations wasn't an emergency according to MSS's standards. John looked at his watch. It showed 7 am and the office of MSS would probably open at 10AM. John was contemplating his options. He could either call around for hours picking arguments with an endless list of reference numbers, or he could go home, have breakfast with his family, take a short nap and then visit the MSS office during office hours and get the help he needed. John chose the easy and diplomatic "wait for business hours" approach, aware that the delay risked letting the suspect out of the country. *"Well in that case, at least there won't be any more shootouts at the airport,"* he said to himself as a reassurance.

At 10 am John Dean walked in at the office and met with the public affairs manager of MSS, Richard Monroe. Richard Monroe turned out to be very helpful, and the following conversation took place:

John Dean:

- I am here because of the murder at the DiMaestro mansion

Richard Monroe:

- Yes, I have heard about it, as it was our team that reported the crime to the police. It is a great tragedy to one of our best customers.

John Dean:

- Well, I understand. How come your security guards appeared at the scene so quickly, did the killer set off an alarm?

Richard Monroe:

- We are unsure about this. Because an alarm went off and when the alarm goes off this causes all the concealed and visible security cameras to send a live feed to our command central, this feed is also recorded. But when the feed went on Miranda DiMaestro was already murdered, and the perpetrator is not seen.

John Dean

- Interesting, any theories on how this happened?

Richard Monroe

- Well, either the cameras were broken, or the killer knew what he was doing. It would seem he remotely deactivated all our security, killed Mrs DiMaestro, and then left unnoticed.

John Dean

- I see. How could this be done exactly?

Richard Monroe

- Well, no system is stronger than its weakest link. Since the security systems were ordered to be controlled remotely, it could be done by guessing the right password. Many people are not very good at picking good passwords.

John Dean:

- I see, so why was the alarm activated then?

Richard Monroe

- We are investigating this now. It was either activated by the same person who deactivated the system, or by a glitch in the system. We'll have to make an internal investigation and get back to you this afternoon.

John Dean:

- Please do; here is my card. Anything else to add?

Richard Monroe:

- Yes, there was an incident earlier that evening with a drunken man threatening the victim, Miranda DiMaestro, via the intercom, so she felt compelled to call security. This event activated the camera feed for ten minutes until our men turned the feed off. Please take this USB stick with that video.

John Dean:

- Thank you. You have been very helpful; please call me later today when your analysis is complete.

Richard Monroe

- Will do sir, good luck with the investigation

After this conversation, John went back to his car to watch the video from the earlier incident at the DiMaestro Mansion the night before. He could see a drunken man on the street cursing and kicking an empty plastic bottle. John immediately recognised the man *"Oh my god it's Michael Fuller!"* he said to himself, falling back into his chair struggling to decide what to do.

Chapter 17 Thomas Anderson Finds Some Contradictory evidence

M eanwhile, Thomas Anderson was searching the house for any data that might hint the team in the right direction. He did find a few pieces of very counter-intuitive evidence. Apparently, Antonio DiMaestro had sent a series of threatening E-mails to Miranda DiMaestro over the last few months, and from this correspondence, it was clear that their relationship was stormy. But, in the latest text messages found in Miranda DiMaestro's phone, the tone was different. Apparently, Miranda had prepared a romantic night for Antonio when she interrupted by her murderer. Since Thomas was not an expert on stormy relationships or any relationships for that matter, he decided to take this contradictory evidence to the perpetrator profiling support function of the CSMI. What he also put on his to-do list was to check the technical integrity of the inbox and the cell phone to check if these messages were when the timestamps indicated.

While investigating the house, Thomas also found some of the concealed security cameras in the building. Unfortunately, all the wirings led to a locked room, and Thomas did not feel like tampering with the crime scene by picking a lock without discussing the matter with the rest of his team. Thomas kept looking for clues but was unable to find any. A bit later in the day the stolen property department had done their review of the items in the building and concluded that four of the paintings were on their list of stolen artworks.

Thomas Anderson decided to call James Locker:

James Locker (half asleep):

- Hi, Thomas, what are your findings?

Thomas Anderson:

- Seriously mate, were you sleeping?

James Locker:

- Of course not, what are your findings?

Thomas Anderson

- Well, several; apparently Antonio sent a lot of threatening E-mail messages to Miranda and yet it seems like he was the one she was meant to meet with. What would you make of that?

James Locker:

- Well, that does not necessarily mean more than that they were fighting, and now they were trying to reconcile. What else?

Thomas Anderson:

- Apparently, the place is full of concealed security cameras. They are all wired to the same locked room. I decided to not pick the lock until after we have discussed it at the team meeting. Oh, and the stolen property team was here. They found out that four of the paintings were registered as stolen.

James Locker:

- This discovery is significant; possessing high value stolen art is enough to send an international arrestation order through Interpol. Finding this Antonio DiMaestro guy must be our top priority. I will handle it with Barry.

Thomas Anderson:

- Excellent, and one more thing, can you request a trace for Antonio's phone last night?

James Locker:

- Of course, leave it to me and the BITCH. See you at 3 pm.

Chapter 18 The 21st August Staff Meeting

At 3 PM the same day the team gathered to summarise their findings and decide how to move on. Everyone except Barry was gathered in the same depressing room that James Locker had held his inauguration speech in the day before, James started the proceedings:

- Well, let's summarise the case this far. We have a murdered woman Miranda DiMaestro. We have her shady husband Antonio DiMaestro who was supposed to meet up with her last night. What we know is that they did not meet up for a romantic meeting. Furthermore, the killer entered the mansion and bypassed the advanced security system unnoticed. E-mail correspondence states that Miranda and Antonio have been fighting lately. Antonio's phone was in the neighbourhood at the time of the crime. We have found four pieces of high-value stolen art in the mansion. The case is clear, Antonio must be our man.

Samantha Robinson:

- Yes, the evidence points in that direction, but there are several issues in this case that don't feel right to me.

James Locker:

- I see. Can you please share your thoughts with the group on this matter?

Samantha Robinson:

- Well, my issues with the case are this:

- The murderer's choice of weapon and killing method. This murder was a calculated murder, done by a professional, and not a crime of passion. If Antonio killed his wife due to calculated reasons why would he text her and ask her to set up a romantic evening? The smartest thing to do would be to get an alibi and let a hitman do it while he was far away.

- If he chose to kill her and has the mental presence to deactivate the building's security before doing so, why on earth would he have his phone turned on. If he was unaware that cell phones act as 24-hour tracking devices, why did shut down the phone shortly after leaving the scene?

- As for my findings; well I was talking to the neighbours accompanied by Assistant Johnson and Baker. We found out was that no-one heard any gunshots. Considering Miranda was shot six times, this indicates the use of a silenced weapon. One neighbour mentioned a drunken man standing outside the house swearing and muttering for at least 10 minutes before finally leaving. The neighbour called Mosman Scrooge Security, to have the nuisance removed from the neighbourhood. They had already received a call on this matter from Miranda and were on their way.

James Locker:

- Okay, communicating with MSS is John's responsibility, so don't worry about that. As for your objections to Antonio DiMaestro being the killer, what is your theory?

Samantha Robinson:

- That someone with vast resources is trying to set him up, perhaps a rival who has been unable to get to him.

James Locker:

- And the stolen art?

Samantha Robinson

- Well, those pieces seem to have been there for a long time; Antonio is probably guilty of this.

James Locker:

- Interesting, Well I guess you should talk to the Organised Crime department, as they might know if Antonio had any enemies. Oh, and can you contact Miranda's relatives and friends back in Colombia? Your file says you are the best Spanish speaker in the team.

Samantha Robinson:

- Well, I am not fluent in any way, but I'll give it a shot.

James Locker:

- Moving on, Thomas you have already reported your findings to me. What's new?

Thomas Anderson:

- Nothing. I was unable to pick the lock to the locked room in the mansion. Some of the guys from the forensics team also tried and failed. Whatever is hidden in there it must worth a lot. We'll get back there in due time and blow the lock off with explosives, but we can't-do that until we have swept the house for evidence. We'll probably do it tomorrow afternoon or Friday morning.

James Locker:

- Well, we certainly don't want to ruin the evidence and have Antonio acquitted from a technicality. Proceed when you are finished with the forensics. Moving on to Adam; how is the search for Antonio going?

Adam Smith

- Pretty bad. At first, the Organised Crime department refused to help me because I didn't have clearance to access their investigations. So, I asked Barry for permission, but he was stalling it and questioned why I even needed the files. Instead, I visited the reception of Antonio's import/export business. They told me he was still abroad. Apparently, Antonio is still avoiding us since the Lopez Investigation.

James Locker:

- The Lopez investigation?

Adam Smith:

- Oh yeah, you were not part of that case as you were home "sick." The last case we had before our Asia trip. A professional killer killing a guy in a warehouse owned by Antonio DiMaestro's company. Unfortunately for our killer, the place had video surveillance. Even more unfortunate for him he was unable to dodge bullets when he was a gunfight with the airport police. He got shot several times and died on the way to the hospital. With the suspected killer dead, we transferred the case to the Organised Crime department.

James Locker:

- I see; Antonio only gets more and more interesting! So, you have not been able to find out about his whereabouts then?

Adam Smith:

- That's correct, even after I got clearance from Barry to access the DiMaestro file, I got nowhere. The last observation the Organized Crime department have of him is more than five weeks old.

James Locker:

- I see. Well since both you and Samantha have business with the OC department go there together. Two brains are better than one.

- Oh well, we have been saving the best for last, John what's your findings.

John Dean had been sitting all the way through the meeting fearing for when it was his turn to speak. He could not decide on how to act with information and evidence that Michael Fuller was outside the DiMaestro mansion drunk and threatening Miranda via the intercom. If John destroyed the evidence, he could be charged with evidence tampering which at the least would lead to immediate dismissal and at worst could lead to jail time. But if he told the others about Michael's behaviour and it turned out that Michael was innocent, he could lead the investigation in the wrong direction. He decided to confront Michael before sharing his knowledge with the team.

John Dean:

- Well, I spoke with Richard Monroe, manager of public affairs, at Mosman Scrooge Security. He was a helpful fellow, but the facts, he provided us with makes this investigation more complicated.

James Locker:

- Well, complexity is a part of the job, the reality is never easy, but it's our job to put complicated facts together into a smooth case.

John Dean:

- Okay here is the deal. The killer knew how to deactivate all the security systems remotely, so there is no trace of him on the surveillance tapes.

James Locker:

- It would be natural for Antonio DiMaestro to disable the security cameras if he indeed is the killer. He must have the access codes to the remote access of his house's security.

John Dean:

- I am sure he does. But here is the strange thing, straight after the killer left the house, he remotely activated the alarm. The security company could see the corpse of Miranda on their screens but no trace of the murderer. It seems like he wanted the body to be found as quickly as possible.

James Locker:

- Strange indeed, what about the drunken man who threatened Miranda over the intercom, any trace of him?

John Dean:

- Well MSS activated the feed to all the cameras and thus their recording function straight after Miranda's call. I am looking through all the feeds, but I have not had any vision of the threatening man yet.

James Locker:

- Keep looking; his identity is necessary to verify.

James Locker:

- That's it for now unless anyone has any objections? I release a press statement in an hour giving some minor details to the media and stating that our primary suspect is Antonio DiMaestro, but that we are also looking at other solutions to the case. Does anyone have any objections to this plan?

The procedure seemed reasonable to the group, and no-one had any objections. They agreed to conduct daily meetings at the same time every day, and the meeting was over.

Chapter 19 Michael Fuller & John Dean Form an alliance

Michael Fuller had spent the entire day drinking and listening to music. Because of this, he was blissfully unaware of Miranda DiMaestro's death. Michael was very drunk when John Dean called to remind him about their planned meeting. *"Damn what he sounded upset,"* Michael thought for himself before checking his watch. It was 4 PM, and John had requested a meeting at the local pub near John's house at 7 pm. Michael realised that he would better sleep for a while and have a shower before meeting with John Dean as it would be hard to convince someone to help him while he was stinking of alcohol and his eyes were blood-red. He set his alarm for 6PM and went to bed for a nap.

Before he fell asleep, he was considering the option just to walk away and let things be. Financially it would not be a big deal. He had lots of money from working in a high position as well as all the annual leaves he had saved up that would get paid out now that he had quit his job. Furthermore, his house was worth a lot since he had inherited it from his parents who in turn had bought it long before the property bubble had hit Sydney. If he sold his house, he could live a comfortable life somewhere else and still leave an inheritance to his daughter. Oh yes, his daughter if he stepped down now, he would finally have the time to repair their relationship. But then Michael got his resolve back, he had been wrongfully accused and had lost what he loved the most in the world. He would find the person behind this bullshit and have him hanged! Satisfied with his resolve he fell into a few hours of slumber.

Meanwhile, John Dean sat in his office and felt very stressed. Officially he was working on reviewing all the surveillance tapes to see if he could identify anything leading to the identity of the unknown drunken man who had threatened Miranda DiMaestro. Knowing that this man was his former boss and friend Michael put him in a terrible mood. He would have to deliver the videos with commentary at the staff meeting the day after, but if he was sure about Michael's innocence, he could tamper with the videos a bit, so they became too blurry for precise identification. Doing this was a safe procedure, but it would only buy him time since blurry videos could be sent to a subcontractor who was an expert in getting a clear picture. *"However, since the others seemed pretty fixated on Antonio DiMaestro, they might overlook the option to have the picture made clear,"* he thought and decided to go with that option.

In his family life, he also suffered from a lot of stress. His daughter had epilepsy and had seizures regularly. Either he or his wife had to stay home with her during these periods which cost them money and career opportunities. His wife had stayed home with his daughter during most of the seizures as John had assured her that he was in the frontline of getting a promotion to a detective's rank and thus get a sizeable well-needed pay raise. Now that he so clearly had been sidestepped and not even asked to be the provisional detective, it became apparent for the Dean spouses that his career opportunities were dull, and his wife was upset over having forsaken her career for his failed ambitions.

John Dean finally made up his mind. He had decided to embark on a course of action which was not in line with his ambitions or morals, but his struggling finances and the disappointment over being sidestepped had dulled his senses. John decided that if Michael Fuller wanted help from him, he would have to pay for it. He copied all the data he had available on Antonio DiMaestro to a USB memory stick. There was a lot of data at this stage since the Central Sydney Organized Crime department, CSOC, had opened their files on Antonio DiMaestro for the CSMI during the ongoing murder investigation. John copied all the data on the Miranda DiMaestro murder as well as the video of Michael Fuller outside the DiMaestro mansion the same night.

They met at the sports bar near John's house, and John started the conversation:

- You look shit mate; how much have you been drinking the last few days?

Michael Fuller:

- I have had a few...
- ...bottles of...
- ...Whiskey.
- You don't look that well either?!

John Dean:

- That's correct I was called up at 230 this morning by Mosman local police due to murder, and what is worse is that you are somehow involved.

Michael Fuller:

- Me? How on earth would I be involved?!

John Dean:

- Well, you called on the murder victim's intercom and threatened her. A few hours later she was found dead, shot with six bullets...

Michael Fuller:

- What are you talking about?

- I was looking for Antonio DiMaestro. Some woman at his house responded via the intercom. She was speaking poor English, so I got annoyed, but I did not threaten her. Someone murdered her?!

John Dean:

- Yes, that was Miranda DiMaestro, the wife of Antonio DiMaestro. Furthermore, I did a trace on your phone for the actual night, and you were staying in Mosman until 1230. How do you explain that?

Michael Fuller:

- Well, I had a drink at the local pub watching a game, was it 1230? It feels like I left at 11 pm.

John Dean:

- Well, your phone connected to the base station that connects the DiMaestro mansion until 1230. The estimated time of the Miranda DiMaestro murder is 1215. You better give me a reasonable explanation of why you contacted the DiMaestro mansion in the first place.

Michael Fuller:

- Okay wait a sec; I just need to go to the bathroom.

Michael Fuller went to the bathroom; he was sweating heavily, and panic spread like a plague across his body. He had been drinking heavily for almost 48 hours straight with little or no sleep. His vision was fading, and Michael saw the shadows around him moving. He could hear the dark voices around him speaking in a foreign demonic tongue. *"This is why I need my job back, to keep me from drinking too much and giving my life a purpose,"* he thought. Without a purpose his life was void and black, he had been alone for so long, so he forgot how it felt to feel something for another human being. Although Michael loved his daughter, it had been so long since they hung out and did something meaningful, so he had forgotten how that love felt.

Michael could feel how the shadows tried to claim his soul, but he would not let them, he would fight back. He stuck his fingers down his throat and vomited into the toilet. Afterwards, he took a gulp of mouthwash which he had in a miniature bottle in his pocket. Michael threw it away after use; he had decided that he would not need it again. He went back to John, who was sipping on a beer to pass the time.

Michael Fuller:

- Sorry about that, could you please put that beer away?

John was looking at Michael for a second and realised that this was not his battle to fight, so he complied and left the almost full schooner of beer at the bar.

Michael Fuller:

- Thank you, I just realised that I needed to get my alcohol problems in check.

- To understand my reason for going to the DiMaestro mansion, you need to know the actual reason for my resignation.

- I did not resign because of liver problems but because I was set up.

- Barry got tipped off that I was storing large quantities of cocaine at my house, cocaine that I supposedly stole from the crime scene of the Lopez murder. Antonio DiMaestro owns the warehouse where Lopez was killed, and I have been making inquiries about him on my spare time as I am not satisfied with the case being handed over to OC after the alleged killer, Angelo Ramirez, was killed at the airport.

- Apparently, I asked too many questions and was causing trouble as someone found it a good idea to waste a lot of cocaine to set me up.

- Barry then got tipped off by someone and sent two guys he knows from some shady security company. They found the cocaine, 3.5 kilos to be exact, in my house with my fingerprints on it, and they gave me two options: Either signing my resignation or facing charges in court. I decided to sign my resignation. Barry then handed me the cocaine and told me to destroy it in his private bathroom, which I did.

John Dean:

- Fascinating story Michael, but sadly alcohol-induced paranoia. Barry wouldn't let you get away with this unless he was involved in a conspiracy against you. If Barry were involved in a plot against you, he would not let you destroy 3.5 kilos of cocaine.

- If Barry were an honest cop, he would have forwarded this case to the internal investigations, and you would be facing a long-term jail penalty.

Michael Fuller:

- Well, Barry is a very particular person. For him, appearance is everything, and the image of the CSMI is his baby, and he loves it more than anything. Barry does not care for justice or truth as long as everything looks good. That's why he chose to cover it up. You do realise how embarrassing it would be for the department if it's leading and the most famous detective was charged with serious drug charges?

John Dean:

- Well, you might be right; Barry is a fucking retard. I am not convinced, but I might help you for old friendship's sake on one condition.

Michael Fuller:

- I am listening.

John Dean:

- I am broke, my marriage is crumbling, and my daughter's condition is worsening. I need money Michael, and I know you are rich.

Michael turned red of anger and disappointment. His did not feel like his short stint as a sober alcoholic had turned out for the better. Michael felt desperate for a drink, he could see the bottles in the bar, and they were calling him. He regained his composure and replied.

Michael Fuller:

- John, this is outrageous! I thought you were my friend during all these years, and now you do not believe in me at all. Instead, you are offering me help in return for money. You have fallen from the man I used to know.

John Dean:

- Well, I guess we both have. But your word changes nothing. I need money, $10,000 to be specific that will keep me afloat for a while. Don't see it as a bribe; see it as helping a friend in need. If things improve, I promise to pay you back.

Michael Fuller:

- And if I don't pay?

John Dean:

- Then this meeting never took place, I won't turn you in, but I won't help you either.

Michael Fuller was contemplating his options. The evidence against him in the Miranda DiMaestro case was not enough for a conviction, but god knows what other proof could be fabricated if there was a conspiracy against him within the CSMI. Could John Dean be the one behind it all? Well, that seemed unlikely, because if John were in it for the money, he would make a lot more from selling the stolen cocaine, than from blackmailing Michael. Money was not an issue for Michael as he owned a large beach house near Palm Beach. The house was over-dimensioned for his needs, and he rarely went to the beach anyway. As $10,000 wasn't a lot for Michael, he decided to accept John's offer.

Michael Fuller:

- Okay, I accept your offer, shall I transfer the money right now?

John Dean:

- No, that would be traceable. I'll come by your house tomorrow afternoon with the files, make sure to have the money ready in cash.

They agreed to meet up at 5PM the following day, and they separated for the evening. John Dean was filled with worries while travelling home. For sure his economy was saved for at least six months if he got the money. He could finally get back on track with his mortgage. But how would explain this sudden influx of money to his wife? And what if he got caught? Most of all he was worried about his human development and his downward spiral down into the darkness he had spent all his life trying to fight in society. He had seen a lot of police officers join the force for all the wrong reasons. Some had enlisted for the lust of violence, and they regularly used excessive force when making arrests. Some had joined for the desire for power and authority, and they routinely harassed and threatened people for the rush of it. Finally, some officers had joined to get a badge and a carte blanche to skim the other criminals for money. He suspected that both Thomas Anderson and Adam Smith were in the latter category and used their badges to get free drugs and hookers.

John Dean reckoned that they probably only did drugs when they had a few days off work as there were random drug tests in place among police officers, but his opinion about them was clear; they just reeked of corruption. Now he could place himself in the same category as Thomas Anderson and Adam Smith or even worse. Because something was very wrong with Michael's behaviour this evening, and if he were left unchecked, he would do a lot of worse things than stealing drugs.

Chapter 20 Adam Smith and James Locker Playing Video Games

I t was Thursday evening, and James Locker and Adam Smith were meeting up at Adam's place to play the yearly instalment of the Aussie Rules Football game. From a gameplay perspective, the game was utter rubbish, but as both Adam and James were hard-core AFL fans though they still saw the game as an excellent opportunity to experience those massive victories over their rivals, that never experienced when they played Aussie Rules Football in reality. Since Adam, was the better video games player of the two he beat James every game, which brought him joy, but also a bit of frustration.

Adam Smith:

- Hey, mate; you better start focusing! It takes half the pleasure of beating you when you are not even trying!

James Locker:

- Oh, sorry man, I am a bit off my game today. I guess I am over-thinking things.

Adam Smith:

- I see. Awesome thoughts, lame thoughts or plain strange ideas?

James Locker:

- Well, I was considering changing my name to get a new start in life.

Adam Smith:

- But why on earth would want a new start?

- You just landed a promotion, you fucked half of Asia during your holiday, and despite being over 30, you are neither fat nor ugly. You lead a remarkable life I reckon. Learn from me and be awesome as well.

James Locker:

- So, you are happy with life then?

Adam Smith:

- Yes of course! I get fed, paid and laid. What is there to whine about?

James Locker:

- Well, you might want to get loved and appreciated for who you are?

Adam Smith:

- Look, if I wanted to listen to emotional whining when playing video games, I would get a girlfriend and play with her.

- Here are two shots of absinthe bottom up and harden up James.

After sculling the shots, James realised that Adam was not the right person to share his complex inner thought with, which was good as Adam undoubtedly had a point. Sometimes it was better just to keep things simple. Fuelled by this insight, James focused and spent the evening trying to beat Adam in that damn video game!

Chapter 21 Friday Afternoon and Antonio DiMaestro Still at Large.

The last staff meeting of the week took place on Friday afternoon. A few new pieces of evidence came up, but James Locker reckoned that none of the new evidence was of such value that it was motivated for the team to work overtime during the weekend. The report from the forensics team stated that they had found DNA from four different people in the mansion, two males, and two females. The two women DNA were identified as the housekeepers, Kim-Ji-Wo who worked in the estate three times a week, and the late Miranda DiMaestro. The housekeeper had a sound alibi for the evening and no apparent motive for killing her employer so James decided that she shouldn't be kept under surveillance.

The two male DNA was a more significant issue. One of them was from Antonio DiMaestro which was natural as he supposedly lived in the house. The second male DNA was more important to follow up upon. It could be from the Killer if Antonio was not the killer or it could be from whoever visited the house in the last few days.

Fortunately, they had managed to get access to the security room of the building with the mainframe. In the security room, the investigators found a large amount of money as well as minor amounts of cocaine, clearly indicating what kind of business Antonio DiMaestro was doing. As expected, all the feeds showcasing the actual murder had been remotely deactivated, but apart from that, there were security feeds for a long time back. The group decided that these feeds were important and the work to go through them was assigned to Samantha Robinson and Thomas Anderson, a task they both seemed happy to receive.

Considering the DNA from the unknown man Adam Smith and John Dean were assigned to find alternative killers. The main priority was to identify the man who called on the intercom and threatened Miranda DiMaestro, but they were also to make inquiries among Antonio DiMaestro's business contacts to find out if he had any enemies who wanted to set him up.

Chapter 22 Friday Night Laser Tag Session

Since the work week was over, Thomas Anderson and Adam Smith decided to spend their Friday night playing Laser tag. They did this now and then and tonight's session was of great importance to get their skills up for the Sydney laser tag championship held the following week. Accompanying them this week was Samantha Robinson who Thomas Anderson had persuaded to join their team for the upcoming championship. Since they did not want any team members, who sucked they decided to give her the necessary training before the games that mattered.

After three games they decided to take a break, and they had the following conversation.

Adam Smith:

  - Three games: three first places; I am indeed still the king of laser tag.

Samantha Robinson

  - Oh, Adam, you are so sexy, I am getting all wet.

Adam Smith

  - Uh really?

Samantha Robinson

  - Yeah, not from you, but from sweat. Running around with a toy gun is more fun than I imagined. Next week will be awesome.

Adam Smith:

- Yeah, you are better than I thought, I feared we would be stuck with a feeder just because Thomas wanted to make a move on you, but you might get better than him.

Thomas Anderson:

- Hum, I did not bring her as a lame pickup attempt, I brought her because we need four players for the championship next week so that it will be you and I, Samantha and James.

Adam Smith:

- James??! He sucks worst player I have seen!

Thomas Anderson:

- Well, that's because of his colour blindness, James can only play well when he knows the people he is playing with, he does not function at all in mixed teams.

Adam Smith

- We'll see about that. I got to go; I am getting laid tonight!

Adam Smith smiled with a huge smile.
Thomas Anderson

- No, you are not. You are just making up an excuse so you can leave with three consecutive wins. I am not buying that one, we'll keep playing my stamina is better than yours.

Adam Smith:

- Oh really? Look at this text!

Adam Smith handed over the phone to Thomas to show an SMS conversation he had with a woman. The entire dialogue consisted of different smileys, question marks, and exclamation marks. Not many words were written.

The last message from the woman was a question mark, followed by Adam's response an exclamation mark

Thomas Anderson:

- What the fuck is this? It looks completely retarded. How does this mean you are getting laid tonight?!

Adam Smith:

- Well mate, she is a psychologist, so she listens to people whine about their feelings and stuff all day long. So, when the urge comes all she wants is sex; and I am happy to provide.

Thomas Anderson:

- That is beyond retarded. Do you.

Samantha Robinson interrupted Thomas Anderson:

- Oh god! Thomas, why do you even care if this woman exists or not? But yeah you can't leave yet, Adam, we'll have to play a final game to determine the winner of tonight, and I am going to show you some girl power if you are up for it?!

Adam Smith:

- Tough words indeed, I accept your challenge!

They went in, to play a final round before Adam Smith had to leave to meet his booty call. To Adam's surprise, he got beaten by Samantha. Thomas Anderson finished second with a small margin, and Adam Smith got by his standards a humiliating third place.

Thomas Anderson:

- Ha-ha psyche out. The great master of laser tag beaten big time by a girl. How does it feel?

Adam who had a very red face from the physical exertion yelled:

- Shut up! You suck nine out of ten games, and besides, she beat
  you too!

Adam cooled down for a while, and then he added

- Anyway, I am leaving now; I am getting laid tonight. Good luck
  with that.

After this outburst that caused everyone to look at him; Adam quickly
left the venue.

Thomas and Samantha decided to have another drink and went to a
couch to have a chat. After a while, she leaned her head towards him and said:
Samantha Robinson:

- You know he was right about one thing; you do suck at Lasertag.

Thomas looked at her with sad eyes and said nothing.
Samantha Robinson:

- But he was also wrong about one thing...

Thomas Anderson:

- Okay, and what would that be?

Samantha Robinson smiled at him and said:

- Well, you are getting laid tonight.

She pulled the surprised Thomas Anderson towards her, and they kissed
passionately.

Chapter 23 An Insight into the Killer's Mind.

The killer was lying in bed looking at the sleeping woman next to him. She was the most beautiful thing he had ever seen. When she touched him all the pain in his mind, all the horrible things he had seen and experienced was healed, and he felt like a whole man. They would be the perfect couple, maybe even start a family someday.

But there was a big problem, that could prevent this dream from happening. The Killer was not free, he was a slave, and although he tried his best to control his destiny, he just could not. For instance, this was the first time in weeks he was able to be with her. All because of another man who decided his fate and played with his life like he was a puppet. He hated that man above all else, but for now, that man was out of reach.

The Killer looked at his watch. He would soon have to leave her. Again! How he dreaded the fact that he could never spend the whole night with her and wake up to see her smile. She had accepted his explanations as to why he could never spend the night with her. It was always work-related, and she said she understood. Which of course she did not. Oh, if it were only work-related reasons, he would quit his job tomorrow just to wake up to see her smile.

The Killer got dressed and contemplated his options. He knew that if he smothered his mistress while she was asleep, he would finally be free of the bondage and the strong connection he felt to her. Maybe he would even come by the following day and see her corpse. She would be the most beautiful corpse he had ever seen. The Killer cast this thought aside, as he felt appalled by the thought of never being able to see her wake up with a smile on her face with the morning sun reflecting on her hair. The Killer's biggest dream was to witness her wake up and the thing that kept him going. Without this dream he might as well put the gun, he had used to kill Miranda DiMaestro to his head and blow his brains out. He smiled when he thought about how shocked everyone would be. Sadly, he would not be able to see it himself which took most of the fun out of it.

He decided to neither kill her nor himself tonight and instead he chose to leave her a note to explain why he had to get off this time. It read *"Dear Rebecca; it breaks my heart to not be able to see you wake up this morning. Sadly, bad things came up; things that I don't want to trouble you with. Rest assured that I have a plan for how to make it you and I together forever. I love you and hope that you feel the same for me. Your's Forever JP"*

He left the apartment and faced his fate of yet another day of tormenting captivity, unsure of when he would be free to see her again.

Chapter 24 Boozing at James' house

It was Saturday the 24th of August 2013 and James Locker decided that it was time to get drunk. He had felt the alcohol withdrawal all week, but today he was energised and could not see any reason why he should not drink. He decided to call his friends Thomas and Adam to come over as it felt better to drink in a group, and they had a lot of talking points since their Asian holiday. He started off by calling Thomas.

James Locker:

- Hey, mate, how are you doing? Up for some boozing and hunting tonight?

Thomas Anderson:

- I don't know mate; I am seeing this awesome girl, I don't want to go after any other women for the time being...

James Locker:

- Seriously? You have been back in Sydney for one week, and you have been working long shifts, how did you manage to meet someone?

Thomas Anderson:

- Fate has its ways; anyway, I don't want to speak about it for now since I don't know where it's going.

James Locker:

- Fair enough. So, are you seeing this mysterious woman tonight, and if not, does she mind if you go out boozing with your friends?

Thomas Anderson

- I am not seeing her tonight, and I don't think she minds if I hang out with you guys.

James Locker:

- Ha-ha, that's because she does not know Adam. Anyways come to my place at 7 PM. I have already bought the drinks and the snacks, a man got to celebrate his promotion after all.

They hung up, and James Locker contacted Adam who did not need any form of persuasion for a Saturday night boozing and hunting session. Adam and Thomas arrived at James's place at 7 pm, and they realised that he was already drunk. Adam Smith decided to bring up the issue:

- Dammit, James! How are you supposed to go out boozing and hunting in this state with the Responsible Service of Alcohol rules being in place?

James Locker:

- Well mate, my plans for tonight is a lot more awesome than going to RSA licensed venues. You know exactly what I am talking about.

Thomas Anderson:

- Well, that's Adam territory, and since when do you do drugs?

James Locker:

- Are you kidding me? I am drinking alcohol which evidently is more dangerous than most illegal drugs you'll find lying around. And besides these antidepressants, I am taking would be classified as narcotics if they were not backed by doctors and wealthy pharmaceutical companies.

Adam Smith:

- That's my man! Bitter, believing in conspiracies and a party animal at the same time! Can it get better? Pour me a big one!

Adam sculled a shot of absinthe and several hours of excessive drinking commenced. They were playing video games where the loser was forced to drink a double shot of absinthe. Considering the shock, the body experiences after consuming 60 ml of a beverage with an alcohol content of 70 % in one gulp Thomas who was the least alcoholic of the three could not handle his round, so he went to the bathroom where the poison came out the same way it came in. When he returned, James was looking at him with crazy eyes and began to talk.

James Locker:

- Hey, Thomas, have you ever thought about how it would feel to get shot? I have...

Thomas Anderson:

- Probably highly unpleasant and possibly lethal, I prefer ignorance.

James Locker:

- Well, the pursuit of knowledge and freedom is essential for me, and I only feel free when I am living on the edge.

While saying this; James handed the slightly shocked Thomas Anderson a pistol. James continued to speak:

- You see I have always wondered how it feels to be shot, but I just can't make shoot myself and that's where you come into the picture. You have a gun I want YOU to shoot me.

Thomas Anderson:

- Are you fucking insane?! I won't do that; you might die.

James Locker:

- I might, but it's not likely since I am wearing body armour. As long as you are steady on your aim, we'll both be fine.

Thomas Anderson:

- You are crazy; there is no way I am doing that, no matter what you say.

James pulled forth a second gun from his pocket and aimed it at Thomas. James Locker

- Well sadly mate; it's either you or me. Since I am wearing body armour, I would prefer to be shot, than shooting you.

Thomas was sweating heavily, and the panic caught a black grip over his mind. He perceived James as deadly serious, and he did not want to risk his life by turning his back to James and disobey his request. Thomas decided to go ahead and shoot. He lifted his gun and focused his aim before firing. The bullet was stopped by James' body armour, but the force was still enough to knock him to the ground. Thomas' and Adam's gaze met, and they both felt shocked by the event that had just occurred. Suddenly James jumped up and laughed:
James Locker

- Ha-ha fooled you guys! Thomas, you just shot me with a blank bullet; you did not think I would let you shoot me for real?

Thomas Anderson:

- No, I wasn't; look at your body armour there is a hole in it!

James looked perplexed putting his finger in the hole of his body armour; he grew pale for a while before regaining his composure. Finally, he spoke.

- Holy shit! You are right; I better stop drinking! But the night is young, and I am not going to bed yet! Adam can you get us some free cocaine, I know you have sources

Adam felt very uncomfortable when James brought up the topic. He was not supposed to know about this; as this was a thing between Adam and Thomas. But it was true as owning a police ID was a great way of getting an occasional bag of free cocaine, ecstasy, weed or whatever they fancied for the night.

Scoring free drugs as a police officer was all about knowing about the environment and not becoming too greedy. Thomas and Adam had settled for asking for freebies once or twice a month. It was the perfect equilibrium between police and drug lord they reckoned. If they asked for too much, they would become a liability and probably have an "accident." If they were strict and did their jobs; they would arrest the drug dealers and maybe get a minor staff appraisal, but that was worth far less to them than having free drugs whenever they liked. Neither Adam nor Thomas were drug addicts, so an occasional gram of coke every now and then was enough to fulfil their needs.

Adam was unsure of how to respond to James. There was a possibility that James was only testing them and knew nothing about their drug habits and how they acquired their drugs. Adam Smith decided for an approach and started talking:

- What you are suggesting is an interesting idea, James. I did not know you were using cocaine but if you could recommend a way for us to get it for free; it would indeed bring an extra dimension to our party tonight.

James Locker:

- Oh Adam, please! I am not an expert on how to get free cocaine from drug barons, but I suppose you ask them for a small cut to look the other way. So here is what we do: the principal drug lords in Sydney are Antonio DiMaestro, Salvador Allende, and Miguel Vasquez.

- I suppose none of you knows where Antonio DiMaestro is since he is wanted for murder and you probably would not be stupid enough to take bribes from him when his operations are in the spotlight.

- This leaves us with Allende and Vasquez. Who do you think has the best girls and the best cocaine?

Adam Smith:

- Well, we have not spoken to Vasquez for months so he would be more inclined to help without considering hurting us.

Thomas Anderson:

- Well none of them is dealing with prostitution though.

James Locker:

- Hey, mates get real! Every drug baron with self-respect always has an array of girls available. The fact that they are not actual prostitutes just makes them hotter. Who does not dream about a hot night with a Latin American femme fatale?

Adam Smith:

- Woo. It sounds awesome mate! But how would we convince them to let us touch their girls? I mean we don't have that much on them.

James Locker:

- Don't worry about that. I'll sort it out! Just point me in the direction of their place, and I'll lead the way.

Adam Smith:

- Well, I know Vasquez has a place at Potts Point, but we better get a cab there as it would be stupid of us going down for drunk driving.

James Locker

- Awesome! Let's go!

Chapter 25 Corruption at Kings Cross

The gang arrived at Kings Cross around midnight. It was a chilly and rainy evening not suitable for a real party, but since it was a Saturday night, there was still a lot of action around them.

James Locker sometimes thought about the bizarre realities of the legal system and how the governments of men needed an enemy either real or constructed to legitimate their power. In the specifics of in the war against drugs the government was victimising a group of people because they were committing a victimless crime, the crime of using a product that in the long run might be harmful to them and reduce their value as citizens. But the main issue was that for most users the concept of being arrested and getting a criminal record was a far worse liability for his or her future career prospects than the usage itself brought to them.

Apparently, James Locker and his friends did not share the legislators' opinions on drugs, but ironically, they and the organised crime were the only ones who profited from the current situation. The organised crime earned a lot of tax-free benefits possible only possible due to the legislation, and corrupt police offers were making money as they could have a slice of the pie without upsetting the balance too much.

After a short walk, they arrived at the Vasquez venue which looked very inconspicuous from the outside. For those who knew about the place, it was the place to go for buying anything illegal. Vasquez supplied contraband ranging from various drugs, weapons, and chemicals used for bomb making. Adam called on the intercom, and two very rough looking guards came out. One of them was known as Marko, and Adam had been in interacting with him in the past.

Marko started speaking:

- Puta de Madre! What are you fuckers doing here, and who is that guy?

Adam Smith:

 - This is James, and he has a special request for you tonight.

Marko:

 - Fuck off; you are getting nothing from us, now scram!

For the second time, this evening James shocked his friends with his behaviour as he instead of saying something pulled his gun and hit Marko in the head with it thus breaking his nose. He quickly turned around and aimed the gun at the head of the other guard.
James Locker:

 - Okay, that's step one of creating understanding. Adam and Thomas: Disarm them.

Adam and Thomas decided to do as directed. As it turned out both the thugs had firearms. These firearms were most likely unlicensed ones as Australia was not like the USA when it came to gun laws.
James Locker spoke again:

 - What do we have here? Illegal guns?! More than enough to have you imprisoned for a while and then deport you from the country. Provided that we can't link any of your guns to any serious crimes, in which case I can assure you that your stay in Australia will be long and unpleasant!

 - However, I only care about this kind of behaviour when I am grumpy, so provide me with some free cocaine and some awesome Latina pussy, and I'll let it pass for now.

Marko lying on the ground with a broken nose realised that James was a man not to be trifled with, but he was unsure on how to keep this psychopath cop happy. Marko had the approval of his bosses to give minor handouts to people that were causing minor trouble if the donations were far less than the cost and effort of just silencing the person. So, if some bum junkie came by and thought he would get something for free by blackmailing them all he would get was a portion of lead. With police officers, it was different as a dead policeman was terrible for everyone's business, and his organisation was not robust enough to wage a full-scale war against the police in Australia. He swallowed some blood from his broken nose and started talking.

Marko:

- You sure got some nerve fucker. Oh well, have some cocaine. I guess it's the only way for you to feel like a man, you fucking maricon. As for girls, there is a brothel around the corner, I know because I fucked your mum there last week.

Marko handed a bag containing five grams of cocaine to James, who smiled at him and started to talk.

James Locker:

- Oh, how happy I am to get half of what I asked for. You were not very courteous or service-minded though, so I give you an F for presentation. And I give you this for your comment about my mum.

James kicked Marko with full force in the face smashing some teeth out and knocking the Colombian unconscious. He turned to the other thugs who was sitting with a gun to his head and started speaking

James Locker:

- You see, that's what happens if you don't give me excellent customer service.

- I'll let your buddy live for now, but you better give me better service.

Fabio Swallowed and said nothing while James Locker continued speaking.

James Locker:

- I know you don't keep women here. But I also knew your boss has access to some smoking hot women. So, if you provide us with these women as well as cigars, fine liquors and a spa I will surely praise your excellent customer service.

- Now call your boss and let me talk to him.

Fabio was not eager to call his boss about problems in the middle of the night. Miguel Vasquez was a severe cokehead who was always close to anger when his henchmen bothered him with unpleasant news. He has been particularly prone to violence when he was orchestrating large coke filled orgies at his mansion in Watsons Bay, a short trip away. For situations like this, however, with his friend lying unconscious badly roughed up, he preferred disturbing his foul-tempered cokehead boss, rather than the drunken psycho standing next to him with a gun pointed at his head. Fabio grabbed his phone and called the number that Miguel Vasquez had told him to only call in case of an emergency. After a few signals, Miguel Vasquez picked up the phone.

- Who the fuck is this, why are you calling, and how did you get this number?

Fabio:

- It's Fabio sir. There is an emergency at the Potts Point warehouse. Some drunken psychos who claim to be cops are here. They knocked Marko unconscious, and they require talking to you about women and fine liquors.

Miguel Vasquez:

- Are you fucking kidding me? What clowns, are these people? We are not even dealing with the ladies or fine liquors.

Fabio:

- I told them, but they wanted access to your private stash, Marko argued, and they beat him to pieces...

Miguel Vasquez

- Tell them to shoot you; you fucking coward! Would save me the hassle!
- Ah, fuck it put them through.

James Locker:

- So, I finally get to talk to the big boss huh?

Miguel Vasquez:

- Who the fuck is this, and what the hell do you want?

James Locker

- Yet again the same bad language and lack of customer service approach.

- To answer your questions, I am James Locker from the CSMI. We are investigating the murder of Miranda DiMaestro which appear to be mob-related.

Miguel Vasquez:

- Yeah, I have heard about it. But that shit has nothing to with us. We are at peace with the DiMaestro cartel, and Miranda was a worthless bimbo that meant nothing to their organisation anyways.

James Locker:

- That's true. Although I am sure, Antonio would not agree...

Miguel Vasquez:

- That fucking wimp just got her to show up to the public. To create an image of being legit. He fucks everything that moves, Although I have found out that he has been away for a long time and is presumed dead. Anyway, what the fuck do you want?

James Locker:

- What I want is simple. I want in on the high life of organised crime. I don't give a shit about money, but I want some great booze and some awesome Latina pussy on my dick tonight. I have heard you are arranging massive freaking orgies in your mansion on Saturday nights.

Miguel Vasquez:

- I see. What if I just choose to kill you and have the problem solved?

James Locker:

- Well, you could try, but if you succeed it would only cause you more problems. Or contemplate this: three police officers from the CSMI go to the mansion of an alleged drug lord and go missing while investigating a mob-related murder. Not very good for business.

- So yeah, enough of this bullshit. We'll swing by your place in 30 minutes. Have the girls and the good stuff ready.

Miguel Vasquez:

- You indeed have cojones; I like that. Prepare yourself for the freakiest night of your lives!

Using his persuasion skills, James managed to get Fabio to drive them to the Vasquez mansion. About the same time, Marko woke up from his beating with the worst headache of his life, having learned the lesson that one should never mess with James Locker's mum!

Chapter 26 A Tired Reflection by James Locker

After the craziest night of his life, James was finally home at his place at 3PM the day after. His headache was horrible, and he knew that he would not be very productive in the following days. James felt ashamed over his behaviour, and he feared what had happened to him. For sure he had some crazy nights in his youth, but at the age of 32 and with a distinguished career ahead of him, he should focus on other things than promiscuity and bizarre sex games.

The night before had certainly been an adventure beyond everything he had experienced before. But it was the darkest and most twisted paths of human nature he had encountered. The extended sex orgies of last night were so far away from the love between two humans as it could be. He thought about the famous expression by German philosopher Nietzsche *"When you stare into the abyss the abyss also stares into you."*

How had this happened to him? A year ago, he had been living with his love, planned a wedding and lived a very normal life far away from the perversion of darkness. Less interesting in many ways but also a lot happier as ignorance of the dark is bliss. After Emily Luong had disappeared with some of his money to never be seen again his entire world had fallen apart. What had happened that fateful night? What clues to the mystery had he been unable to see? James did not know the answers to these questions, and since he would never find out, he should move on with his life.

James felt exhausted and was shaking from the hangover from last night. He was thinking about how his friends must have perceived him. It couldn't be pretty. His memory was very vague from the evening, but he remembered getting shot and beating someone up. He could however not have been shot as an untreated gunshot wound would have killed him, and he was alive with no visible injuries except a sore foot and a bruise on the right shoulder.

James realised that he would get no answers today and all he wanted was to sleep a lot to wake up feeling a lot better the day after hopefully. He went to the bathroom and had some of the pills his psychologist had prescribed him. After a while, he felt very sleepy and fell into a deep dreamless sleep.

Chapter 27 An unwelcome visitor in the night.

It was a chilly evening, and the Killer was having a conflict of interest. He knew that his enemy; the man who stood between him and his dream of freedom, James Locker was sleeping very deep in his bedroom. He could see him from his position outside the bedroom window. But what would he do? The Killer knew he could break in and put some bullets in the head of his sleeping enemy, and it would be over. But did he want it to end that way? Did he want to kill a man who was oblivious of what he had done? It hardly seemed ideal.

The Killer thought about Rebecca. She was the most beautiful human he had ever met. The light in her eyes when their gaze met. Her sparkling teeth when she smiled at him. How their hearts were beating at the same pace when they made love. She was the definition of heaven for him, and he would do anything to live in that world knowing that it would last. It pained the Killer that he could never tell her what he had done and expect her to understand or forgive. But if he could forgive himself and complete what he had to do; he could be candid and forthcoming to her about things in the future.

The Killer's dream of a different future was worth more than anything else to him, but to make it happen he would have to make James Locker disappear; permanently. He picked the lock to the door and made his way into James's room. The Killer was looking at his enemy, who almost seemed unconscious. Hah, that fool is so afraid of what he is and his dreams that he uses heavy drugs to get a dreamless sleep.

In a way killing James Locker would be an act of mercy. A man that was so afraid of his inner self that he sedated himself just to get away from his dreams was more dead than alive anyway.

The killer aimed his gun at James Locker. But he could not take the shot. Not now, not under these circumstances. James must know before he dies. He must face what he had done before going down into the abyss! He would

96

leave a message, however! He went to the bathroom and painted the following message on the mirror using blood. *"I am watching you! / JP!"* Then he left the building and vanished into the night.

Chapter 28 An Unpleasant Monday morning.

When James Locker woke up in the morning, he saw the bloodstained writing on his bathroom window and freaked out. Not knowing how to react he walked around confused in his house losing all grip of time and room. James woke up from this state when Barry Itch called him to find out where he was. He told Barry Itch what had happened and soon the entire team was there to document the crime scene and find any trace of the perpetrator. James suddenly felt a lot of discomfort over the fact that his colleagues were there. In case this was related to his still very blurry memories of the weekend, he could be deep in trouble if they discovered the truth about his mafia connections. Why had he even taken those steps last weekend it was an awful idea, and it could cost him everything.

As his manager, Barry Itch took James Locker apart for a quick chat:

- Such a wretched way to wake up. Do you think this is a real threat just a very sick joke?

James was considering his options and decided that honesty was probably not in his best interest. After all, coming out clean about his drug use and mafia connections wouldn't improve his prospects.
James Locker:

- I have no idea, sir. I have not received any threats on my life or wellbeing before this event.

Barry Itch:

- Okay. Do you think it could have a connection to your current case?

James Locker:

- That would not make any sense. Why would the DiMaestro murderer, come after me? I know nothing in this case that is not common knowledge.

Barry Itch:

- Well whoever the perpetrator is, he or she does not necessarily know about your lack of knowledge. How would you like to proceed?

James Locker:

- Let's do nothing for now; hopefully, the forensic team will help us by finding some valuable clues.

Barry Itch:

- If that's your wish. Although I prefer taking threats to our officers more seriously.

James Locker:

- I see your point, but let's put it this way: Whoever did this shall not succeed in taking our focus away from what's important; which is getting justice for the victims and putting the bad guys behind bars!

Barry Itch:

- I guess you are right. Will you hold the meeting this afternoon instead?

James Locker:

- Yeah, no worries, it takes more than a sick joke to get my focus broken!

After Barry Itch left, James had a private chat with Thomas Anderson:
James Locker:

- Hi Thomas. Can I ask you for a favour that we will keep between ourselves?

Thomas Anderson:

- Of course, James. What do you need?

James Locker:

- Can I ask you to install two hidden security cameras in my house and don't tell anyone but me of their existence and location?

Thomas Anderson:

- Sure, I guess, but why keep it a secret?

James Locker:

- Well because I have a feeling that whoever did this will do something similar in the future, and I want to find out who did it.

Thomas Anderson:

- So, you think it's someone on the team?

James Locker:

- Not really, but I don't want to rule anyone out.

Thomas Anderson:

- Fair enough. I will install them later this afternoon when the last tech has gone home. Do you want the remote access as well?

James Locker:

- Yes, that is my plan.

Thomas Anderson:

- Sure, you'll have full access to the systems tonight. Do we meet at the team meeting this afternoon?

James Locker:

- Yes. Let's go to the station right away, so we don't disturb the others.

They were walking towards the exit when one of the technicians on the team, Police assistant Vinnie Chung, approached James.
Vinnie Chung:

- Sir do you want us to check the basement as well? The door to the basement is locked, and the lock has no signs of being picked.

James Locker:

- Don't worry about that, I lost the key over eight months ago, and I have not been there since. Nothing of interest down there anyway.

Vinnie Chung:

- Understood sir. You'll get the report by the 3 PM staff meeting.

After this conversation, James and Thomas went to the office to commence with their respective tasks in the DiMaestro case.

Chapter 29 Michael Fuller Follows a Lead

Michael Fuller had not been passive since his meeting with John Dean a few days earlier. From his many years of service in the police force, he had acquired many contacts, which could fill him in on the latest news from the underworld of Sydney. Most of the connections were hostile and needed persuasion. Unfortunately, as a civil person without authority, he did not have much bargaining power over these individuals. A few of his contacts, however, had had their lives saved by the quick and efficient work of Michael and those people were forever grateful to him. From one of these contacts, Michael learned that Antonio DiMaestro had met an escort named Jessica Hall a few years ago and that Antonio was so emotionally attached to her that he had made her his protégé. The contact did not think this was due to love but due to the possessive nature of Antonio DiMaestro; the man disliked sharing. When it came to taste in women; however, the contact praised Antonio as Jessica apparently was an extraordinarily beautiful woman.

Michael Fuller decided to contact John Dean to ask why he had not been informed about Antonio DiMaestro's mistress. After all, John Dean was handsomely paid to provide him with information.

Michael Fuller:

- Hi, John. Something new to tell me?

John Dean:

- Yes, there is. Someone broke into James Locker's house and left a scary message.

- "I am watching you/ JP" written in blood on his bathroom mirror.

Michael Fuller:

JAMES LOCKER THE DUALITY OF FATE

- Wow. That is strange and scary. Do you have any clue who did it?

John Dean

- None yet. But it did have an impact on James; he has been even more cloudy and distant than last week. I seriously doubt his leadership as well.

Michael Fuller:

- Well, you might be right, but there is nothing we can do about it now. Any more clues on Antonio DiMaestro?

John Dean:

- No, but I gave you everything I yesterday so why you are calling again?

Michael Fuller:

- Because you didn't mention that Antonio DiMaestro had a paid mistress, Jessica Hall, she seems quite relevant to the investigation, both as a witness and as a suspect.

John Dean:

- Thank you, Michael. This comes as news to me. But this information can be quite helpful for our investigation. Who is my source?

Michael Fuller:

- Forget about it. Is no-one doing their job under James? I will contact her myself. Hopefully, she'll help me out better than you do.

John Dean:

- Is that wise, considering your current situation?

Michael Fuller:

- Well, I had to resign due to "health reasons." What is the BITCH going to do?

John Dean:

- Don't say I did not warn you.
- Got to go. Talk to you later.

Michael Fuller was in an awful mood when he thought about the news he got from his old team. What was going on with James Locker? How could such a sharp mind overlook that Antonio DiMaestro had a mistress? What about the break-in at James's place? Michael was getting convinced that something was seriously wrong with James and he made a mental note that he should investigate it as soon as possible.

Michael felt very sick from the alcohol withdrawal, and he could not think straight anymore. *"So much for not drinking to keep a clear head,"* he muttered to himself. But after speaking to that gold-digging bitch Jessica Hall, he would have some drinks. One of his favourite bars in Sydney was on the same street as her apartment, and they had some great whiskey blends. Last time he went there he believed that he had met his soul mate. Sobering up next to her the day after, he had realised this was not the case. Still, it was a good memory, and since he had no obligations anymore, he might as well drink all night and hope for the best!

Chapter 30 An Unexpected Text Message

The time was around 1130PM on Monday the 26th of August 2013. Jessica Hall was lying in the bathtub when she got a text message. She struck the foam away from her perfectly symmetrical face to be able to read it better. It was an SMS from Antonio DiMaestro. The message said that he missed her and wanted to see her tonight. She was shivering from the idea. Just a couple of hours ago she had been visited by a very unpleasant and rude man who identified himself as Michael Fuller; Police detective from Central Sydney Murder Investigation department. He had looked old and ragged, but the news he brought and the questions he had asked were a lot more intimidating. Apparently, Antonio DiMaestro's wife was killed a few days ago in her home. The ragged old man had wanted to know what she knew, and he had flamed her with a variety of accusations. *"What right did that bitter old man have to judge her?!"* Jessica felt outraged when she thought about it.

Jessica did not know much about Antonio DiMaestro. She had arrived in Sydney two years ago from the small outback city of Tamworth after graduating high school to either make it or break it. Her dream was to have a breakthrough in media or acting, and she had been attending an acting school when she first came to Sydney. At first, she had lived a decent life doing some occasional modelling gigs and some shifts as a waitress. As Jessica had dreaded serving drunken idiots to make tiny scraps of money, she had quickly started looking for another line of work which could utilise her two strengths her great physical beauty and her elegance/ sense of fashion. She had decided to go into escorting to make full use of her strengths. Jessica had worked for a high-end escort agency, and her dream had been to meet well-versed gentlemen who could appreciate her beauty and entertain her with their charming tales. She was disappointed though, as most of her clients were drunk and rude assholes who just happened to be rich. But Jessica couldn't quit as she had acquired expensive tastes and did not want to go back to a regular job. Working as an escort, Jessica had felt like a prisoner in a golden cage.

One day Jessica's life had turned around for the better. That was the night she had met Antonio DiMaestro. He was the perfect gentleman, and after having an excellent dinner full of charming tales, she had felt a strong connection to him and enjoyed the prospect of having sex with him. Later that night they had gone to his suite at a 5-star hotel nearby, had some more champagne and then made love all night. For the first time since she started as an escort, she had enjoyed sex, and he gave her multiple orgasms that night. What she liked even more and would never forget was the day after when he had surprised her by serving breakfast and told her how beautiful and unique she was. She had been very moved by this gesture and started crying. He had comforted her and said that her days as an escort could be over and he would love to help her if she wanted to take the step.

The deal was that Antonio gave Jessica $2,000 tax-free per week and provided her with a centrally located apartment. Antonio's only conditions were that she was always available when he needed her and that she never contacted him or asked him things about his life. Furthermore, she was not allowed to see anyone else. After a while, she had seen the not so pleasant sides of Antonio, and she had realised that he was a psychopath, and the sweet things he said while he was in the mood was just empty talk. Still, she followed the contract instead of walking away or second-guessing his motives as this suited her. She could live without love as she had never experienced it, and it was better to have lots of money and occasional steaming hot sex than to live with some average annoying man.

But receiving Antonio's text was very unsettling. Jessica had not heard from him in six weeks, and she had wondered where he might be. She knew the rules of their relationship, but it had been challenging for her not to contact him to find out his whereabouts. Now when Jessica was supposed to meet Antonio, she was terrified. If Michael's claims were true, he might be coming to hurt her. Then again, Michael, the man who had visited her was an alcoholic, and Jessica could tell that he had severe withdrawal symptoms. He simply didn't seem trustworthy, and she would not betray Antonio, who had done so much for her, just because of some disgusting old alcoholic. She put on his favourite clothes opened a box of high-quality chocolate and then lay in bed waiting for him to sneak up on her. Doing this was his favourite game, and gosh she wanted to play with him tonight!

Chapter 31 From the Killers Point of View

The Killer was overjoyed when he finally managed to hack and disable the security cameras in the building where Jessica Hall lived. Since he did not have the code for the system, this had proven to be a difficult task, but he had managed to nail it with a computer virus that made security cameras overwrite their current view with a later recording 30 minutes later.

The Killer was a bit disappointed that there was no security camera in Jessica's apartment. He had thirty minutes to kill before it was time to strike and he would love to watch her last thirty minutes alive. He was considering talking with her before he killed her. Would that be difficult? He had chosen to not say anything to Miranda DiMaestro, but it had hurt him a bit that she never knew why he killed her. Then again, since the Killer did not believe in life after death what use would his victims have for that knowledge? Besides, there was another reason to kill Jessica quickly; if she realised that he was going to kill her, she would probably scream her lungs out which would alert the entire neighbourhood of his presence.

The Killer felt good about killing Jessica Hall. He had experienced mixed feelings when killing Miranda DiMaestro as she had seemed to be a more naïve woman who believed in the good sides of her husband. When it came to Jessica Hall, the Killer perceived her as a source of corruption and evil. She was not the greatest of sinners, but she was the kind of vice that nurtured the other ones. As long as there were women like her who served as the prize for evil deeds the spirit of evil would never die. Would men still turn to darkness and do horrendous crimes if this would lead to never feeling a woman's touch again? Most of them would not! But if there were women like Jessica Hall, who glorified evil and corruption through gladly the accepting the spoils without asking questions, evil deeds would always appeal to a lot of people. She would die tonight as a symbol for the damage her egoistical behaviour was creating in the world!

The Killer started the engines of his car and drove to the garage of the building block. He used a swipe key to get in and then parked the car close to the elevator in the building. He took the package he had prepared for Jessica and holstered his silenced revolver under his coat. The lift would be the critical part he thought. If someone saw him in the elevator on the way up, he would just have to cancel his plan for tonight and proceed another night. If someone saw him when he was going down on the other hand...

The thought made him shiver, but since he chose to strike at 1 AM on a Monday night, he hoped that he wouldn't meet anyone in the elevator. He entered the elevator, and he realised his plan was working. He pressed "27" and took the lift up. The hallway of the compound was quiet and empty. He unlocked the door to Jessica's apartment. He snuck in and moved like a shadow. When he came into her room, he could hear Jessica Hall say.

- Oh, Antonio so you finally came, please come and warm me up.
The winter has been so cold and lonely without you

When the killer heard Jessica Hall's voice, he decided to change his plan and tell her everything before she died. He flicked the switch on the lights in the room, and before she could make a sound, he shot her twice in the throat ruining her vocal cords and her ability to fight him. She would be unconscious shortly, but the killer decided to tell the petrified Jessica Hall his story anyways. When he finished talking, he said:

- On the bright side; you will die rich at least."

He then put the package on top of her chest put her arms around the container and shot her in the head with one bullet, while placing the three remaining bullets in her chest. He left the apartment door open so she would be found soon and left the apartment complex undetected. When driving away from the compound, he realised that the time was 1.32 AM. He had fucked up; he certainly hoped that the cameras had not filmed him.

Chapter 32 Michael Fuller Decides to Confront Jessica Hall

It was 2AM, and the whiskey bar was closing. In his drunken mindset, Michael Fuller felt that everyone was plotting against him. He could understand why the mafia was against him, as he had been incorruptible in his quest to find the truth and bring justice to the murder victims. But why had his former colleagues turned their back on him, and who was the mastermind behind setting him up? The questions were many, but Michael knew what he needed to do; he needed to find Antonio DiMaestro.

Michael Fuller always followed his intuition until the end. He knew that his disinterest in listening to the opinions of others made him unpopular among his colleagues; but why would he change? Why would the officer with the best track record in the history of Sydney give in to mediocrity? The talk about him being arrogant and never listening was incorrect, as he sometimes asked for input before he had the clear picture of a case

Now Michael's intuition told him that he should confront Jessica Hall as she was the key to finding Antonio DiMaestro. Michael was certain that Jessica was withholding information, but he was unable to figure out what she was hiding from him. He thanked God that he chose to drink at the pub next to Jessica's apartment as he was in no condition to drive. As Michael approached the elevator to Jessica's apartment, he met two officers from the local district. He knew that he had met them before, but there was a lot of police officers in Sydney so he could not place them. Due to his fame within the force, they recognised him and started talking.

Officer Mason:

- Hi, Michael. Are you having a good night? What are you up to?

Michael Fuller

- Yeah, I can't complain. It has been a good night, and now I am meeting up with a friend.

Officer Johnson:

- Okay. Well, have fun. I heard you quit the force? May I ask why?

Michael Fuller:

- Well, I realised that I was rich, and I felt like doing something else. After 20 years with the police, I want to do something else! What are you doing in this apartment building?

Officer Mason:

- An old woman heard suspicious noises from a neighbouring apartment, and she decided to check what was going on. The door was open, but no one answered when she shouted. She did not want to go in there herself, so she called the police to establish contact.

Officer Johnson:

- Whining oldies if you ask me.

Michael Fuller:

- She has a point, but she should have walked in there herself. Someone might be dying in there from a heart attack right now, and what good is a police patrol to deal with illnesses?

Officer Mason:

- You are right Michael
- Well we better hurry then, this is our floor. See you, Detective.

Michael followed the police officers with his gaze as they walked down the corridor. They entered the apartment where he had met Jessica a few hours earlier. Michael realised that if something had happened to her, he would have a lot of explaining to do. He pressed the "ground" button on the elevator panel and quickly left the building.

Chapter 33 John Dean Arrives at the Crime Scene.

At 250AM John Dean arrived at the crime scene. He did not feel pleased being dragged up in the middle of the night., John did not feel very comfortable at all since his wife had given him a hard time explaining how he had acquired the $10 000 they needed to solve their debt crisis. He had assured her that the money was a loan from Michael Fuller who was wealthy and did not mind helping them out. But she had had several questions on this. Questions like: Why could he not show her the copy of the promissory? Why had he received the money in cash and not via bank transfer? Her suspicions were hard for him to bear since he doubted the course he had chosen when he decided to sell out his integrity as a police officer to Michael.

When John arrived, he was approached by Officer Mason.

- Good day, sir, the crime scene has been secured. How would you like to proceed?

John Dean:

- Well, I guess you guys are not specialised in crime scene forensics so I would like you to guard the apartment until my team arrives.

Officer Mason:

- Understood sir. Oh, and one more thing. There was a bizarre coincidence in the elevator on the way up here.

John Dean:

- Okay, tell me.

Officer Mason

- We met Michael Fuller who was meeting a friend in the building. He was blind drunk. Didn't he resign immediately due to health reasons?

John Dean:

- Well, I am not supposed to say anything, but his alcoholism WAS the health reason. Now if you excuse me.

John Dean entered the room where Jessica Hall was lying dead. The entire bed was soaked with blood which an indication that the heart of the victim had been pumping for quite some while before she finally passed away. This seemed strange to John, as he could count multiple bullet wounds on her savaged body where one of them was in the head. As John realised that he would get an explanation after the autopsy, and he searched her belongings for an ID card. He found one stating that she was born on the 26th of August 1993 and thus she was killed on her birthday. "Hell of a birthday," he thought, but then he saw something that was interesting; her name. "Jessica Hall, why does that name ring a bell?" John thought for a while and then he realised the uncomfortable connection

Chapter 34 "Rise and shine Sleeping Beauty."

James Locker woke up from his slumber from someone banging on his front door. Considering the break-in, the night before, his first reaction was fear, and he reached for his gun which he kept in his bedside drawer. Why had he turned down Barry Itch's offer regarding police protection? It seemed like a dumb choice considering the circumstances, he hadn't wanted to appear weak in front of his peers.

James was relieved when he heard Adam Smith's voice calling his name. He checked his nightstand watch. It showed 3.00 AM with an intense glowing light, almost like the time had some magical feeling to it? Hadn't he seen this exact time on the clock not too long ago? Then again, he knew that the human brain was programmed to see patterns, and if someone were looking too much for a pattern, they would see a pattern that did not exist. This trait was usually called paranoia, and James knew that he should try avoiding it as much as possible.

James put on his pants, holstered his gun and went to open the door. He saw Adam who looked puzzled.

Adam Smith:

- Finally! Rise and shine Sleeping Beauty!

James Locker:

- Hey, Adam. What's going on? Why are you knocking on my door in the middle of the night?

Adam Smith:

- That question is closely related to my question; why are you not answering your phone? We have been trying to reach you for 50 minutes.

James Locker:

- Really?

Adam Smith:

- Yeah really. And I have been knocking on your door for 10 minutes as well. I was even considering breaking in, to check you out, but then I remembered your *"please shoot me"* incident from this Saturday and decided not to.

James Locker:

- That night is blurry to me. What the fuck happened.

Adam Smith:

- Well, you were drunk, and you insisted that either Thomas should shoot you or you would shoot him. You thought that we were shooting blank bullets, but in reality, your body armour had a hole after that shot!

James Locker:

- Oh shit, I better stay off the piss! Where are we going?

Adam Smith

- To the Central Business District.

James Locker:

- I see, why was this case assigned to our team? We already have a case.

Adam Smith:

- Well, because the central command thinks this case relates to our other case.

James Locker:

- Got it. Oh well give me a second, and I'll be good to go.

Having said this James got dressed, and they commuted to the crime scene in Adam 's car as James felt too sick to drive. James considered the option to use some of the leftover cocaine from the weekend to clear his mind up, but he realised that once he followed that path, things would go downhill. James checked his phone, and as Adam had told him, there were a lot of missed calls. Why didn't he wake up from those calls? And even stranger, why did he stay asleep for ten minutes while Adam was banging on the door? Could it be the antidepressants he was using that put him in such deep sleep? James had needed them to regain his energy after the heavy partying during the weekend, but was it worth the side effects? He must have been sleeping for nine hours straight and yet he was exhausted. After this thought, James fell asleep and slept for the rest of the drive.

Chapter 35 James Locker Arrives at the Murder Scene

As the last members of the team James Locker and Adam Smith arrived at the crime scene. James was surprised that a very young single female could afford a place like that, as it was a luxurious two-bedroom unit in the CBD overlooking the Sydney Harbour. John Dean greeted them as they arrived:

- Hello, gentlemen, running a bit late, are we?

Adam Smith:

- Well someone had to wake Sleeping Beauty up, not the easiest of tasks.

James Locker:

- Well, I had some trouble sleeping, so I consumed a sleeping pill. But hey we are here now, so let's not waste any more time on snide remarks!

John Dean:

- Well, you better stay alert James. It's the second time you have been late to a crime scene in one week. Protocol states.

James Locker

- Well, the contract says a lot of things; for starters, that a subordinate should focus on his work and not the time management skills of his boss. I know I am late, and I don't need you to complain about it.

John Dean:

- Oh, I'm sorry. Understood sir!

James Locker

- So now, show me what you have and tell me what you know.

They walked into the bedroom where the corpse of Jessica Hall was laying. James felt a sense of shock when his gaze met her cold dead gaze. He knew this girl from somewhere he had met her before. But from where and when did James ever meet her? His extreme headache was killing him, and he could not focus. Suddenly, he felt very nauseous and went to the toilet to throw up.

Adam Smith approached Thomas Anderson.

- Gee, I wonder what's wrong with James, first he came late for work and then the concept of throwing up when seeing a corpse. He has been in this job for what? Eight years? He should be able to handle it by now, and by the way, this is a relatively clean crime scene.

Thomas Anderson:

- Valid point. A real waste of such a beautiful young woman. This is very strange, the second young and wealthy female gunshot victim a week.

- Considering the demographics of murder victims and how they are killed. This seems like a highly unlikely event.

Adam Smith:

- Yeah, it does not look like there was any struggle either, do you think it's the same killer?

Thomas Anderson:

- I prefer to speculate, but central command seems to think so, as they dispatched our team to the site although we already have a case.

- What troubles me was James reaction; I saw recognition in his eyes. He must have met this girl before.

Adam Smith:

- I find it troubling that you overanalyse people's eye movements. But let's say you are right, what's the problem?

- Oh, here he comes let's ask him.

Thomas Anderson

- Hey, James! Are you alright? Have not seen you vomit after witnessing a murder victim before. Was anything special with this one?

James Locker:

- I don't know. Her face seemed familiar, but I can't tell from where. What do you know about her?

Thomas Anderson:

- Her name was Jessica Hall, and she was 20 years old. She was initially from Tamworth, but after taking her High School Certificate, she moved to Sydney.

- Oh, and her taxed income and assets were meagre, so there is something fishy about her staying in an apartment like this.

James Locker:

- Oh, Tamworth. That makes sense my sister moved out there some years ago when she married Eric. I have visited her a few times since then. I must have seen this woman there somewhere.

After said this, James remembered where he had seen Jessica before. He had seen her in a school theatre play in Tamworth three years ago. She was a stunning beauty at the stage in that lousy play, and he had felt shame for feeling attracted to her. Partly because she was so much younger than him but also since he was engaged to Emily Luong at the time. He knew that he should not have felt any shame at the time since he did not act on his feelings. And biologically there was nothing strange about being attracted to 17 years old girl as she was a fully matured lady at the time. Hearing the voice of Adam awoken James from his thoughts.

Adam Smith:

- Look what I found! A couple of thousand dollars in cash, hidden among her underwear. I think this woman was an escort, the kind that is out of range for our sorry police salary range.

Samantha Robinson joined in on the conversation

- I would beg to differ. Most of the clothing in the wardrobes are very conservative and not very sexy. Why would an escort have that much traditional dresses?

Adam Smith:

- Hey, Sammy, remember that you are the only woman working in the unit, so don't expect any useful input on your latest fashion statements.

Samantha Robinson:

- Well from a man who has worked for five years and never received a raise I would not expect any beneficial input at all. What do you think about it, Thomas?

Thomas Anderson:

- I think your sense of fashion is excellent and you are by far the most attractive person in this room.

Samantha Robinson:

- Thank you, Thomas. It's a relief to me that you are not into necrophilia.

James Locker:

- Okay. Enough of this. I am heading to the office and will be co-ordinating our efforts from there. John, you will check the videos and surveillance systems of this building. I saw a key card panel when I got here so that one would register anyone entering or ex-iting the building. Thomas, can you check the computers and elec-tronic media for clues. The rest of you. Knock doors in the build-ing ask everyone, and I mean everyone if they have seen or noticed anything suspicious in the last few days.

- Oh, and I need a volunteer to go to Tamworth and question Jessica Hall's family and friends to find out if anyone knows why someone would want to have her killed.

Adam Smith:

- Okay, I'll go. This will give me a chance to see James' sister again. Yummy!

James Locker:

- Okay, but no inappropriate ideas, otherwise her husband will shove a pitchfork up your ass.

Adam Smith:

- Yippy! A freaky threesome with some creepy farmers! This can almost be better than the last weekend. See you in a couple of days.

James Locker:

- I am not even going to comment on that idiot.

After finishing up at the crime scene, James started walking towards the police station. He struggled to understand this case. It was highly uncommon that women were killed in this fashion. Most female murder victims were killed by jealous and impulsive partners or ex-partners. If it indeed was the same killer as with Miranda DiMaestro the killer certainly did not fit the typical profile. Antonio DiMaestro was still the primary suspect in the Miranda DiMaestro case, but the man was nowhere to be found. Organised Crime had been looking for him for almost two months now since the Lopez case, and they had come up empty-handed. With suspected drug barons the problem was not usually finding them but connecting them to the crime so why and where was Antonio DiMaestro hiding?

James Locker felt that his headache was preventing him from thinking clearly and decided to have a nap at his office as soon as he got there. While James felt ashamed sleeping at work, he was not useful to anyone with a headache this severe.

Chapter 36 Trouble with the Bitch

James Locker was sleeping a lengthy dreamless sleep when he woke up by a twitch. Someone was knocking on his office door. He checked his wristwatch which indicated that the time was 8 AM and thus he had been sleeping four hours straight since he entered his room.

James opened the door and faced Barry Itch. James Locker's first feeling was annoyance. The meeting with the BITCH was supposed to be eight hours after each new murder case, and yet here he was less than five hours after James had left the crime scene. From Barry Itch's body language James Locker understood that this was not going to be a pleasant meeting.

Barry Itch:

- How are the cases going? You won't catch many criminals sitting here, rolling your thumbs.

James Locker:

- Um, that is correct sir, but someone must coordinate the team. I reckoned that since we are working on two cases simultaneously, we needed to divide our resources, and I need to organise everyone. Why are we working on two different cases and how do we know that the cases are connected?

Barry Itch:

- Well to answer your question. The reason you got assigned this second case is that high command is convinced we are looking for a serial killer since it's very uncommon for young women to be killed this way.

- I am here to question your reasons for being in your office. That is weak leadership, and since no-one is working on the DiMae-stro case during the night, you don't need to be here, when you are much more useful on site.

James Locker:

- Understood. I am still very new to the leadership and responsibility aspect of police work. Michael Fuller was a great detective, but he was not the kind of person that made other individuals grow.

Barry Itch:

- I know how Michael Fuller was. Although I did not agree with his leadership principles, he achieved excellent results, better results than anyone else.

- Now it's time to step up a level James. I want my eight-hour report in two hours!

After Barry Itch had left the office, James felt the panic and the shame take his grip on him. Summarising eight hours work in two hours was not an easy task even though it was doable as the initial crime scene report was not an extensive report.

James could not understand what made him this tired all the time? After all, he had taken sleeping pills every night the last week early on to get a good night's sleep. Most of the nights he slept like a baby and some of the nights he woke up around 3AM. But even those nights he would objectively get enough sleep if he went to bed at 8 PM? Maybe it was the performance anxiety that drove him crazy, after all leading a crime unit had been his dream ever since he joined the force and now it could slip between his fingers if he did not improve his performance.

James Locker realised that if it were performance anxiety that weighed him down, the best option would be to not think about it all, but instead carry on performing the duties he performed as Police Inspector under Michael Fuller.

James Locker took a deep breath and reassured himself that this day would be a day to shine. Feeling this way, he made the necessary phone calls to acquire the information needed for compiling the eight-hour report.

Chapter 37 Lunchtime chat between Thomas Anderson and Adam Smith

After many hours of dedicated work, the dynamic duo Thomas Anderson and Adam Smith decided to go for lunch. Since they hadn't eaten since the day before they decided to go for a cheap Asian buffet. After satisfying their worst hunger, they began talking.

Thomas Anderson:

- You look extremely tired Adam. You look like you have not slept in days. How do I know that you are not the one who killed Jessica Hall? It would explain the bags under your eyes...

Adam Smith:

- Now I feel very insulted! I would never kill such beauty. Such a waste for the sake of mankind. I would rather fuck her dry.

Thomas Anderson:

- Well, a girl like that would not even consider fucking you. You fat fuck. That would be your motive.

Adam Smith:

- Well true as that may be, there was still no sign of sexual violence. Why would I kill someone for getting rejected and fuck her afterwards?!

- Oh, this sounds wrong to me, I am not into necrophilia. I fucked two women that were alive and kicking this weekend, and one of them last night.

- You, on the other hand, seem to get nothing. Do you have any confessions to make Thomas? I am sure James would appreciate, if you gave his career a boost by turning yourself in.

Thomas Anderson

- I've told you several times already. I made passionate love with a remarkable woman last Friday.

Adam Smith:

- Picture or it did not happen!?

Thomas Anderson:

- Goddammit. I am not going to tell you who it is until I know where it's going!

Adam Smith:

- I see. "I respect that" Anyway here is the picture of the psychologist and me.

Thomas Anderson:

- What the fuck? A picture of a hand, a dick, and a pussy. What the hell is this?

Adam Smith:

- I would call it proof. As you can see it's my lower arm with my watch on it and my penis; and as you can guess it's the pussy of my date.

Thomas Anderson:

- I can't understand why I am always hanging out with you. Where is the picture of her face?

Adam Smith:

- Why would I have a picture of her face? What would that prove?

Thomas Anderson sighed loudly and then commenced the conversation

- About proof. Did you see the test results from the blood on James' mirror?

Adam Smith:

- Yep, I saw it. A great relief. It was the same DNA as one of the two male samples in the DiMaestro mansion. At first, I thought it might have something to do with the way we handled the Vasquez cartel last weekend,

Thomas Anderson:

- You might call me crazy, but what if James Locker has finally snapped and is the killer? I mean why would the killer otherwise come by James' house paint the bathroom with his blood but otherwise do nothing?

Adam Smith:

- Well, I am buying tickets for the lottery dreaming about the jackpot even though the chance is 1 in 72 million. So, I am not going to call you crazy...

- But your hypothesis seems highly unlikely and how would you verify it? By going to the BITCH and telling him about your insane theory and request to have James DNA tested? It's more likely to get you fired than solving the case.

Thomas Anderson:

- Hmm...

- I know a better way.

- Considering the amount of blood, we found in the bathroom, whoever it belongs to must have a big cut on his body. So, if James indeed is the killer, he would have a big cut somewhere. The easiest way to find out would be to make him come along to the gym, and that way check out his body in the sauna afterwards.

Adam Smith:

- Let's do it. If nothing else to beat that lazy bastard; I have not seen him at the gym for ages!

Thomas Anderson:

- Great, I figure out some great reason to have him tag along. Let's head to work now; I have some things to prepare for the 3PM meeting.

Adam Smith:

- Great, make sure to tell me what you find; I am heading to the airport for my flight to Tamworth now.

- It will be great. Hitting on some outback women and "solving" the case.

Thomas Anderson:

- "I am sure you will succeed."

Having finished their meal and their conversation Thomas headed back to the station to complete his tasks for the 3 PM meeting, while Adam headed for the airport.

Chapter 38 A Dilemma for James Locker

In two stressful hours, James Locker managed to compile a satisfactory eight hours report to send to Barry Itch and the high command. He was not satisfied with the result as it had the characteristics of something done in a hurry. But, the most critical task at hand was to get the report out; so, the continued police work had a direction that was imperative for the first 24 hours of a case. After all the reports would be rewritten and audited several times before going up to court.

James checked his E-mail and found a new piece of evidence: the blood painted on the mirror in James' house matched one of the DNA samples found at the DiMaestro mansion. The relief was that he was just looking for one man. If the one threatening him had been another person, he would need to find two separate perpetrators, which would divide his attention. The dilemma was to find this man. Theoretically, the killer could be someone from the Vasquez cartel who wanted to send him a message because of his behaviour against them the last weekend.

When thinking about his behaviour the weekend that passed, James was angry with himself. Why had he put himself in this situation? He was so close to obtaining his career goal at the age of 32, and now that his feelings for Emily Luong finally were fading, he knew that he would have excellent prospects of finding a new love. Still, he was risking all of this for a crazy night out; and he could not understand why?

James thought about a second scenario for why the killer had broken into his home; that there was a connection between him and the murders. This scenario made him uncomfortable, and James could not understand how he was connected to any of this. He had never met Miranda DiMaestro before, and as for Jessica Hall he had seen her once before but never spoken to her. As for the principal suspect Antonio DiMaestro, James knew that this man had been of interest for another murder investigation a while ago, but James was on sick leave at that time and had not participated in that investigation.

Finally brushing these thoughts aside, James prepared himself for the 3 PM staff meeting.

Chapter 39 The 27th August Team Meeting

The time had come for another staff meeting, and as usual, the first session after a new case was crucial as everyone needed a general idea of where the case was going. Every member of the group was present except Adam Smith who was on the flight to Tamworth where he was supposed to find out if Jessica Hall had any noteworthy enemies from the past. With everyone present, James Locker decided to start the meeting.

James Locker:

- Good afternoon everyone, thank you for coming.

- After discussion with Barry and the High Command, we have decided to focus on the theory that this murder and the murder of Miranda DiMaestro are connected.

- Please report your finding, let's start with you, John.

John Dean had feared for the staff meeting, but he managed to keep his composure. John knew he was in big trouble if someone found out the extent to which he had been sabotaging the investigation. John had handed Michael Fuller sensitive information. Furthermore, he had not shared his well-founded suspicions against Michael and finally he had stolen money from the crime scene. Since it was too late coming out clean, he had to continue on the chosen path, and the corruption manifested in his body by making him feel very nauseous. John realised he had been stuck in his thoughts for too long when James spoke to him again:

- John? Are you okay? Say something.

John Dean:

- Sorry, sir. Just feeling exhausted with all this stress and my daughter being sick and all.

- Anyway, I have not found out much. We believe the murder must have taken place between 1230 and 2 am. Most likely closer to the latter as the neighbours heard noises around 130 and that was the reason the police got arrived at the crime scene

- But here is the catch. There are security cameras in the building, and one camera is overlooking the corridor on level 27 where Jessica Hall's apartment is located. But no-one is seen entering or leaving Jessica's apartment during this period.

James Locker:

- I see. Are there alternative ways of getting to the apartment?

John Dean:

- Not from the outside. There is a fire ladder down the corridor, but if the killer entered that way, he or she would still be visible on the surveillance tape. Theoretically one would be able to get into the apartment via the ventilation shaft, but that is a very long shot as that would be implying the suspect climbed from another level to reach her apartment undetected.

James Locker:

- It could also imply that the killer is one of her neighbours as they would have a much easier route to climb. It's an unlikely scenario but investigate it anyway.

- How do you know that the cameras were not turned off by the way? After all, that was the procedure of the DiMaestro murder.

John Dean:

- Well, that would create a black spot on the surveillance tape, but I did not see any. Besides the security officer for the building would be alerted if the cameras went down.

James Locker:

- Well, I guess you are right. Keep looking through the feeds and see if you can find any discrepancies. Oh, and have another chat with the security officer. He might have seen something.

- Moving on, Samantha what do you have to report?

Samantha Robinson:

- Well, two interesting things.

- I spent the day talking to Jessica's neighbours. No one had seen anything, but one of them had heard Jessica Hall argue with a drunk man a couple of hours earlier.

James Locker:

- This testimony is very compelling since Miranda DiMaestro also argued with a drunken man a few hours before her death. If this man is not Antonio DiMaestro, this could be another lead.

- Samantha, can you go back to the neighbours and ask how the conversation sounded? I believe there would be a different tone when you argue with a stranger compared to when you argue with someone you know.

Samantha Robinson:

- Sure, sounds like a plan boss.

James Locker:

- Great, what was the second point of interest?

Samantha Robinson:

- Well, the killer left a package at the crime scene, on top of Jessica Hall's corpse. We opened it and found an expensive necklace inside. I took it to a jeweller, and he estimated that it is worth at least $100,000. Considering how expensive the necklace is, I reckon we should be able to trace whoever ordered it as there are only a few jewel shops that deal in this price range.

James Locker:

- Samantha. You are a dream to have as an employee. Take a picture of the piece and leave the original in an evidence locker. I am sure you know what jewel shops to visit.

- Moving on to Thomas, what do you have to report?

Thomas Anderson:

- Well, quite a few things:

- The building manager indicated that Antonio DiMaestro owns Jessica Hall's apartment. A text message on Jessica's mobile phone shows that she was expecting Antonio to come, the night she was killed. Furthermore, I have checked the electronic swipe key log to the building. Antonio entered the building via the garage at 0101am and left the building at 0129am. I have requested the location of Antonio's phone from the telephone company, but they are yet to get back to me.

James Locker:

- Damn that we don't have the same resources and rights as the Federal Police. Then we could just trace his phone and find him in no time!

- No matter, I am sure the fucking snake was there, but where is he now? We need to find him fast.

Thomas Anderson:

- We don't know James; Antonio is a ghost, no-one has seen him for over a month.

Samantha Robinson:

- Sorry to interrupt, but I don't think Antonio is the murderer. If he was the killer why would he make all this effort to avoid the security cameras, and yet walk in using his own swipe key, and with his mobile phone turned on?

James Locker:

- Well, you do have a point, but he is still our only clue unless we find the mysterious drunken man.

- Anyway, this concludes our meeting. Keep working on your assigned tasks. I will contact the federal police to see if we can get a permanent trace on Antonio DiMaestro's and his associates' mobile phones.

- Now let's wrap this off and get back to work.

Chapter 40 Barry Itch Feels Frustrated

Barry Itch put down the eight-hour report he received from James Locker and felt the frustration overwhelm him. It was not the findings per se that disturbed him but the presentation. To Barry, a perfect presentation was everything, and he expected clean results every time. He had been frustrated with Michael Fuller's sloppy works for ages, and he had hoped for improvement now that he finally got rid of Michael but instead the reports he received from James, was even worse. It was like the report was written by someone fresh off the ship and the poor writing was unacceptable for Barry

Barry reflected over Michael and wondered if he had done the right thing when he let Michael off the hook for the cocaine charges. Barry had been very lenient to Michael and settled for his resignation instead of taking him to court. Barry hoped that Michael Fuller would not do anything stupid now that he had received this favour. Barry had had some thoughts about whether it was morally correct to let Michael go, but morality was less critical than perfection, and at least the reputation of the department remained unsullied.

Barry was thinking about his past relationship with Michael. It had been a mostly negative relationship. Barry Itch had been dissatisfied that Michael would not adapt to his professional standard, often delivering sloppy reports or showing up with a hangover. Barry had on several occasions reassigned the worst employees from the other murder investigation teams to undermine Michael's performance so he could get rid of him. But Michael had just kept performing despite having the far worst team members of all the groups. Barry Itch was impressed by Michael's performance despite his other objections.

Barry studied on James's report again. Barry decided to go easy on him for now. James Locker was not a star like Michael Fuller and with incompetent misfits like Adam Smith, Thomas Anderson, John Dean, Vinnie Chung and Oscar Lee in his team, it was unrealistic to expect excellent results from

James. Besides Barry understood why he was known as the BITCH to his subordinates and he did not want to grow that myth more than necessary!

Chapter 41 Muscle Flashing in the Sauna.

The time was 8 PM, and James Locker and Thomas Anderson had just finished a boxing class at the gym, and they were now sitting in the sauna. James had been a bit hesitant about going to the gym since he had not worked out for a long time. Thomas had convinced him with the motivation that he was seeing his mysterious date later the same night and wanted to look pumped up for the occasion. Thomas was thinking about his conversation with Adam and his hypothesis that James might be the one who wrote on his own bathroom mirror with blood. Thomas needed a way to see all of James's body to figure out if he had any significant wounds. Thomas decided to start off with some idle chatter:

- Look how fit I look today; I hope it will be good enough for my date...

James Locker:

- Feeling a bit needy today, are you?

- Your body is toned. I am sure that if you fail, it will because of something else.

Thomas Anderson:

- Well... Thank you, I guess.

James Locker:

- Yeah. Why do you keep it a secret by the way? There is only one woman it can be, Samantha Robinson. A good catch if you ask me

Thomas Anderson:

- Hmm, why would you think it's Samantha that I'm seeing?

James Locker:

- Well, it's quite easy. You see, I know you well enough to realise it must be someone I know; otherwise, you would just say the name and show a picture.

- Secondly, I know you have a crush on her.

- Thirdly, I know you are picky and the other single women I know... Well, they are not that attractive.

Thomas Anderson:

- Okay then! You are right. I am seeing Samantha.

- I guess your deductive skills is why you got promoted in the first place...

- But please don't tell other people. I want to tell them myself when the time is right.

James Locker:

- No worries mate. Your secret is safe with me.

- Besides, it will be a lot of fun seeing how frustrated Adam will get before he figures out who you are seeing. Sure, he will claim not to care, but his inquisitiveness will keep him awake at night.

Thomas Anderson:

- Great you should get on the horse as well! Show me your muscles big fella.

James Locker:

- Okay. You mean like this.

James flexed his arms chest and core. He was still in decent shape although he had lost a lot of fitness in the last year. James was by no means a wreck, but his body no longer gave him an advantage on the dating scene either.

Thomas Anderson:

- That's a great body man; a lot of people would crash a lot from such a long absence of training. Now flex your legs, back, and bum.

James Locker:

- Okay... That seems a bit strange...

Thomas Anderson:

- Don't worry mate. See it as a great opportunity to get input and feedback. I am as good as a personal trainer but a lot cheaper.

James Locker:

- Okay, I guess it can't hurt to show it all off. Well, don't expect to see my erected penis though I am not into that kind of stuff.

Thomas Anderson:

- I am happy to hear that. Well looks good, A month of hard training and we'll have you back on the dating scene again!

James Locker:

- Thanks. Yeah, it would be a good idea, the "dating" in Asia felt very fake. Maybe some more exercise and training can help me sleep as well

Thomas Anderson:

- Great.

They sat silently enjoying the heat of the steam sauna cleaning the pores of their bodies. Thomas noticed that James looked like he was in deep thoughts and decided to find out what was on his friend's mind.

Thomas Anderson:

- Hey, James, you seem like you are in serious reflections, what are you reflecting over?

James Locker:

- Yeah, it's a thing that has been bothering me for a while.
- Thomas, can I ask you something?

Thomas Anderson:

- Yeah sure mate, what's on your mind?

James Locker:

- How do you feel when you stand in front of a mirror?

Thomas Anderson:

- Oh, I don't think very much at all. I am happy with my looks.
- What about you?

James Locker:

- Oh, I have thought about it for a while. Sometimes mirrors make me uncomfortable. It's like an obsession, a splinter of my mind and the world feels unreal. It's like I am watching my reflection, but I can see another person. And sometimes when our eyes meet, I can see into his soul. And I can feel it's very dark and ugly.

Thomas Anderson:

- Okay, James, I am not sure what to say about that. I guess it's natural to be dissatisfied with yourself if you have been alone for a long time.

- But see it this way; you are above the 50 per cent mark compared to the general population. So, your looks are not an issue for you; it's an asset.

- You are hotter than Adam, and he gets laid all the time. Oh, and so did you, so you are worrying for nothing.

- You also have a great personality; otherwise, I would not want to hang out with you. So, don't worry, the right one will come your way.

James was not satisfied with the answer he got from Thomas as his looks were not the issue to him. Then again it was hard for him to describe the problem, as he was not able to put the finger on it himself. James decided to absorb the positive things Thomas had said and quit the negative thought patterns. Why think about questions without an answer? Asking questions that could not be explained only lead man to insanity or religion, which were two sides of the same coin. They finished their session, and James headed home while Thomas headed to Samantha's place.

Chapter 42 John Dean gives Michael Fuller a time frame

John Dean sat at the pub drinking and contemplating his options. He knew that his wife would not be happy as she perceived his frequent pub visits as an escape from sorting out their problems. In the past, it was, but for the last weeks, the pub visits were because he had involved himself with Michael Fuller. John knew that he was not in this for the truth or justice but merely because he had fallen for the temptation to take money from Michael. Now he had to keep supporting Michael even though he seriously doubted Michael's intentions and sanity.

Michael showed up thirty minutes late unshaven and wreaking of booze. John realised that it would be difficult making any sense with him, but he decided to try anyway. Since John had known Michael for a long time, he knew that he would have to keep a friendly but decisive approach if he wanted his message to be received.

John Dean:

- Hi Michael. Great that you could make it. Are you having a good night?

Michael Fuller:

- Yeah definitely, I was talking to a foxy lady down at my favourite waterhole, and then I realised I had to see you as well. Oh well, I got her number, and you are married, so I guess you won't be here all night?

John Dean:

- Well, it'd be nice if we could avoid it.
- I might as well be straight to the point; a problem has arisen...

Michael Fuller:

- Yeah, I have heard...
- The gold-digging bitch is dead.
- Will be hard to find Antonio now...

John Dean

- Well, that complication is the least of our problems. What is worse is that you were threatening her at 9 PM and then lingered in the area until 2 AM when you decided to go to Jessica's apartment apparently to pick another fight but left instead when you realised the shit had hit the fan.

- What do you have to say about that?

Michael Fuller:

- That you should stop monitoring my phone, you don't have the rights.

John Dean

- I am sure I don't have the right to hand you information from our investigation and covering up for you either. So now tell me the truth what were you doing there?

Michael Fuller:

- Okay, relax. You know that I told you that I followed up on the lead with Antonio DiMaestro's mistress?

- Well, that bitch Jessica Hall was his mistress. She even lived in a flat owned by him. And she must have seen him recently because why would he otherwise let her live there?

- But yeah, she got offended, and we argued but no threats involved.

- After that, I went to my favourite whiskey bar in the city. I drank a few too many, and I got angry...

- So, I decided to confront the bitch for real, but when I saw Mason & Johnson stepping off on the same floor walking towards the open apartment door of Jessica, I realised that something was wrong, so I panicked and went home.

John Dean:

- Well, there is a complication. Security cameras filmed you arguing/threatening her at 9 pm. The picture is too bright for me to blur it out this time, so I can't help you when Samantha or James decides to follow up on the lead...

- And once you become a suspect, they will most likely require a trace on your phone, and we are both in trouble!

Michael Fuller:

- God dammit can't you do anything?!

John Dean:

- Well, I can stall it as much as possible. Here is my plan. I'll lock down the video files with a biometric password. After that, I will get an urgent message saying that my daughter got an epileptic attack. Then I will become unreachable on the phone for a while.

- Should give you until Monday considering how bad things are running.

Michael Fuller:

- Great John. Appreciate it; you are such a great friend.

John Dean:

- Of course, Michael, that's who I am.

- A tip to get you in the right direction. The blood we found at James Locker's house matched one of the male DNA-s we found at the DiMaestro mansion.

- I have some more files for you to read through. Make sure to delete them as soon as you read them; it's not good for us if they are found on your computer.

Michael Fuller:

- Hmm, interesting thank you.

- Well, I hope my foxy lady friend waits for another night. Now that I have another lead, I'll better stay sober for a while.

After Michael left, John sat for a while thinking about if he made the right choice sharing his suspicions about James' supposed break-in. Chances were that Michael would do something even stupider than confronting the mistress of Antonio DiMaestro. And John was still unsure of Michael's innocence. The only indication that Michael wasn't the killer was that he was drunk at 9 PM and blind drunk at 2 AM according to Officer Mason and Johnson. To bypass the building security, the killer must have been sober an hour earlier. Then again, Michael was an alcoholic, and he was no doubt a genius so if anyone could pull off these murders while being drunk it would be Michael. John realised that he had to help Michael regardless of his innocence. If Michael went down, he would take John with him in the fall, and that scenario was not appealing at all...

Chapter 43 Bedside Talk between Samantha Robinson and Thomas Anderson.

Thomas Anderson lied next to Samantha Robinson and was stunned by the moment. Samantha was so beautiful, and he had dreamt about this time for so long. While Thomas, was satisfied last weekend it felt even better now, as this was the second time. Thomas felt that anyone could get lucky once but being with her for the second time was a seal of approval showing that they were heading in the right direction. But had he pleased her enough? Thomas felt like he didn't get Samantha all the way, and that feeling was discomforting. As if she could read his mind she started speaking:

- Don't worry Thomas you were surprisingly good for a man.

Thomas Anderson:

- For a man?

Samantha Robinson:

- Well, I guess you know that I am bisexual?

- It's mixed feelings because I am a lot more sexually attracted to women, but at the same time, I am a lot more drawn to the concept of a relationship with a man.

Thomas Anderson:

- Interesting. Never heard anyone say that before...

Samantha Robinson:

- Does it put you off?

Thomas Anderson:

- Nope, we are both adults, and I don't mind you having a sexual past. But what you are saying is fascinating to me. Please tell me more.

Samantha Robinson:

- Okay... Here is the deal

- My best friend Rebecca and I were best friends for a long time. Eventually, we could not resist each other any longer, and we became a couple. No-one has ever touched me like she did, and I have never felt those heights of sexual pleasure with anyone else.

- But we never loved each other; it's only friendship and an extreme attraction.

- Anyway, we realised that we both wanted children and families in our future and since we are both bisexual men are the way to go.

- Besides I have a heterosexual mindset, it's just that the attraction to her is so strong.

- And finally, I don't like the gay scene at all. I don't think people should categorise me to like transsexuals and specific music and fashion just because I am attracted to my best friend. That is just not me.

Thomas Anderson:

- Well, that's interesting. I never thought about it that way. I just assumed that all gay people liked the same things as if it was genetically predisposed.

Samantha Robinson:

- Yeah but anyway I want to take it slow with you, for now, Thomas because I like you, but Rebecca needs me as well. She has fallen for some jerk who calls himself JP. I have told her to dump him as he seems to be away for weeks at the time, but she claims he is a wonderful man despite this. And what do I know? But I like to be able to comfort her in any way, and that means sexually as well.

Thomas Anderson:

- Okay, I understand... Thank you for being so open with me. Hopefully, my jealousy will not come in the way.

The conversation kept Thomas sleepless for a long while. He was confused and did not know what to do. He had never felt this way for a woman before. Thomas had been in a few relationships in the past, but those had been short and based on convenience and not on strong emotions. Here he had the first woman in his life that it felt magical with and she was a lot more attracted to her friend than she was to him.

Thomas felt that they had an excellent connection and if he could only look past his ego and valour what they had and could have in the future it would be worth it? Thomas decided that he would pursue a relationship with Samantha and happy with his decision; he fell into a cozy sleep.

Chapter 44 The Killer Struggles with the Monster Within

The Killer heard his phone buzz. It was a text message from Rebecca. The message was *"Hey JP, Sorry but I cannot see you tonight. I am not feeling too well, and it would be a shame to spread my germs. See you some other night"* The killer put down his phone. He just knew she was lying. That bitch! He loved her, and yet she was fucking other guys. He could feel his vision pumping and the anger raging all over his body. She should pay. She should pay dearly! Then the Killer calmed down, and he saw things clearly again.

When reason prevailed, the Killer realised several things. For starters, he realised that he didn't know whether Rebecca was lying. Statistically, it was more probable that she was with another guy than her being sick. But even if she was with another man who was he to blame her? After all, he was always away and distant telling her lies about his life to fill the gaps. He would love to be honest with her, but he could not entrust her or anyone else with his secret.

The Killer realised that even when it came to faithfulness, he was failing Rebecca miserably. Since they first started seeing each other, he had sex with several other women. The Killer would not feel any guilt on this matter though as these actions had not been his choice. He would never choose to be with another woman than Rebecca; she was his everything, and yet he had been. This behaviour was because he was not free, and he hoped that he soon would win his freedom. What if his plan failed and wouldn't bring him freedom? Well, he would not live the rest of life as a prisoner so soon he would be free in one way or the other, even if it would be the freedom of death. The Killer assured himself however that his plan was fail-proof and continued with the next step off it.

He turned on his computer and hacked into the CSMI networks. He would like to know how their investigation was proceeding. It seemed like, everyone was oblivious to his existence. Their ignorance was both satisfying for the Killer as it proved that he had made the perfect crimes, but it was also uninspiring as it took the thrill out of the game he was playing. He opened the file on James Locker. That fool would need to pay the ultimate price, but he had to go last. The Killer wanted James to realise why he had to die, all of this would be pointless otherwise.

The killer made up his mind. He would leave the police another hint and then he would wait a few days before moving on his next target. This was as he felt sorry for his next target that didn't deserve to die. Because of this he would leave her a few more days to live and maybe fate would ensure her survival this way. The killer created a new entry in the police case file and wrote the following text *"Great work officers, I know everything you know now. Good luck with finding me! /the Killer"*. After doing this, the Killer felt thrilled and satisfied as he went to bed.

Chapter 45 Breakfast Talk Between Thomas Anderson and Samantha Robinson

After a night of passion Thomas and Samantha decided to have breakfast at Samantha's favourite café on the way to the police station. She noticed that he was in deep thoughts and felt very curious about what he was thinking about. As Samantha had an inquisitive personality and was not a big fan of beating around the bush, she decided to ask him:

- You seem to be in deep thoughts this morning? May I ask what's on your mind?

Thomas Anderson:

- Sure.

- It's about the case. I have thought about it a lot, and I feel a bit ashamed.

Samantha Robinson:

- Okay. Why is that?

Thomas Anderson:

- Well, this is the thing, the two best officers I have seen in my career, Michael and James both told me that the key to solving a murder case is to follow one's intuition when it points in a direction.

- In most of our cases, my intuition leads nowhere, I just do the tasks that I am assigned to and let the others solve the case.

- But yesterday my intuition pointed me in one direction, and it was incorrect, and now I feel ashamed of my thoughts.

Samantha Robinson:

- Well, you don't need to feel ashamed just because you were wrong. Trial and error is the most common scientific method, and most hypotheses turn out to be incorrect. But even being wrong can often lead to progress if one acknowledges being wrong.

Thomas Anderson:

- Well, I am not ashamed because I was wrong but because I suspected one of my closest friends. I suspected James to be involved as it makes no sense that the Killer broke into his place to leave a threatening message

- So, I reckoned this. James Locker has problems with his mental health, so I thought he might have hurt himself in a bout of insanity. This theory would explain all the blood and the message on his bathroom mirror.

- But to lose all that blood one must get a big wound and when I checked James' body in the sauna yesterday, I could not see any injuries at all.

Samantha Robinson:

- Well, I understand why you feel ashamed over suspecting one of your closest friends, but I must admit I find James' behaviour suspicious as well.

- But I also find this case very strange. The Killer seems to be a calculating genius who bypasses security systems and kills with precision while at the same time being psychotic madman painting a room with blood. A very tricky person to get a profile on I reckon.

Thomas Anderson:

- Seeing it that way, James' can't be the one we are looking for anyway. The Killer is obviously very sharp when it comes to computers while James would hardly be able to change the time on his mobile phone without help.

Samantha Robinson:

- Oh, I did not know of James' technological dyslexia. Is he so terrible?

Thomas Anderson:

- No, I was exaggerating of course, but he would not be able to outsmart me and the security systems at the crime scenes.

- Oh, anyway let's head to work, we are getting late.

Chapter 46 Michael Fuller Breaks into James Locker's House

M ichael sat in his car outside James 's house. He wondered why he had driven all this way and what he would hope to achieve through breaking in and examining the house. The way John had described the break-in at James' home, the break-in seemed very suspicious, and Michael wanted to check out the place himself. But then Michael considered the downsides of the plan. As his situation was right now all he had done, was visiting the murder victims looking for Antonio DiMaestro. He could explain this to a court if he became a suspect in the killings. But how would he justify breaking into James' house? It was apparently a felony as he had no business being there. Could John be trying to set him up and if so, what would his motive be? Michael could see no reason why John Dean would try to set him up, as he had everything to lose in that scenario.

Michael suddenly felt the alcohol withdrawal kick in with full force. He became extraordinarily restless and felt how his mind was all over the place. Since he realised that he would not be able to make a rational decision in his current situation, he decided to go with his gut feeling. His gut feeling was excellent and what had made him a very successful detective. Now his gut feeling told him that answers were to be found inside James' house.

Michael went in through picking the lock of the back door of the building. Although Michael wasn't an expert at lockpicking, it was easy to pick the lock, and Michael was amazed that James had taken no means to tighten security.

Michael went in and walked towards the bathroom. He could tell that the bathroom was thoroughly investigated as it was a lot cleaner than the rest of the house. This was a disappointment to Michael as it was a lot harder for him to get an intuitive feeling for a room once someone else has worked through it. Michael's intuition was the reason he always wanted to be the first on a crime scene, to see the crime scene in its rawest form. Seeing pictures or reconstructed scenarios did not have the same effect on his mind. Michael Fuller went back to the lounge room of the house. This room had also been swept for evidence but as there was no indication that whoever broke in also visited the lounge room. Michael found this clue interesting. Why had the intruder gone through the backdoor straight the bathroom to leave a message without even checking the other rooms? As the intruder most likely was the Killer this was an armed and very dangerous man; judging from all the blood in the bathroom also borderline psychotic. Why was a man like this afraid to check out all the rooms and why didn't he kill James as he did with Jessica Hall and Miranda DiMaestro? Michael walked towards the hall again. He tried opening the door to the basement, -but it was locked. Michael remembered this from the report from the break-in had read earlier during the day. *"James Locker told us he could not find the key, but the basement would not be relevant to the investigation as he had not been down there for ages."* Michael saw something very naïve in this formulation. For all, they know the basement might be the solution, and Michael was curious about WHY they were unable to find the key. After all, there was a chance that whoever broke in went down to the basement and then brought the key with him by mistake. If that were the case, the basement would be the room where Michael's could find important new clues.

Michael picked up his lockpick set and was just about to start picking the basement door lock when he heard a voice and footsteps outside heading towards the backdoor. It sounded like a discussion, but he could only hear one of the voices possible due to the conversation being over the phone. Michael did not recognise the voice, but he realised that whoever it was, it would not be a good idea for him to be there in case the person entered the building. Michael was unarmed and if the person he heard talking were the Killer his life would be in danger. It could also be a neighbour or someone from a security company, and then he would be in trouble as he had no business being in James' house. Michael moved as quickly and silently as he could and exited the building via the bedroom window. He then got into his car and drove away, knowing that he had been very close to a very problematic situation. While driving home, he got stuck on a detail from the conversation he overheard *"Hi Rebecca! It is JP speaking. How are you today?"* Rebecca was the name of his daughter. It was also a common name, but still, he could not get the connection out his mind. Who the hell was this guy JP, what was he doing outside James' house and what did he want with Michael's daughter? It blackened for Michael's eyes for a few seconds, and once he got back to his senses, he was driving off the road heading towards a tree. He braked as hard as he could, but it was not enough to avoid the collision. The car crashed into the tree, and Michael was knocked unconscious in the accident.

Chapter 47 Phone Call Between the Killer and Rebecca

The Killer was sitting at home full of anticipation. He had spoken to Rebecca a few hours earlier, and tonight they were catching up. He had swallowed his disappointment from the night before, and he could feel the butterflies tingling in his stomach. This love was way better than any drug he had ever tried, and he had tried them all. He saw a mental picture of Rebecca's smile and knew that if his plan succeeded, he would be able to see it on a much more regular basis. His daydreaming was interrupted by a phone call. It was Rebecca on the other line.

Rebecca:

- Hey, JP. I am so sorry I'll have to cancel our date tonight as well. My dad just crashed his car and got a severe concussion. I'll have to go and visit him at the hospital.

The Killer

- Oh god. That's terrible, how and where did this happen?

Rebecca:

- I don't know how, but I suspect it has to do with my father's alcoholism. Damn him I've told him many times to never drive while drunk! He is a police officer goddammit he should know better!

- Oh, sorry for getting that angry, it's not appropriate I guess

The Killer:

- That's alright. You have told me enough about how absent and uninterested he was during your upbringing, so I understand your anger towards him. What hospital is he at?

Rebecca:

- He is at Auburn Hospital; he crashed against a tree at Olympic Park. I am heading there now.

The Killer:

- Okay. I am close to that location. I can drive you home after your hospital visit. It can be tough for you getting back home with public transport after such a severe event.

Rebecca:

- Thank you, JP. That's very thoughtful of you. But it will probably take some time before I am done, you don't mind waiting there?

The Killer:

- Don't worry about it. I'll just stay at the pub watching a game. And for your safety, I'll drink soft drinks tonight.

Rebecca:

- Thanks. You are the best. I'll call you later then.

After hanging up, the Killer felt confused and disappointed. Disappointed that his excellent evening plans with Rebecca were ruined for something as depressing as driving her home from the hospital and comforting her in case her father's concussion had left any permanent damage. No-one had forced him to give her this offer, but it was the right thing to do. Partly because he believed that this was something a regular guy would do but also since it was a way for him to find out if she was honest with him or not. After all, she was highly unlikely to go on a date with some guy at a hospital cafeteria, so if he picked her up at the hospital, she must be going there to see someone who got suddenly injured. In that case, it seemed likely that the injured one was her dad. So, the Killer felt that he had picked the right course of action for the evening, given the sad circumstances.

But the killer also felt confused. He knew that Rebecca's dad was Michael. But what had he done in the Olympic Park area of the city? That would be at least one-hour drive from Michael's house in Palm Beach, and no-one is going on such a long ride without reason. The Killer suddenly felt very frustrated that Michael was not behind bars. He really should be in jail considering the cocaine and everything. Michael was a loose cannon, he was unpredictable, and it was impossible to know what he knew since he was not filing anything. On the other hand, Michael added some valuable tension to the game, so his existence was welcome in that sense.

The Killer was dying to know why Michael Fuller was in the neighbourhood today. Both James and Adam were living close to Olympic Park, but it seemed highly unlikely that Michael would have contact with any of them. Unless... Michael was investigating the nightly visit, James received on Sunday night and decided to investigate it himself. If so, Michael was signing his own arrest warrant, and the plan was working even better than the Killer had ever imagined that it would. There could be a complication, however; if Michael saw him outside James' house earlier during the day. The Killer decided that this was not a real problem as Michael would have a harder time explaining what he was doing out there than he would.

Chapter 48 Rebecca visits Michael Fuller at the hospital

Michael Fuller woke up a few hours later in the intensive care unit of Auburn Hospital. The first thing he saw was Rebecca who was holding his hand. Michael had a severe headache, and he could not remember what had happened. Michael realised that he must have hit his head badly in some way; But how? Michael realised he would get to know soon enough, so he opened his eyes again and started talking:

- Hi, Rebecca, it's so good to see you. Where am I, and what happened to me?

Rebecca Bell:

- Well, I am listed as your emergency contact...

- You are at Auburn Hospital you had a rough car accident, crashing your car into a tree at Olympic Park.

Michael Fuller:

- Oh yeah, I was following up a lead out there, can't remember which now.

Rebecca Bell:

- Following up on a lead? Samantha told me you resigned over a week ago stating health reasons. Everyone at the police station thinks that management paid you a redundancy package to get rid of you due to your alcohol problems.

Michael fought the urge to tell Rebecca about how someone had set him up by placing cocaine in his house. After all, the last thing he wanted to do was to involve Rebecca in his troubles. He loved her although it felt like she disowned him by changing to her mother's maiden name as soon as she turned 18. Telling her the truth about his dismissal wouldn't be a good thing. Either she would see him as delusional, and their relationship would take a turn for the worse or she would believe him, and that might put her life in danger.

Michael felt that he was up against a powerful adversary and that he was lucky to not be in custody. Michael decided to admit his alcoholism and withhold the actual reason for him leaving the police force.

Michael Fuller:

- Yes, you are right. My alcoholism was in the way of my career, but it's still a shame what happened because I was always the best detective at the department. Also, my job was the only thing that kept my alcoholism at bay.

Rebecca Bell

- Well, it's a shame you valued your job that much. Both I and mum needed you at home you know. But no point lingering in the past, I will try to forgive you someday.

Michael Fuller:

- Thank you. It's a shame that you don't want to join me on my upcoming trip to Scotland; it would be an excellent opportunity for us to catch up and get to know each other better.

Rebecca Bell:

- Well. This event with you in the hospital has made me doubt that decision. Maybe I should go away on a trip with you to get to know you better. I mean you could have died today, and life is too short to carry a grudge...

Michael Fuller:

- Let's hope you still feel this way when I get better, so something good comes out of this mess.

- I am feeling exhausted now; can you get me a nurse so I can get some sedatives?

Rebecca Bell:

- Yeah sure. Please get better. I'll see you soon.

As Rebecca left Michael started thinking about what she had said about him always putting work first and neglecting his family. His dedication to his work was like a curse, and although he had had the best intentions, it had all ended up in misery.

Michael had dedicated his life to fighting evil and crime, but now when his career was most likely over, he doubted that he had made any difference. It seemed clear to him now that the opposing force to evil was not vindictiveness and duty but love to the people who meant the most to him. In his successful crusade against corruption, he had failed to achieve what mattered the most, making the people closest to him feel loved and happy. Because of this, his life was a failure despite his successful career. Now that his career had gone down the drain, he could make a choice. Either he could choose to desperately try to restore his career, or he could focus all his energy and will on making people around him feel appreciated and happy.

Michael decided to go for the latter. It would feel strange during the adaptation period, but it was the only way for him to ever find peace and happiness. Happy with his decision Michael fell into a blissful morphine-based mindset before falling asleep.

Chapter 49 Adam Smith Meets Janelle Wynyard in Tamworth

Adam yawned. His day up in Tamworth had neither been exciting nor given anything valuable to the investigation. His tactic for the day had been to announce the murder of Jessica Hall in the local radio station and that everyone that could leave any useful information was welcome to come to the local pub/diner to share this information with him. The problem was that Tamworth was such as small and uneventful town, so a broadcast like this just made everyone come by and hand in useless statements just for the thrill of meeting one of the big city policemen. Adam hated that he would need to transcribe and file all these useless statements for the case file.

During the day, Adam got a clearer picture of how Jessica Hall was. He had received a few old pictures where she looked considerably better than she had done dead in her apartment. She was hot, and Adam felt that her death had been a waste.

For a while, Adam Smith fantasised about asking for a trip to Colombia to so he could investigate the life of Miranda DiMaestro in search for clues as well. This trip would be awesome; he would do shitloads of cocaine and hit on every hot South American woman passing by! The problem was that the high command would never approve of the time and travel expenses that such a venture would consume and besides Adam could not speak Spanish.

Adam kept philosophising about life and different trades one could pick and how the occupation was perceived. Adam noticed that two different risky trades were viewed opposite in the ordinary perception; the trades of prostitutes and soldiers.

Both occupations had an increased risk of death and injury. For prostitutes, the most significant threats were sexually transmitted diseases and serial killers while soldiers faced the danger of getting shot in battle and post-traumatic stress. Adam would enjoy both trades, and prostitution would be safe for him, as it was unheard of female serial killers who targeted male prostitutes and Adam would never have sex with a man. Sadly, the market for male prostitutes targeting the female market was tiny, and he just did not have what it took. Being a soldier, also seemed like a viable option but apart from the killing people aspect, he could get those kicks from being a police officer in Sydney. As a policeman, he could get laid more and did not need to stay in a barrack with 15 other sweaty guys most of the time.

When it came to the perception of the trades, Adam could not understand why prostitutes had such a bad reputation. After all, they provided a service for a lot of lonely men who would not get laid otherwise. Soldiers, on the other hand, were glorified with public holidays and stuff but all they did was to go third world hellholes bombing the shit out of the natives using superior weaponry. Adam reckoned that would be a lot of fun to do this, but he could not see the glory in it, or why the government spent billions of dollars on this as it did nothing to improve the lives of its everyday citizens.

With 15 minutes left of the workday, Adam Smith saw Janelle Wynyard, the sister of James Locker, coming to the pub. He could feel the blood flowing to his lower regions as she was still hot. The fact that she was the sister of James made her even hotter as Adam had fantasised countless times of being getting to know a relative of James on a deeper personal level. Adam did not know what it was in the concept of banging the sister of a friend that was so hot, but he guessed it was the replay value. If Adam fucked Janelle Wynyard, he would be reminded of her every time he saw James, which were most days. For the same reason, it would be a terrible idea to have sex with someone's ugly sister as he did not need those reminders. She walked towards him and started speaking to him.

Janelle Wynyard:

- Hi, Adam! Long-time no see. How are things with you and James these days?

Adam Smith:

- Well, I am bored as hell, this place is a shithole! But in general, life is good.

- With James, things seem to be picking up. We finally got him laid, and he even landed a promotion.

Janelle Wynyard:

- Oh, that's great to hear. So, he is a detective now then? Who is this woman anyway?

Adam Smith:

- Yes, Detective James Locker. It's a lot of women, not just one he has been ploughing like a king lately!

Janelle Wynyard:

- Okay, that seems unlike James, but I will keep my judgment to myself.

Adam Smith:

- Well, he finally learned from the Master. Speaking of which when are we banging? Still married to the farmer?

Janelle Wynyard:

- Well, there is a higher chance that you will win the $50 million OZ Lotto jackpot than I will sleep with you...

Adam Smith:

- I see, well I will get back to you when I have done that. Would be so awesome to bang the sister of James'!

- But hey, I need something to write in my transcript, so James knew we met today. What can you tell me about Jessica Hall?

Janelle Wynyard:

- Well, probably the same that everyone else. Very beautiful, but a very vain and shallow personality. Not a personal favourite, but I guess the world would be boring if everyone were down to earth.

Adam Smith:

- Okay, so nothing new then...
- But you know what. I have a perfect solution for you, me and James.

Janelle Wynyard:

- Okay, and what is that?

Adam Smith:

- Simple. You confess the killings of Miranda DiMaestro and Jessica Hall. You'll be imprisoned in Sydney, so you'll finally get out of here. James will keep his promotion as he solved the case. I'll visit you in prison and have sex with you.

Janelle Wynyard:

- Oh my god, the same old bizarre Adam. So, retarded so it's funny. Oh well, I will consider it. After all, who would not sacrifice a great marriage and a good life, for a life in prison and having sex with you?!

Adam Smith:

- Thanks! Always nice seeing you. I am leaving for Sydney now, but you should come by and party someday. We are stepping things up a level; last weekend was legendary!

Having said this Adam left the bar and hitched a ride to the airport for his flight to Sydney.

Chapter 50 Thomas Anderson Requests Technical Assistance

It was Thursday the 29th of August 2013, and Thomas Anderson entered the office of Barry Itch. He was going to ask Barry if they could enlist one of his former university friends as a resource for the case. The reason for this was that hacking of the CSMI computers that occurred the night before.

While Thomas did not like to request help as Information Technology was his specialty, he still felt compelled to do so as it was better for him to acknowledge he could not match the skills of the Killer, than failing and letting his failure come at a steep price. Thomas had spoken to the most skilled IT person he knew, Wayne Bruce, who recently had sold his social media network company to Facebook for $1 billion. Having sold his company Wayne was not busy, and he was intrigued when Thomas described the case to him. Since money was not an issue for Wayne, Thomas had persuaded him to help for free, forfeiting his usual excessive consultancy fee. Now all Thomas had to do was to sell this concept to Barry.

Thomas Anderson:

- Hi, Barry. Thank you for seeing me. I have a special request for you regarding the hacking of our systems.

Barry Itch:

- Hi, Thomas. I don't know if I should applaud your initiative or complain that you are not following the chain of command. As you know, James is your supervisor, and I prefer if detectives make the requests for their specific teams. Would be too many people running back and forth to my office if every employee went straight to me.

Thomas Anderson:

- I know that, but the reason I am going straight to you is that I don't want to use the official channels as whoever we are dealing with has access to everything we got.

- Whoever we are up against have excellent computer skills, as he managed to outsmart the security systems at the crime scenes and managed to hack into our system. Unfortunately, he is better than I am and that's why I am suggesting a different solution.

- Have you ever heard about Wayne Bruce?

Barry Itch:

- Well, the name rings a bell. Is that the IT billionaire who was in the newspapers last month?

Thomas Anderson:

- Exactly. I gave him a brief summary of the case giving out any classified details. He was intrigued and is happy to do some pro-bono work for us.

- But the thing is... whoever we are up against will probably try wiping out his trace if he knows we are after him. So, we need to conduct an undercover operation where Wayne Bruce is given access to our files and clearance to do whatever it takes to identify the killer.

Barry Itch:

- Well, Thomas, I don't like what you are proposing, but you have a point. However, I don't trust people before I have met them. Can you ask your friend to come to my office later today? I will make my decision then.

Thomas Anderson:

- Thank you, sir. I'll give him your contact details and tell him to call you straight away.

Thomas left the room with a feeling of relief and frustration at the same time. It was great that Barry Itch was considering his proposal. These were exceptional circumstances, requiring specialised solutions. But what worried Thomas was that the rumours would start spreading at the station when the chief of CSMI meets up with a famous IT billionaire the day after the police system was hacked.

It would be obvious what Barry and Wayne were discussing, and if the Killer got to know about this meeting, he would understand the purpose of it. Regardless, this was a victory for Thomas no matter what. Thomas would just have to hope that the Killer would not know about the meeting and that Barry would be sensible enough to realise that Wayne was particularly useful when it came to solving difficult IT problems.

Chapter 51 James Locker faces insomnia

James was sitting on his couch looking at a televised Rugby League game. He was not highly involved in this game as he was not a fan of either team nor had he bet any money on the match. So instead his thoughts drifted away. They had been unable to figure out the identity of the drunken man due to a strange move by John Dean. For some reason he had password protected the video showing the corridor outside Jessica Hall's apartment with a biometric password. The biometric password would not have been any problem if John was in the office to unlock the file, but unfortunately, he had to look after his daughter after one of her epileptic seizures.

James was contemplating the situation: was it possible to open a password with a biometric lock without the person being there? Maybe Thomas knew a way to bypass a biometric password, but that would only show everyone that he did not trust John. John had promised to be back by Monday and considering James was not planning to put in any work during the weekend. Leaving things unresolved and blaming John for not progressing on the drunken man clue suited James well, and he decided to leave things for now.

James was bothered by the hacking of the CSMI networks by the alleged killer. What kind of a person would leave such a message and make that much effort just to mess with their minds? Most killers did everything they could to get as far away from the police as possible, but this one seemed to want their attention which was very strange considering how the murders took place. Murderers looking for attention would usually kill their victims very conspicuously to make the media pay attention to the case. These cases had received some media attention, but not as much as they would if the killer murdered to get media attention.

But could the message be personal and aimed at one of them? Whoever that person was he or she had hidden it very well during the briefing today, and James had not seen anyone affected by the message.

And who was the man who came by Barry's office in the afternoon? He could be some computer consultant hired to investigate the intrusion into their systems but if that was the case, why didn't Barry involve James in the process? Did Barry mistrust him?

Knowing he could not resolve his work-based issues now, James changed scope to a more personal problem, his sleeping issues. He was considering his options when it came to his prescription drugs. The problem for him was that either he took the pill slept like a rock and woke up around 3 AM in the night still tired although he had slept enough, or he did not take them and had insomnia all night. James was unsure which option he preferred, but he would discuss it with his psychiatrist at his next session the coming week. James disliked these meetings as he considered them to be a lot of expensive talking that just made him feel bad about himself. Or as Adam Smith had put it: *"Going to a psychologist is like going on an expensive date, with an ugly woman, who does not want to fuck."*

James took up one of the pills from the jar and studied it for a while. Did the pill look different than before? He could not put the finger on what the difference was, but his intuition told him that something was strange with the pill. For a second, James considered bringing the medicines to work to ask someone, but he pushed the thought away, not wanting his colleagues to know what medicines he was taking.

Knowing that he would not be able to sleep tonight, James Locker felt very restless and wanted to do something. The problem was Thomas had not picked up the phone, and James did not fancy the concept of hanging out with Adam on his own. Since James Locker had lived in Sydney all his life, he had other friends in the vicinity as well, but since most people he knew had settled down and reproduced there was not anyone who would want to go out on a Thursday night.

James Locker realised that he could not drink every time he felt bored or lonely as that would be the end of him. Lacking better things to do, he decided to visit the police station gym at 9 PM. His gym session with Thomas Anderson the other night had been inspiring, and maybe the solution to better mental health was better physical health? Happy with his decision James Locker left his house for a drive towards the police station.

Chapter 52 Adam Smith stumbles across a clue

It was Friday the 30th of August, and Adam was watching sports at a bar in the Central Business District close to the police station. He was annoyed that neither Thomas Anderson nor James Locker wanted to join him. Tonight, was a big game as it was the 23rd and final round of the AFL deciding whether Sydney Swans would reach the finals or not. Not that Adam was a big fan of the Swans, but he was a great fan of drinking and tonight it was a 50/50 chance that it would be an awesome party and that was odds he liked.

Adam reflected on the reasons the others had given to not join him. Apparently, James Locker had been at the gym four hours straight last night before he finally collapsed from exhaustion. A four-hour gym session seemed like a bizarre thing to do between 9 PM and 1 AM, but since James Locker had assured him of his presence in the Central Sydney Laser Tag championship the following day, Adam did not worry too much about this. But when it came to Thomas who apparently was hanging out with his mysterious hook-up, Adam could not stop thinking about it, and it drove him crazy that he did not know who he/she/it was.

Adam Smith was thankfully interrupted from reflecting further when Officer Mason came up to his table.

Officer Mason:

- Hey, Adam, how have you been? I heard you pissed off the BITCH severely recently?

Adam Smith:

- Hey, mate! Yeah, that's correct. The punishment he gave me should be reported to the United Nations Human Rights department as a cruel and unusual punishment! Five daylong sessions with Barry's wife Wanda Itch AKA the WITCH.

Officer Mason:

- Hmm... Five sessions at the workplace equality seminar sound like the typical punishment for sexism in the workplace?

Adam Smith:

- Well, it's still a cruel and unusual punishment! Anyway, I will get drunk tonight since tomorrow is going to be woeful anyway.

Officer Mason:

- Don't get Michael Fuller drunk, because then you won't make it out of bed tomorrow.

Adam Smith:

- What about him?

Officer Mason:

- I saw him blind drunk the other day. In the elevator when we headed to your latest crime scene. I told John Dean about it, but he did not seem to care.

Adam Smith:

- Well, no-one cares about Michael Fuller; he is an arrogant prick! Good riddance I'd say.

- By the way, what's your first name Officer Mason? I have never heard you say it?

Officer Mason

- That's because I always use Officer Mason. It works wonders, with the ladies!

Adam Smith:

- Great do you want to be my wingman for tonight?

Officer Mason:

- I would be honoured to Agent Smith!

A few hours later Sydney Swans had won the game and qualified for the finals. Adam Smith and Officer Mason celebrated this with an epic night of boozing and hunting, a night that is not covered by this story.

Chapter 53 The Killer Experiences a Delay.

The Killer sat in front of his computer, bored and a bit frustrated. Since he was planning to frame Michael Fuller for the murders, his convalescence in the hospital was bad news that forced the Killer to postpone his plans. In theory, this would be the best time to plant all the evidence against Michael. But the Killer was not finished with his plans, and he had not reached his goal which would finally give him freedom. James Locker was his final target, but he felt no satisfaction in killing him if he did not understand why he had to die.

The Killer was looking at the file he had made for his next victim. He did not enjoy the prospect of killing her. But it had to be done, as it would send a message for James that would finally make him understand. Once James understood it would be a pleasure to kill him. The Killer could not put the finger on why it was vital for him that James understood who he was, but it was just the way things had to go, it was an obsession he had, and the only way to get rid of it was to follow it to the end.

The Killer was thinking about Rebecca. She was hanging out with her friend Samantha Robinson, from the police academy, tonight. The Killer had a feeling that they had been more than friends once from the way Rebecca spoke about her. He did not feel compelled to find out more as he did not mind if she had romantic connections in the past. Although he was considerably older than Rebecca, she was still 21 years old and probably had several romantic relationships from her past that he didn't need to know about. From what Rebecca had told him she was playing Lasertag with her Samantha, which seemed like an odd thing for two girls to do a Friday night, but he did not mind. He would love to join them, but sadly it was too dangerous. He knew that Samantha was one of the police officers that was investigating his murders and it would be a great thrill to stand face to face with her while she was oblivious to whom he was. But it would be dangerous, as the excitement might go to his head and blow his cover. He could not risk all that for having fun.

Finally, the Killer decided to just rest for a couple of days. He would need to gather all the energy he could muster for the grand finale where his plans would unfold so he could use the rest. He went to bed and immediately fell asleep.

Chapter 54 A Vivid Dream

James Locker woke up and felt excited and nervous at the same time. For the first time in nine months, he was going on a proper date. James had been a bit sceptical about online dating, but Thomas Anderson had persuaded him that it was a great way of seeing people and getting to know them in a relaxed environment one on one. The woman he was meeting today was named Vanessa Ward and was almost a perfect manifestation of all his desired traits in a woman. Would she be his perfect match for him, and would he be a good match for her?

James picked her up at her place, and they drove south to a deserted beach in the Royal National Park south of the city. It was late August, so the beach was empty, but it was a sunny and pleasant day. They spoke for hours, and James felt how their souls connected when he held her hand. When the sun set, he kissed her. It was a truly magical moment. He spoke to her:

- Oh, Vanessa, this day has been so beautiful. I can't wait to see you again.

Vanessa Ward:

- James, I would love to be with you as well. But I can't.

James Locker:

- But we are perfect for each other why are you turning me down.

Vanessa Ward:

- You know why.

James Locker:

- You... Don't Exist?

She disappeared in front of James Locker's eyes, and suddenly he recalled a phrase from the Matrix *"Have you ever had a dream that you were sure were real? What if you were unable to wake up from that dream? How would you know the difference between the dream world and the real world?"* The phrase felt very authentic to him at this moment when he woke up alone at a beach and could not understand how the day had only been a dream.

Chapter 55 Pre-Talk Before the Central Sydney Lasertag Championship

J ames Locker arrived at the Lasertag arena in Darling Harbour 30 minutes late. He found his friends and Adam immediately approached him:

- Hey, mate you are late! A damn good thing I anticipated something like this happening and picked our meeting time an hour early.

James Locker:

- Well, a good thing I predicted you doing something like that, so I did not come here too soon...

- No, but I am sorry mate I went to a beach in Royal National Park and completely lost track of time.

Thomas Anderson:

- Oh yeah, the date from the online dating site, how did that go?

James froze for a second when Thomas asked him about the date. When had he told Thomas about it and what had he said to him? James decided to play along:

- Well as it turned out, she was not at all what I expected. I guess my mind got carried away before. I should learn not to have as high expectations.

Thomas Anderson:

- Well, we all live to learn, I understand why you feel that way though, you showed me her profile and pictures. The profile was like it was written towards you and the images. Damn, they were hot.

Samantha felt a bit jealous when Thomas was speaking like that about another woman. Most of all she felt curiosity, and she decided to join in on the conversation:

- Hey, Guys that chick sounds incredible. Can I have a look at her as well?

Thomas Anderson:

- Of course, she can, right James?
- Check it here on my phone.

Samantha checked the profile thoroughly. She did not put much emphasis on the written text as she did not know James well enough to determine whether the person described would be a good match for him or. But she looked carefully at the pictures. There was something wrong with them, but she could not put the finger on what it was. Somehow the person seemed familiar to her. She decided to not mention anything to the group but instead have a talk with Thomas about it later.

Samantha Robinson:

- Yeah, she looks hot, sorry it did not work out for you. But looking at it positively if you can get dates with a hot chick like that you are still an attractive man James, so don't let I push you down.

Adam Smith:

- Yeah, there is a sound to the title Detective Locker isn't there. But fuck this; it's annoying to talk about chicks none of us managed to bang. Let's talk Lasertag tactics.

Samantha Robinson:

- But I already know everything about the tactics for this arena; I went here with Thomas and my friend Rebecca last night.

Adam Smith:

- Seriously? A hot friend? And you did not invite me?

Thomas Anderson:

- Well, she's attractive and taken, so that's why we did not invite you to come along.

Adam Smith:

- Seriously? So, you are banging Samantha's hot friend? Strange development considering how much you fancied Samantha before.

Samantha Robinson:

- Oh please, Adam; you are the only one who would draw that conclusion.

Adam Smith:

- Oh yeah, I am special and so on...

- That used to be a compliment, right? These days you are supposed to use the word "special" when talking about retards and stuff! I would be offended if someone said I was special to them...

James Locker:

- Oh well, Adam, I am sure you don't need to worry about being called special by anyone. But please share your unique Lasertag tactics with us.

After this Adam spent 5 minutes explaining various Lasertag tactics to the group. They sounded advanced and sophisticated when Adam described them but all in all, they could be summarised with *"run around in circles to confuse your enemies and then shoot them in the back."*

Chapter 56 You Are Taking This Far Too Serious.

After listening to Adam Smith's tactics walkthrough, it was time for their first game in the tournament. As they entered the arena, James was paralysed and entered a trancelike state. Lasertag was no longer a match for him, this was for real, and he had to fight to survive! The panic gave him a massive surge of adrenaline that temporarily increased his potential, so for the 15 minutes duration of the game, James was clearing the house with the opposing team. The price he paid, however, was steep as it instead of being a fun competitive Saturday pastime turned out to be a fight for survival in James' mind. When the game ended James Locker collapsed on a couch outside the arena, his shirt was all wet, and he was hyperventilating. Adam was the first to speak to him.

- Hey James. I never thought I would say this, but man you are taking this far too seriously.

- Very impressive performance though you outscored the entire opponent team yourself and we are through to the next round, five wins to go!

James was unable to respond to this as he was still confused and felt very sick from the adrenaline leaving the body. Samantha noticed that James seemed very ill, so she tried establishing contact with him:

- Hey, James, are you alright? What happened there?

James Locker:

- No, I am feeling sick can anyone drive me home?

Adam Smith:

- Feeling sick? Come on man you would not have swept the entire opposing team by yourself if you were not feeling great. Have a drink to calm down; the next round is in 30 minutes.

Samantha Robinson:

- Adam! Can't you see he is not feeling well at all? Don't worry about it. I'll drive him home as this game means more to you than it means to me.

Adam did not respond to this as he knew that Samantha Robinson was right. He found the events extremely confusing though as he certainly had not seen this scenario coming. He decided that this was not a fight to take so he accepted and encouraged Samantha's decision instead.
Adam Smith:

- Okay Samantha, you are right. It's much appreciated that you are sorting this mess out, James hope you will feel better soon.

After this conversation, Samantha and James headed to her car so she could drive him home.

Chapter 57 James Locker Opens to Samantha Robinson

S amantha was driving James home after the incident at the Lasertag place. She was curious and worried about the behaviour she had witnessed. None of it made any sense to her, considering all they had been doing were playing Lasertag.

Rebecca thought of ways to approach James, and she realised that the best way to make him open, would be to pretend to have been through the same situation herself. Since they did not know each other that well, it was likely to work, and James Locker was not in a state of mind where he would question what she said. While it was not morally correct lying about her mental health, she did so to help James out.

Samantha Robinson:

- I know what you are feeling; I have had similar episodes in my past. It's like the weight of the entire world is crashing down on me.

James Locker:

- Oh really? You have never told me about this before.

Samantha Robinson:

- Well, I guess I felt ashamed to talk about it. I do not want to be perceived as a crazy woman; people would not take me seriously if they did.

James Locker:

- That's what I am feeling! I was depressed when my ex-girlfriend Emily left me nine months ago. I did not function well at all. But then I got medication from my psychologist. It's called Xenopropsyche, and it's doing wonders for my mental strength. I mean I have never been doing this well at work as I have been the last nine months.

Samantha Robinson:

- Okay, I have never heard about that brand before. Any idea why you are getting worse now?

James Locker:

- Can I say something to you in confidence?

Samantha Robinson:

- It depends on what you are going to say. All I can promise you is that I will not try to benefit at your expense.

James Locker:

- Well, that's good enough for me.

- Well to be honest with you, Xenopropsyche is not precisely an antidepressant.

- It's a mixture of antidepressants and antipsychotics. The reason for telling everyone it's an antidepressant is because people can accept and understand depression while insanity scares the shit out of them.

- And no-one should judge me for things I cannot help, and it has not affected my work. I have been doing great at work.

Samantha Robinson:

- I can't argue with that statement you have been doing great. Reaching the detective rank at the age of 32, not many persons advance that quickly.

- But you still have not told me why you think you are getting worse now.

James Locker:

- Well as effective as Xenopropsyche is at improving my work performance it has once great disadvantage for me as well. It shuts me down completely emotionally. I don't want to live the rest of my life like that, so that's why I am trying to stop it. But when I don't, I take it I get severe anxiety and insomnia.

Samantha Robinson:

- Well, I see where you are coming from, but you should not make decisions like that without consulting your physician. Resume taking them as prescribed, and you'll be okay.

James Locker:

- Well, I guess you're right. But the pills have seemed different recently. I can't put my finger on it, but something has changed. And the effect has changed as well. I took several pills last night, and the entire day has been like a dream.

Samantha Robinson:

- Well, maybe your pills were replaced by whoever broke into your house Sunday night?

- Tell you what, hand me some of your pills and some of your hair. I know a guy in the forensics lab that owes me a few favours. We can do it all anonymously, and we can do a toxicological screening as well.

James Locker:

- Can't argue with what you are saying. Here you go.

Samantha Robinson:

- Great. I'll get back to you with the results as soon as possible.

- Oh, and are you sure I should drive you home? Maybe overnight observation at the hospital would be a better choice?

James Locker:

- Yes, I am sure.
- Thank you for the offer though.

A while later Samantha dropped off James at his house. She would have preferred dropping him off at the hospital, but he did not want to, and she didn't want to force him to go. It was strange though as he seemed very un-confident and insecure most of the drive, but when questioned whether he wanted to go home or to the hospital he seemed very sure about his choice.

For the 15 minutes that passed rejecting to go to the hospital, he spoke very casually about the AFL game he saw the night before and the upcoming finals for the Swans. Samantha Robinson had never witnessed anyone switching from broken to normal in that short time before and she was un-sure how to perceive it. She checked her watch. Samantha would still be able to make it back to the Lasertag championship before the semi-finals, and it seemed likely that Adam Smith and Thomas Anderson would make it that far without her. But now she was more interested in following up on this lead than playing child games.

Samantha's reason for getting James' hair wasn't to do a toxicological screening but to compare the blood from his bathroom mirror with the DNA of his hair. Of course, she would make toxicological testing as well, but that was so she would have something to show James if he asked her about it. Samantha called her contact, and after some intense persuasion, she managed to get him to meet her at his laboratory at the University of New South Wales in two hours.

Chapter 58 Samantha Robinson Meets With Gerry Livingstone at the UNSW Forensic Lab.

S amantha arrived at The University of New South Wales and was observing Gerry Livingstone, her former professor in forensic criminology and the man she had a short affair with a couple of years ago. Physically he was a lot older than her and not very appealing, but she remembered that he had fascinated her a lot as a person back then when she was 20, and he was 40. Being a descendant of the legendary explorer David Livingstone mostly known as Dr Livingstone, Gerry Livingstone had been quite an adventurer himself in his younger years, although not even close to reaching the fame of his famous ancestor.

They had met on many occasions, and the concept of seeing a married man had been an extra spice at the time for Samantha Robinson. Sexually, Garry was never much of an adventure; Samantha's exciting sexual experiences had come later when she met Rebecca. She approached him with the classic phrase they always used.

- Dr Livingstone, I presume?

Gerry Livingstone:

- Hey, Samantha, great to see you too. Although it was tough to explain to my wife why I had urgent work at 10 pm a Saturday night!

Samantha Robinson:

- Well, at least you are honest with her this time.

- No, but seriously your help is much appreciated.

- I am working on a lead that could expose a significant security breach of the police force. But I can't proceed without knowing the facts; otherwise, I might ruin my whole career.

Gerry Livingstone:

- I see. I assume you don't want to share the details with me?

Samantha Robinson:

- That is correct. But that's for your sake as well; you are not supposed to work outside the official channels either.

Gerry Livingstone:

- That's true. So, tell me, Sammy, what is that you need from me?

Samantha Robinson:

- Well it's three things basically

- I need you to run a DNA matching test on this blood and this hair.

- I also need you to run a toxicological test on this piece of hair.

- Finally, I need to know if this pill is Xenopropsyche or if it's something else.

Gerry Livingstone:

- I see. Since you only need an indication, I can do the quick sample test which is invalid for court since it has a significant margin of error. It's enough to give a clear indication though. It should take about two hours. I will also run a standard drug test on the hair you provided

- As for the pill, I can't help you for now with the chemical analysis as I am not a pharmacologist. But I have a friend at the university who is, and I can ask him as soon as I see him

Samantha Robinson:

- Great thank you. It's unfortunate that I will have to wait to know about the pill, but I appreciate that you are helping me out, nonetheless.

Gerry started performing the tests, and while the lab equipment performed the tests, they had some downtime which they spent talking about old memories. Samantha was fascinated by the fact that attraction felt so different with different people. When it came to be an exciting character Gerry Livingstone was probably one of the most attractive individuals in the world to her. She loved his stories and his intellect and the charismatic way he had of speaking which transformed the banalities of life into the most extraordinary adventures. Physically, however, she had never been attracted to him and the sex they had back in the day was just her way of keeping him seeing her. After all, every human relation was about giving and taking, and she knew his main reason for meeting with her was the sex although he must enjoy her personality as well, otherwise he would never be as entertaining and charming as he was towards her.

Physically, things had been great with Rebecca, but they had been and still were best friends primarily. She had never experienced emotions like jealousy or overwhelming love with Rebecca and the fact that they both dreamt about families and kids in the future made them a poor long-term match. Most of all, Samantha shunned the concept that she was expected to join the entire gay subculture just because she was attracted to Rebecca. The gay culture had never appealed to her, and she could not understand the peer pressure on bisexual people to be perceived as one group. Heterosexual people had a lot more freedom in that sense, and that freedom was something she loved.

Samantha thought about Thomas. Could he be the man for her life? It had started off right, and he was the most balanced choice even though he would never be as charismatic and intelligent as Gerry and never as sexy as Rebecca. Since Samantha knew that one could never get everything one wants in one person, she was still excited to see how things would turn out with Thomas. Once the tests finished, Gerry gave his report:

- Well, I have run the DNA tests now, and there is a 90 per cent probability that the hair and the blood are different persons.

Samantha Robinson:

- Okay, that's a relief! I was suspecting that a colleague of mine was crazy and lied about a break-in that occurred. But this proves that it did happen, so even though I feel ashamed over not trusting my friend, I am still happy that he's okay.

Gerry Livingstone:

- Okay. A close friend of yours?

Samantha Robinson:

- No, not in that way. I am seeing a guy now though.

Gerry Livingstone:

- Well, congratulations Sammy! But I have some bad news about your other friend. It seems like he has a bad drug habit, specifically towards cocaine.

Samantha Robinson:

- Okay, I did not see that one coming!

- But can you take the hair to the pharmacologist, nonetheless? I need to know what else they can detect in a full scan.

Gerry Livingstone:

- Sure, I'll get onto it.

Samantha Robinson:

- Thank you, Gerry, for everything, you are a good friend. I will
not forget this.

Samantha left the University of New South Wales more confused than
before. She had suspected that James was crazy, but not that he had a cocaine
addiction. Hell, she had nailed the *"How to identify a drug user"* course at the
University and still she had not seen any symptoms of cocaine intoxication or
cocaine withdrawal in James. Maybe the tests were wrong or gave an unclear
indication? Or maybe James was a casual user, and his use would be easier to
hide from the colleagues.

Regardless, Samantha now knew that her boss was a cocaine user, which
was a felony in New South Wales. But what would she do with this knowledge? If James were crazy, it would have been an easy choice to report him
as it would be in everybody's best interest that he had received proper help,
with someone else overseeing the team. But with cocaine addiction, it was
different. Michael was an alcoholic and was forced to resign due to this. But
was that the right leadership choice? Michael Fuller was the best detective
the city had ever seen, so getting rid of him was a sketchy choice. Samantha
found it amusing that Barry Itch in his eagerness to get rid of the alcoholic
Michael had replaced him with the cocaine-addicted James.

Samantha decided to not act on her knowledge about James Locker's cocaine usage because she liked him. Another reason was that Samantha had
nothing to gain and everything to lose from turning James in. If they indeed
believed her and James later got caught in the drug test, she was unlikely to
get rewarded as it seemed unlikely that they would promote her after such a
short tenure with the police. But if a drug test cleared James of her allegations
Samantha had made a lot of effort and all she had made was a fool of herself
and a personal enemy in James.

There was indeed a significant risk that James would be cleared if Samantha forced a drug test upon him. James could go free because cocaine was
detectable for up to three months in hair tissue but only up to three days in

urine or blood tests. Since the only legally applicable tests were blood tests, James Locker was highly likely to be cleared of any wrongdoing.

Samantha considered if she was going to share her thoughts and concerns with Thomas. Samantha decided to share her concerns with him at a later stage, as she realised that he was not as involved in work as she was and if she brought up work a Saturday night, it would only annoy him.

Instead, Samantha decided to send Thomas a text message wishing him a good night. Her message read. *"Hi Neo. I got James home safe and sound. Sorry for not returning to the Lasertag arena afterwards but I got obsessed with a lead that I wanted to follow-up. I won't bore you with the details now, but I'll tell you all about it tomorrow when we play bowling. I hope you won the championship without me and had a great night of boozing with Adam. XOXO Sammy"*

Chapter 59 A Revelation of the Killers Ultimate Plan.

The Killer woke up. The sun was shining outside his window, and he felt great satisfaction with his life. All his plans had worked great this far: James was a broken man, and soon it would be the time to strike. His plan involving the replacement of James' antipsychotics with psychedelic drugs seemed to be working. It had been a pleasure for the Killer to make up the fictional profile of Vanessa Ward and then tricking James to go to that deserted beach for a "date." The fool had been sitting around there for hours believing he had found his soulmate when he was speaking to the thin air or more accurately a manifestation of his subconscious. The most ironic of it all was that the pictures of "Vanessa Ward" were pictures of Emily Luong that the Killer had edited to be unrecognisable. The Killer had also made the profile to match Emily Luong personality and interests as far as possible. The idiotic James was thus on an imaginary date with his ex-girlfriend oblivious of this ruse.

The Killer had a theory that James' mental problems were because he was living in denial about what happened to Emily Luong on that fateful night nine months ago. The Killer had not forgotten! He had been passive for far too long before he had decided to act about one and a half month ago. Unfortunately, James had gone on a holiday just the day after the Killer had put his plans into motion, which was a frustrating drawback at the time, but it did not matter in the long run. Now he experienced another delay with Michael hospitalised, but hopefully, Michael would recover soon.

The Killer reflected over how he felt about Michael. To summarise it he had never liked the man. But Michael was not the primary target, but it was necessary to frame someone for the murders otherwise the Killer would never be able to sleep sound at night always fearing that his past would catch up with him.

There was no shame in setting Michael up. The Killer perceived him as an arrogant and selfish piece of shit who had always neglected the needs of others especially those of his daughter Rebecca in his pursuit of glory and "justice." Michael's drinking problem was most likely because of the hole inside him that all addicts had, and sending him to jail at least gave him a chance to sort out his priorities in life.

The Killer looked at the file he had made on his next victim, Emily Luong. Not the Emily Luong he once knew and loved, but another one. The two Emily Luong's had very little in common except for their names, but the Killer reckoned that the name would be enough to tip James' mind over the edge so that he would finally understand. What if James did not know? Well, the killer could not possibly be more transparent, so in that case, he would have to kill the oblivious James anyway which would be a very unsatisfying but still acceptable outcome.

Since the Killer could not proceed with his plans today, he decided that it would be awesome to see Rebecca instead. They usually did not meet in the daytime, but he felt that he was willing to take the risk to look at her eyes glitter in the sun with the wind in her hair. After witnessing the "date" between James Locker and Vanessa Ward the day before; the Killer felt that a real meeting with Rebecca at the same beach would be awesome, so it was worth the risk of detection. He called her, and she accepted his invitation. Feeling happy the killer bought the best picnic basket money could buy and picked up Rebecca for an awesome day at the beach.

Chapter 60 An Excellent Day at the Beach

The Killer and Rebecca went to the same secluded beach in the Royal National Park where he had witnessed James Locker's "date" with Vanessa Ward the day before. Even though this Sunday did not feature the excitement of breaking his enemy down it had some features which the Killer valued even higher. It offered the feeling of tranquillity, belonging and love. The Killer admired the features of Rebecca in the sunlight. She had a beautiful face with her blonde hair glittering in the sun with blue eyes matching the colour of the sky and slim and a very feminine body. The Killer reflected that if she would make it as police in the future, she would probably have to build some muscle so she would be less frail; nonetheless, a slim and very feminine woman was what he had in front of him now, and that's what he wanted. All in all, they both had a perfect time when they spoke, kissed and enjoyed the variety of flavours and drinks in the picnic basket. For the sake of this story, the following dialogue is the most important.

Rebecca Bell:

- JP this has been such a beautiful day, you were indeed at your best today.

The Killer:

- Well as one should be, when wooing a woman as unique as you are to me. And you have not experienced my best yet; the night is yet to come!

Rebecca Bell:

- Oh... you are such a teaser.

- Another good thing is that my father has left the hospital. Apparently, he was not as badly injured as they first thought so they reckoned it would be easier if he rested at home for a few days

The Killer:

- That is excellent news; I noticed how worried you were when I drove you home the other day.

Rebecca Bell

- Yeah, I was, he is my father after all...

- You know I was so disappointed when you left for four weeks, it felt a lot like how my dad treated me during my upbringing

The Killer:

- I understand what you are saying. And I missed you a lot as well, but I was abroad working for four weeks, not much I could do about it.

Rebecca Bell:

- Yeah, I know. You work for the government with some secret project and so on. And that's fine I am thrilled by the mystique and games as well, but I just feel that if we are going to have a long-term relationship, we must start being open to each other.

The Killer:

- Yes, I agree with you. Tell you what; my current project will probably finish in a couple of weeks. After that, I will go back to normal police work. But I must warn you. I might be very busy in the weeks to come and difficult to get in touch with.

- But I will make it up to you; look at this I have made reservations for us in a luxury hotel suite tonight.

Rebecca Bell:

- Oh, that's amazing. Wait a second your last name is not Pierce?

The Killer:

- No that is correct; it's just a name I use. I did some research on my ancestors. I found one named Aaron Pierce who was an adventurer in the 19th century, and he lived the most inspiring and exciting life one can imagine. I feel like him when I use his family name, while my real family name only makes me feel old, dull and tired.

Rebecca Bell

- Hey JP, you are not that old! But don't worry I'll keep calling you Pierce if that what it takes to keep you interesting and attractive.

The Killer:

- Thank you, Rebecca. I am planning to change my name to Pierce soon. But hey let's head back to the city. The luxury suite is waiting for us.

After saying that, they headed back to the city for a night to remember in the luxury suite.

Chapter 61 Thomas Anderson and Samantha Robinson Go Bowling

It was Sunday the 1st of September and the first day of spring. The season had little relevance for Samantha and Thomas as they were playing ten pin bowling indoors. He usually went to the venue with Adam Smith and ended up with a hungover since they both were competitive and kept playing and drinking for a long time. With Samantha it was a bit different, Thomas still wanted to win, but the main point was not winning but only being with her. After two rounds Samantha's score was 248 VS 224 for Thomas.

Samantha Robinson:

- Oh, Thomas, I am winning; this is not a good weekend for you sports wise.

Thomas Anderson:

- Tell me about it. The two replacements we had to get for you and James from the team we eliminated in the first round were not able to pull your weight. We got eliminated in the semi-finals. Adam got spastic and made a fool out of himself.

Samantha Robinson:

- Well, I had to get James home, he was unwell.

Thomas Anderson:

- Yeah, I know that. Adam, on the other hand, thinks that James is a cry-baby and that you let us down by not coming back straight away.

- But don't worry about it. Adam acts out sometimes, then he goes home sulking for a while and then everything is fine; he is not the kind of man who carries a grudge for long.

Samantha Robinson:

- Okay. What do you think?

Thomas Anderson:

- Well, I am disappointed we lost but not disappointed with either of you.

- I am curious though; what lead were you following up on last night? Working on a Saturday night does not seem healthy I prefer if you are not the female version of Michael.

Samantha Robinson:

- Don't worry I am not.

- But I got hunch last night that I needed to check out. I thought "What if whoever broke into James Locker's house replaced his anti-depressants with something else?"

Thomas Anderson:

- I see. What did you find out?

Samantha Robinson:

- Well, he could not determine the contents of the pills as he was not a pharmacologist. He also tried matching the blood from the break-in with the DNA from James Locker's hair. They did not match. But he did find out that James Locker had cocaine addiction from the concentration of cocaine in his hair. Do you know anything about this?

This question made Thomas uneasy. He could lie and say he knew nothing about it. But then he would be lying, and Thomas was hoping that Samantha was the woman he would be happy with in the long run. If she were that woman, she would not judge him too harshly if he admitted he did cocaine with James and Adam the weekend before.

Being honest was a great leap of faith as he had no idea how she felt about the use of recreational drugs. Thomas knew Samantha well enough to know that sitting on the fence. I.E., admitting that he knew about James' cocaine usage and at the same time condemning it would not work with her. She would only see him as a: hypocrite. Hesitantly Thomas decided to tell her about what he knew.

- Well, Sammy, you might not like this, but I will tell you anyway.

- Last weekend when we were out drinking, we all used significant amounts of cocaine. I am not proud of it, but I am not going to lie about it either.

- I have never seen James as a cocaine addict though as I don't see myself as an addict just because I have an occasional line.

Samantha Robinson:

- Goddammit, Thomas! You are a member of the police. You should always try to uphold the law to the best of your abilities even when you don't agree with it. I can see why you think the persecution of drug users is wrong, but then you should find another employer where your usage is not an as severe breach of the values of your workplace.

Thomas Anderson:

- I don't know what to say Sammy other that I am sorry, and I don't want to lie about who I am to you.

Samantha Robinson:

- That's alright Thomas. On a personal level, I am not angry with you. I am just saying you can't be a police officer and break the law even if the law is stupid. So, I guess that for everyone's sake you'll have to make a choice; not between me and the cocaine but between your career in the force and the cocaine.

Thomas Anderson:

- Wow, Samantha. You do make a lot of sense; I have never thought about it that way.

- But anyway, moving back to James, I have only done coke with him once, and never really seen him as an addict. But I must admit I have done it several times with Adam though.

Samantha Robinson:

- Oh well, at least you are not lying to me. But funny thing none of us saw James as a cocaine addict and still the tests indicate he is.

Thomas Anderson:

- I guess it only shows one can never truly know another person.
- While on the topic I also did some research on James' life today.

Samantha Robinson

- Well, we have a lot of other things in common as well. But tell me what you found out?

Thomas Anderson:

- Well you know the date James spoke about last night.

- I rechecked her profile, and there was something that did not make sense with the pictures. So, I used a photo editor to reverse the changes made to the picture to get the original image. Look at the picture from the site compared to the original.

Samantha Robinson:

- I must admit the pictures are different, but I can't see where you are going with this?

Thomas Anderson:

- Well now compare the original picture with this picture from James' Facebook.

Samantha Robinson:

- It's the same woman, but I am still not following.

Thomas Anderson:

- Okay, I tell you. James went on a "date" from an online dating page with his ex-girlfriend he has not seen in nine months. At least he thinks he went on a date with her. But did he make the fake profile himself or is someone trying to break him down mentally? In both instances, we need to find out as quickly as possible, and I will talk to him about it tomorrow morning.

Samantha Robinson:

- I guess that would be a good idea. This is the strangest case I have ever had.

Thomas Anderson:

- Well from the bright side, you are only 23 years old; continue with your career in the police, and you will face a lot of strange cases.

- But hey let's leave. No point in sitting in a venue without drinking and I want to have a clear head at work tomorrow.

Samantha Robinson:

- Oh, I see. Does that mean you'll go to sleep early tonight?

Thomas Anderson:

- I am not THAT dedicated!

They both smiled and then left for Samantha's place not intending for an early night's sleep.

Chapter 62 A Truthful Story

The Killer was lying awake in bed. He wished he could fall asleep, but he could not. He was too fearful of what might happen if he stayed. It was 2 AM, and in one hour he would transform. Filled with uncontrolled rage which he had a tough time controlling. That would be okay if it were someone else, but Rebecca was not to see this side of him, he feared that he might hurt her.

Rebecca was the last person in the world the Killer would ever want to injure, and if he did, he might as well end his own life. The Killer knew how he would remedy his rage that peaked a 3 AM; by eliminating the source to it. Every night for nine months he had that same vision in front of him at that time of the evening, the sight of James doing horrible things to Emily Luong for claiming that she was unfaithful. He could not bring Emily back, but he could bring her to peace by killing the monster that had killed her. That monster was James. But there was no point in killing James without him knowing why, but it had to be done soon!

The Killer left Rebecca a note explaining that he had to work and that he had left money for the room service they had consumed during the night. It certainly did not feel right to leave her money like she was some prostitute, but it was a far better solution than just leaving her with the bill. He left the hotel and drove home. In two days, this would all be over, with James dead and Michael in custody with ample evidence against him. That if something was an encouraging thought.

Chapter 63 Thomas Anderson Warns James Locker About Vanessa Ward

It was Monday morning on the 2nd of September 2013. James Locker was rewriting a progress report Barry Itch who had complained about some of his other reports. James had not been able to come up with any reasons why he should not rewrite the report. He wrote it poorly, and the trail to the Killer was cold although he hoped they would get some clues when John Dean came back to the office today so they could unlock the video files.

Looking back James was upset that they had not requested new copies from the building management during Friday and then worked on them during the Saturday, but they were all too lazy and unambitious to make an effort. Thomas Anderson walked into James' office and closed the door behind him.

James Locker:

 - Hey, Thomas, good morning. What's on your mind?

Thomas Anderson:

 - Well don't take this the wrong way, but I am worried about you.

 - To be short, did you meet Vanessa Ward from the dating site last Saturday?

James Locker:

 - What kind of question is that?

Thomas Anderson:

 - Just answer honestly, and I'll explain to you in a second.

James Locker:

- Well, to be honest, I did not. I went to the beach where we were supposed to meet up. But she never came. So, I felt despondent and had the picnic by myself daydreaming of a better life.

- I did not mean to lie to you; I just did not want to look like a fool.

Thomas Anderson:

- Well, that's great. You see Vanessa does not exist!

- You see the picture she was using was photo edited. But I recovered the original image. Can you see who it is?

James Locker:

- Oh my god, it's Emily.

Thomas Anderson:

- Indeed. So, tell me, James. Has your obsession with your ex-girlfriend gone so far so you are creating a fake profile for her so you can imagine chatting with her?

James Locker:

- That notion is absurd. Of course, I did not!

Thomas Anderson:

- Very well. Would you like me to find out who did it? It might lead us to the person who broke into your house whom most likely is the Killer.

James Locker:

- Yes, of course, it's scary that all of this would be about me, but I have thought about it myself.

- I suppose you need my login and password for the site so you can trace the messages from Vanessa?

Thomas Anderson:

- Yes. That would be preferred as I don't fancy the concept of hacking the dating site account of my friend and boss.

James Locker:

- Yeah, you better stay away from doing that stuff. My username is JamesLocker81, and my password is emilyluong

Thomas Anderson:

- That would have been easy to hack!

- I will get back to you with an estimate of who is behind the "Vanessa" account this afternoon.

After Thomas left the room, James took a few deep breaths to calm his nerves. He was afraid as it was now obvious to him that whoever was behind these murders also had him in his sights. But how was this the case and James connected? He could not come up with any answers, but he hoped Thomas would figure something out before it was too late.

Chapter 64 John Dean is Taken Off the Case

J ohn Dean was sitting at his desk frustrated and anxious. He knew that he was on the brink of losing everything and that he was powerless to do anything about it. For starters, his decision to take money from Michael Fuller would backfire as the others would find out that he was colluding with Michael.

John considered his options. Stalling the investigation even more by deleting the video files would not do him any good as they would just go to the security companies directly and ask for new copies. Besides John was unsure how he would delete the files without being noticed by the log that registered all changes done to the case file.

John had spoken to Michael, who had left the hospital during the Sunday and was "celebrating" the fact that he had survived his car crash without any serious injuries. Michael had given up his pursuit to find and apprehend Antonio DiMaestro as he finally had realised that there were better things to do with life than chasing ghosts from his past. John had told Michael that they would come by his house and question him as soon as they realised his connection to the crime scenes.

Apart from his professional problems John was also facing personal challenges. He had seen another woman last night, and his wife who was supposed to a double shift had come back early from work, so he wasn't home when she got home. John had faced a hard time explaining why he was not home until 2 AM, and he wondered if it would be better, to tell the truth than making up a story.

Officially John had been celebrating with Michael that the latter had come out of the hospital without any severe damages from his car crash. His wife had told him that he was out of his mind who first took two days off to be with his daughter, and then left her with his sister to go out drinking on a Sunday evening. His wife didn't believe him, and John was worried that this would be the final straw that would lead to divorce.

"More trouble is coming" John muttered when he saw James accompanied by Samantha approaching his. James looked quite angry, and John knew that this was going to be a confrontation.

James Locker:

- Hey John. Please follow us to the meeting room; we need to talk to you.

John was considering if he should argue and ask why they took him off privately. He knew that it would not be a good idea as he had fucked up. Hopefully, they would accept his apologies and move on without question his loyalties or get the idea that he had been collaborating with Michael. John followed his colleagues to the meeting room.

James Locker:

- Jessica Hall was killed the night towards Tuesday. Now on a Monday almost a week later you have been unable to find anything useful on the surveillance tapes, and I would like to know why?

John Dean:

- Well, I told you I could not see anyone entering Jessica Hall's apartment at the time of the murder. I don't know why frankly, but the video seems strange like someone edited it in a way I have not seen before.

James Locker:

- Okay. Samantha claims that you were very unhelpful when she requested your assistance in identifying the mysterious drunken man during the Wednesday. How do you explain that?

John Dean:

- Well, I was stressed from home, and when my daughter got sick during the afternoon, I just closed my files to be with her as soon as possible without worrying about the handover.

James Locker:

- Okay, I see, but that still does not explain why you used a biometric password for the files or why you could not get to the station to unlock the data during the Thursday or the Friday...

- I am sick of your bullshit. Just get your thumb out of your arse and on that biometric password scanner so Samantha and I can work on the files. You are off this case. Proceed to work on the Father Walker case report. Hopefully, you won't fuck that up.

John chose to not respond to James' verbal assault. He unlocked the files and left the room without a word.

Samantha Robinson:

- A bit hard on him hey?

James Locker:

- No, I don't think so. He has spent most of the investigation bitter that I got promoted instead of him. Since he is apparently stalling us, he is better off wrapping up some other case that sabotaging this one.

Samantha Robinson:

- So, what do we do now?

James Locker:

- Well, you better get us some coffee we are not leaving this room before we have identified the mysterious drunken man!

A short while later Samantha came back with one triple shot latte each as this was a task that was going to take a lot of focus...

Chapter 65 The Inner Circle Has a Lunch Discussion

For the first time in a week, the team was making progress. Since James believed someone was compromising the team, he decided to only take his inner circle out to lunch instead of sharing the case with the entire group. A group consisting of James Locker, Adam Smith, Thomas Anderson and Samantha Robinson met up at a dinner serving excellent rump steak close to the police station. After eating their meals, James Locker decided to speak:

- Thank you for joining me today. I will move away from my rule to not discuss work during lunch break as these are extraordinary circumstances.

- We found out today that Michael Fuller had been at both the crime scenes just hours before the murders took place. We discovered this by reviewing the surveillance tapes that John Dean has been investigating the last weeks. Considering how fast we this out, I believe John has intentionally sabotaged our work

- The question is. How do we proceed?

Adam Smith:

- Well, that's a simple one. We got to the high command of the police and request arrest orders for the two of them as they are apparently up to no good.

James Locker:

- Well by principle you are right Adam. Problem is we don't have evidence against any of them that would lead to any convictions at present. If we go in and arrest them now, we are in big trouble in case we can't find the evidence necessary. Bear in mind that these are our colleagues and respected member/ex-members of the force.

Thomas Anderson:

- What if we just have informal questioning with both without bringing up any accusations, that can't bring us any harm?

James Locker:

- Our careers can't be damaged by questioning Michael or John, but there is a problem. If we ask them informally and they are in-volved in the murders, they will have all the time in the world to get rid of all the evidence.

Samantha Robinson:

- So, you are scrapping the Antonio DiMaestro trail then?

James Locker:

- No. He is still of the important for questioning, but there is not even any indication whether the man is alive or not. All the traces we have from him the last month might as well be someone else trying to frame him for the murders

Adam Smith:

- Well, you got the point boss. How do you reckon we should pro-ceed?

James Locker:

- Well, I reckon we should get permission from Barry Itch and the High Command to tap Michael's and John's phones and see where it leads us. It is imperative however that you don't share this information with the rest of the group as we can't tell the allegiances of the other team members.

Samantha Robinson:

- I don't like this North Korea approach, with distrust and spying on your peers, but given the evidence, I am obliged to agree with you.

James Locker:

- Thank you, Samantha. Yes, this is not the usual approach, but extraordinary circumstances require extraordinary solutions.

- Has anyone anything to add?

Thomas Anderson:

- Well, I have another piece of evidence backing your approach. My research showed that Michael is behind the "Vanessa" account on the dating website.

Adam Smith:

- I don't see the big deal; it's obviously a prank. Can it be illegal?

Thomas Anderson:

- Well, I don't think it would be illegal, but it speaks volumes when Michael does it with the intent of breaking James down, don't you think?

Adam Smith:

- Well, I guess you are right...

James Locker:

- Anyway. Does everyone in this room agree on a path of action where I ask Barry Itch for permission to tap Michael's and John's phones and locations for the last two weeks to find clues that will lead us forward in the investigation?

Samantha Robinson, Adam Smith, Thomas Anderson

- Agreed

James Locker:

- Great. I will talk with the BITCH, and hopefully, we'll soon be ready!

Chapter 66 Failed Communication with Barry Itch

I t was Monday afternoon, and Barry Itch was sitting quite content in his office. He had had a good weekend providing him with the best of life. Barry being a high-ranking police director, received a paycheck that enabled him to enjoy the best of life and the weekend that passed had contained all of it both when it came to the company, drinks, and activities. He had enjoyed listening to Wanda complain about how dreadful and horrible it was to have Adam Smith on part 2 of her workplace equality seminar. Although Barry Itch acknowledged the importance of his wife's work, it was still a good feeling for him to let her experience what he had to deal with every day. After all, a lot of his subordinates were lowbrow grunts which apparently had some undefined usefulness in the organisation, but Barry Itch simply could not stand dealing with them. In that way, it was a shame that Michael Fuller had been forced away as he at least was intelligent enough to stimulate the brain and match Barry when it came to intellectuality.

Barry saw James Locker entering his office, and in the glimpse of an eye, his good mood left him. James was a pain to deal with, and he had not met the expectations Barry had set for him. He made a mental note to find a permanent replacement for Michael as soon as possible and demote James to inspector again as he was just too difficult to handle. James approached him and started talking:

- Hey sir. I have some important news to share with you. Please look at the videos I have prepared for you at my tablet.

Barry Itch:

- I see a drunken Michael Fuller arguing with someone...

- Michael is not working here anymore; why are these movies relevant?

James Locker:

- Because the videos show Michael arguing with the murder victims just hours before the murders.

- Furthermore, John Dean didn't report on Michael's presence in these videos although he worked with them for over a week. For Samantha and me, it took two hours. So, he must be stalling at best and actively sabotaging the investigation at worst. I have taken him off the case effective immediately

Barry Itch:

- I see. What you are implying is serious if it turns out to be true. As John is still working for us, it would have to be internal investigations investigating his case.

- With Michael, you can take him in for questioning, but you don't have enough evidence to put him in custody.

- I will, however, get all the clearances needed to tap his phone and trace his position. You'll have the approval tomorrow.

James Locker:

- Is it a good idea stalling this even more? If John wasn't delaying us, Jessica Hall might still be alive.

Barry Itch:

- Well, unfortunately, the wheels of justice run slowly. Now if you excuse me; I have other matters to resolve.

After James left his office, Barry felt uncomfortable. An internal investigation was the last thing he wanted considering how he handled the cocaine issue with Michael a few weeks earlier. This time the threat was real to Barry. If Michael got caught, there was a grave risk that he would drag him down the abyss. But why would Michael kill the wife and mistress of Antonio DiMaestro? Barry had known Michael for over 20 years, and although they have had their differences in the past, this seemed like madness and not at all the Michael he knew.

Barry had experienced difficulties dealing with Michael in the past, due to Michael's impulsiveness, drunkenness, and recklessness. Stealing cocaine from a crime scene matched this description as it was likely that someone addicted to alcohol had an affinity towards other drugs as well. But these murders were very thoroughly planned and perfectly executed, and Barry could not see Michael killing anyone that way. It was also a mystery to him how Michael would practically perform these murders considering how drunk he was the hours before them. Then again alcoholics often could function normally even while drunk, so it was not an impossible scenario.

Barry made up his mind about the *"Michael Fuller being the Killer"* scenario. He did not buy it and as he did not; he saw nothing wrong in refusing James Locker's team the right to trace and tap John's and Michael's phones. He would not run the issue with his superiors, but he would tell James that he had if he came by the day after.

Chapter 67 The Killer makes his final preparations

The Killer sat restlessly in his car parked in Palm Beach one block away from Michael Fuller's beach house. Tonight, was the night to strike, but he somehow would have to convince Michael that it was a good idea to see Emily Luong in Claymore supposedly the worst suburb of Sydney. As it seemed, Michael had given up his quest to clear his name so this would not be an easy task, but he hoped he had precisely the bait needed to fry this fish! The Killer picked up his phone and dialled Michael's number. Getting that phone had been a hassle as every sim card was supposed to be registered with an ID card according to Australian law. He had been able to acquire a sim card anyway, as most things were available for someone willing to pay the right price, but it was still an unwelcome hassle.

Michael Fuller:

- Hello, who is this?

The Killer

- It's a friend.

Michael Fuller:

- All my friends carry names. If you don't then fuck off

The Killer

- Okay then, It's Jordan Palmer

Michael Fuller:

- That's better.

- Although I don't know you, so what do you want?

The Killer:

- Well, suffice to say we have common enemies. James Locker is an infiltrator at the CSMI; he has been working for Antonio DiMaestro all along.

- I know who can help you prove it.

Michael Fuller:

- I don't care about that anymore. I have quit the force for good and put all of that behind me.

The Killer:

- Well, that's a shame because that means in 24 hours you'll be in custody for the murders of Jessica Hall and Miranda DiMaestro. You see they have surveillance tapes showing you at the crime scenes hours before the killings as well as location data for your mobile phone showing that you were in the area during both murders. Just because they failed getting rid of you by planting the cocaine in your house it does not mean they will fail again.

Michael Fuller:

- You have my attention Jordan.
- So, who can prove this conspiracy you are talking about?

The Killer:

- Well, James Locker's ex-girlfriend Emily Luong who lives in Claymore can tell you all you need to know about his shady connections. From there it's up to you.

Michael Fuller:

- Alright, I will play along with your games stranger. How do I find this woman?

The Killer:

- I will text you the address. Go tonight, they are bringing you in tomorrow, and from there it's too late!

The Killer was checking the trace he had on Michael's phone. Soon he would know if Michael swallowed his bait or not. What was his contingency plan if Michael did not take the bait? Well, he could still frame Michael for the other two murders, but it would be difficult going through with the Emily Luong murder. That would be a missed opportunity as that murder was the final piece of breaking James down before killing him. The Killer did not have time to think more about his contingency plan as his master plan was working. He could see Michael moving on his tracking monitor and a short while after he saw Michael's car passing down the crossroads.

It was time to strike. The Killer had studied the Fuller residence for a couple of hours before making the call just to make sure there were no surveillance systems installed since his last visit. There wasn't, but he could still not be sure that there were not any hidden cameras in the building invisible from the Internet. This scenario would apply if Michael had anticipated his plan and installed analogous tape-based cameras. Just in case the Killer decided to wear a mask while breaking into the building knowing that even if detection would mess up his attempt to frame Michael, it would still not lead them to him. He planted the evidence where the masterpiece was the almost two month's old severed head of Antonio DiMaestro. He placed the head on a pedestal in Michael Fuller's meditation room. The severed head on a stand would undoubtedly give any investigator entering the room the impression that Michael had lost his mind. Combined with the other evidence as well as Michael's proved presence at all crime scenes would be more than enough to lock Michael up for good.

The Killer smiled. It was time for the second last kill, and then he would finally be free.

Chapter 68 Michael Fuller Gets a Bad Hunch

Michael was driving on the highway towards Claymore when he realised what an absurd mess, he had put himself in. He was driving his replacement car with a blood alcohol level way above 0.5, a few days after a car crash that demolished his car and could have killed him. He was driving towards a destination to see a woman who supposed to be James' ex-girlfriend and was meant to give him pointers on how to clear himself. But there were too many "if'" in this scenario for Michael to feel comfortable. For starters how did he know that this woman the mysterious caller referred to knew anything? How could he be sure that James was the one behind it all? It could be anyone in the police or even outside for all that mattered.

All Michael knew, was that his life was like the motto on the Australian coat of arms. "Never stand still." He was heading into the night towards an unknown destination, but at least if he were to go down, he would not go down without a fight. If Antonio DiMaestro and his scumbag crew wanted him, they would have to come and get him! He looked at the gun which he had brought tonight. It was a heavy calibre Desert Eagle with a lot of punching power. With renewed energy, he headed towards Claymore in the darkness of the night.

Chapter 69 A Drunken Man at Gunpoint

E mily Wanda Luong was watching an episode of sex and the city while eating a bag of potato chips. Growing up in Claymore, and living all her life there, she did not have much in common with James's ex-girlfriend Emily Dawn Luong. Well except for the name and that they were both of Asian ethnicity. While Emily Dawn Luong had been petite and very feminine Emily Wanda Luong was a horror for the eyes with her features since long ruined by excessive junk food eating, smoking, and childbearing.

Emily was dreaming away while watching the show. All their issues and discussions seemed so unrelatable to her, but it was the charm of the show. It provided her with an escape from reality by showing her an alternative reality that seemed so far away. Emily was both happy and sad that her children were with their father this night. Comfortable as it gave her time for herself but sad as she felt very lonely and was convinced that their father was abusive to them. The court was of a different opinion and thus they had received shared custody after their separation a few years back.

Emily sometimes considered the option of moving out of Claymore so her children would get a chance for a better upbringing and environment. She had a job, and with some extra support from the government, she would be able to afford it. But where would she go? All her friends and family were living there, and somehow it seemed safe and pleasant to be close to her family even though she dreamed of a better future for her children somewhere else.

Emily awoke from her reflections when someone knocked on the door. She was hesitant to open it, but since she lived in a security building, she decided to do so. That was one of the advantages of getting a paycheck instead of welfare, at least she and her children could live well and safe. Emily got terrified when she opened the door. On the other side was a drunken delusional man who introduced himself as Michael Fuller from the Central Sydney Murder Investigation Department. He spoke some incomprehensible nonsense about a conspiracy within the police and worst of all this man was holding a gun in his hand waving it in broad gestures. After a few moments of terror, the man realised that he had come to the wrong house and apologised wryly before leaving. Emily did what anyone would and called the police.

Chapter 70 A Failed Attempt

The Killer saw Michael Fuller go from the building where Emily Luong lived. He was holding a gun in his hand. There could, in theory, be a problem as Michael who was visible on the nearby traffic camera held another gun in his hand than the Killer had used for the murders.

But this disproved nothing as Michael could have several firearms. On the contrary, it showed that he was delusional and aggressive waving his gun like that. The Killer decided that it was time to strike. As it was a security building, visitors were forced to scan their driver's license to enter to keep criminals out of the building. The Killer, however, used an electronic lock-pick on the backdoor instead to get in undetected and proceeded towards Emily Luong's apartment.

He had mixed feelings towards killing her, as she, had done nothing to deserve to die and it was a shame to bereave two children of their struggling mum. Then again, he was not a man that was driven by his morals but by what he felt he needed to do. The Killer knocked on the door and said that his name was Jordan Palmer from the local police. Emily Luong opened the door, and the first thing he did was to shoot her in the head. When the Killer tried discharging his second shot, he noticed that his gun had jammed. The gun jamming was bad news as he was not certain that one shot from such a weak revolver would be enough to kill her. He wanted to make sure she died partly to ensure no loose ends existed but mostly out of pity with the unconscious woman lying on the floor. If she survived that shot, she would get severe brain damage, and that was a fate worse than death.

The Killer could hear police sirens in the distance. There was no time to lose! He ran into her apartment and locked the door behind him. He then jumped down from her balcony and ran to his car before the police arrived. He was far too close to get caught, and he had to get rid of the gun. He drove to the nearby Eagle Vale pond and dumped it in there as he could not plant it in Michael 's house as the police were probably headed there at any moment as he had planted Antonio DiMaestro's phone switched on in there.

When driving home, the killer felt very relieved and pleased with his victory. The news of the death of Emily Luong would surely drive James to insanity. Insanity he would try curing from taking his precious pills. Precious pills that the Killer had replaced with other medicines that would make James' mind worse!

Chapter 71 A Trace on Antonio DiMaestro

J ames Locker woke up in the middle of the night from his phone calling. The caller ID told him that the call was from the Technical Surveillance Department of the Sydney Police. James certainly hoped that they were bringing a significant breakthrough as it would be unnecessary to wake him just to notify him of minor detail.

James Locker:

- Hello, James speaking.

Andrew McLane:

- Hi this is Andrew from Technical surveillance

- We have pinpointed a signal from Antonio DiMaestro's mobile phone. How do you wish to proceed?

James Locker:

- Well, we believe Antonio to be armed and extremely dangerous.

- So, I would suggest that you seal off the block and surround the house. Then send in a tactical squad to apprehend him.

Andrew McLane:

- Great a squad will be going shortly.

James Locker:

- Oh, and where is this place? My team will need to come by to secure any evidence that might be in the building.

Andrew McLane.

- It's in Palm Beach, on Ocean Road.

James Locker:

- Thank you for the call, Andrew. I'll assemble my team and be there as quickly as possible.

After hanging up the phone, James started thinking. Michael Fuller lived on Ocean Road in Palm Beach. So, there were two likely scenarios: either Michael was the Killer and was posing as Antonio DiMaestro as a distraction, or Antonio had decided to come after and kill Michael. James Locker concluded that the most likely scenario was that Antonio DiMaestro was coming after Michael, as it seemed strange that the latter would turn on Antonio DiMaestro's mobile phone in his own house if he wanted to divert attention from himself. Thinking that the life of his former colleague might be at risk James decided to call Michael:

James Locker:

- Hi, Michael. We got a trace from Antonio DiMaestro's mobile phone. It seems he is in the vicinity of your house. I just called to warn you.

Michael Fuller:

- Oh, shit is he coming after me? Yeah, I reckon he might be; I guess I have been looking too much for him lately. Oh, and it makes sense that he would want to kill me after failing to get me convicted in the cocaine set up.

James Locker:

- Cocaine set up?! What the fuck are you talking about? Where are you now, by the way, it sounds like you are in a car?

Michael Fuller:

- Yeah, I went out for a midnight ride; following up on a clue in the shadier parts of town.

James Locker:

- Michael let me make this clear for you. You are not a police officer anymore. You do not have the authority to conduct any investigations on behalf of the police or claim to be a police officer. Just get to your house and meet up with the patrol cars waiting outside. I will be there in an hour.

Chapter 72 Outside Michael Fuller's Home

James Locker arrived outside Michael Fuller's house one hour and 15 minutes later. As he had instructed police surrounded the house and a tactical squad was on standby ready to move in and apprehend Antonio DiMaestro. He went to Michael who was obviously drunk. James decided that it was time to take actions against Michael and his alcoholism as the situation had gone out of hand. He called two nearby police officers from the local police to come over.

James Locker:

- Officers, how did this man arrive here?

Police officer:

- He drove here sir. He claims to be Michael Fuller, the owner of the house.

James Locker:

- Did he drive here you say? So, what are you waiting for? The man is obviously drunk; test his blood alcohol levels for drunk driving.

A short while later the officers came back.

- Sir, you were right he had a staggering 1.5 in blood alcohol level.

James Locker:

- Perfect. You know the drill for severe drunken driving. Lock him up in the prisoner transport car.

Michael was going to protest, but he could not come up with anything to say. He knew what he had done was a felony and that he would probably have to serve a couple of months in jail for it. Michael realised that this was perhaps a punishment long overdue and that he had got away from testing several times by knowing the officers conducting the tests. Feeling a bit shameful all he hoped for was that this would not prevent him from his planned British Islands holiday, departing at the end of the week.

For James, arresting Michael for drunk driving served two purposes. Firstly, it was essential to send Michael a message that he did not stand over the law and should not be meddling in police business. Secondly, it gave him an excellent opportunity to question him about his part in this mess once they had apprehended Antonio DiMaestro. With all loose ends sorted out, James sent in the tactical squad to capture Antonio DiMaestro. A few minutes later he got a response from their team leader over the radio.

Squad Leader:

- Sir, we have found Antonio DiMaestro.

James Locker:

- Excellent bring him out then.

Squad Leader:

- No, I wouldn't do that. We found his severed head on an altar.

James Locker:

- Oh my god! Well just secure the scene, and my team will come in shortly.

Knowing that Antonio DiMaestro was found dead in Michael's house, he decided to make a quick decision. Officially it was a decision to be made by the district attorney, but James was so sure of the outcome, so he did not feel compelled to call the DA at 4 AM in the morning for clearance. He walked towards the prisoner transport car opened the door and said:

James Locker

- Michael Fuller! You are under arrest for the murders of Miranda DiMaestro, Jessica Hall, and Antonio DiMaestro!

Chapter 73 Inside Michael Fuller's House

J ames Locker and his team entered Michael Fuller's home. From looking at some empty whiskey bottles and beer bottles, it looked like the place had been hosting a huge party the night before. James reflected over how dirty and untidy the house was and if that was an indication of Michael 's general decay as a person.

James remembered one year before when he and Emily Luong had visited Michael's 55-year party. The place had looked so different back then. It had been spotless, and Michael had been in his best moods as a host. Evidently, he had been drunk at the time but not the lousy and foul-smelling drunk he had been his last months at CSMI. James wondered if this decay was linked to a certain event in Michael's life or if it was a natural development once someone started taking up the bottle to fill the holes in one's soul. James was interrupted in his thoughts by Adam who began talking to him:

- Hey, James. One can say a lot about Michael's arrogance and
"know better than everyone else" attitude, but the man sure knows
how to party.

James Locker:

- Well, I don't know if I would call it a party, there is no indication
of anyone else visiting this place.

Adam Smith:

- Oh well, I guess there is a fine line between being an awesome
party dude and a pathetic lonely alcoholic. But as long as I stay on
the right side of the line, I am happy.

Thomas Anderson:

- Hey James, what are we looking for in here?

James Locker:

- Well, I want you to check his computer. Try figuring out how he hacked the security systems of the crime scenes. Also, check if you can find any indication on his motives. As it is right now, I can't see any other reason than booze-induced paranoia.

- Finally, it would be good if we find anything connecting Michael Fuller to John Dean. I am sure that weasel was sabotaging our investigation, but it would be good if we could prove it so that we can get rid of him for good

- For the rest of you guys. Look extensively. Anything that could explain his motives would be good. Best of all would be if we could find the murder weapon, but there are no guarantees that he hasn't got rid of that already.

Samantha Robinson:

- James. I have got an idea on how to expose John Dean.

- Send him a text from Michael's phone that he must meet up as soon as possible and that John should bring all the files he got.

- John is off the case, so he does not know that we have captured Michael. By doing things this way, we might catch him off guard.

James Locker:

- Sounds like a plan Samantha. In case he swallows the bait bring Johnson and Baker to the meeting point you decide and confront him!

After saying this James walked around the Fuller Estate trying to get a general overview of the house. He got captivated by a set of pictures depicting what was most likely Michael's daughter. The photos were depicting her from her baby years up to roughly 15. She was a beautiful girl, and strangely enough, she looked very familiar although James could not recall ever meeting her. James moved on to the meditation room, where the severed head of Antonio DiMaestro was sitting on the altar, this seemed very strange to him, but he recalled from the Father Walker case that Michael Fuller had a very vivid interest in the occult. The head was in an advanced state of decomposition, and James reckoned that Antonio must have been dead for weeks.

James was disgusted and really shocked that the Killer turned out to be his former boss, but also relieved as the evidence securing phase of a case would now commence. Although it was painstaking and sometimes very frustrating, it was a lot less stressful than the previous stage where they supposedly needed to find the killer. Especially in cases with serial killers the job was very stressful as they all knew that their lives were at stake!

For now, they would just have to gather as much information as possible before conducting the first interrogation of Michael in the morning. James was considering the option to interrogate him now, but there was no point in talking to a drunken person unless it was an urgent matter.

Chapter 74 John Dean Avoids the Trap

John Dean woke up by the text message tone on his mobile phone. He felt confused as no-one ever texted him in the middle of the night. John was a married man in his mid-forties, and he did not have any friends who texted him drunken text messages during the evening. He reached for his phone and saw that it was a text message from Michael Fuller. The message read the following. *"I am in trouble and need your help immediately. I would appreciate if you could bring some of the investigation material. I would like to meet at the University café in Macquarie Park before you start work. Would 7 AM suit you? PS I am close to catching Antonio DS/ Michael Fuller."*

After reading this text message, John immediately realised that Michael had been arrested and that James was trying to use a fake message to entrap him. Although it made him angry that the police arrested Michael, he felt relieved at the same time as Michael had not agreed to testify against him as the other team members felt obliged to send him this pathetic text message instead. John Dean decided to reply to the text message to show James Locker that John was on top of his games and insult him at the same time. He wrote *"Hey James. I suppose you have somehow arrested Michael Fuller on insufficient evidence and now you are trying to forge some against me as well. Well, it won't work as I would never leave out classified material to unauthorised persons. PS Michael Fuller never communicates through text messages, and he never goes to places that do not sell alcohol. DS /John Dean."*

Satisfied with his answer John Dean decided to sleep for a few more hours.

Chapter 75 A Heavy Reaction

It was 10 AM Tuesday the 3rd of September 2013 and James Locker was preparing the initial questioning of Michael Fuller. They had been unable to find any more interesting evidence at the Fuller estate, but at least they had received the location data from Michael Fuller's phone for the last month and now knew that he had been in the vicinity of both crime scenes at the time of the murders. They were also matching Michael Fuller's DNA against the unidentified male DNA found at both the crime scenes, but the result of this matching was yet to come as they were doing the full scan which was reliable enough for the court. James was distracted from his thought when he received an unexpected call from Campbelltown.

Alan Morse:

- Hello this is Alan Morse from the Campbelltown police station, is this James Locker speaking?

James Locker:

- Indeed, it is, how can I help you, Alan?

Alan Morse:

- Well, we had a woman shot in our district earlier tonight.

James Locker:

- Well, I am sorry to hear that Alan, but Campbelltown is not our jurisdiction. Try with the Western Sydney Murder Investigation Department.

Alan Morse:

- Well, I beg to differ.

- You see this woman, Emily Luong called in at 1 AM tonight and told us that she was threatened at gunpoint by a drunken lunatic who called himself Michael Fuller and claimed to be an officer from CSMI. Apparently, he was raving about a conspiracy in the police force against him before he left.

- We took the call seriously, but when we arrived 15 minutes later, Emily was found unconscious with a bullet wound to the head.

James Locker:

- I see. We'll come by and talk to you as soon as possible. What was the name of the victim again?

Alan Morse:

- Great. I'll see you later today then.
- Her name is Emily Luong.

James Locker:

- Oh my god, I got to go!

Upon hearing that someone had shot Emily Luong, James was deeply shocked. He just could not believe that Emily was shot. It was impossible. But why was it impossible? Horrible images of Emily Luong were sweeping in front of his eyes. His pulse rose, and his vision and hearing became distorted. Adam who was passing by his office noticed James' condition and approached him.

Adam Smith:

- What's the matter James, you look like you just woke up next to a fat ugly tranny?

James Locker:

- They called from Campbelltown; they believe Michael Fuller shot Emily.

Adam Smith

- Shot your ex-girlfriend, Emily?

James Locker:

- Yes.

Adam Smith:

- Well, that's a bummer.

James Locker:

- They want me to come by, but I can't handle this...

Adam Smith:

- I understand that...

- Look this is what we do. We drive you home, and I go with Samantha and meet up with them. Then I will let you know whether it's your ex-girlfriend or some other woman with the same name.

James Locker:

- Yes. Just get me out of here. I need to go home and get my medicine now!

Adam Smith:

- If you say so boss, let's go!

They picked up Samantha Robinson at her desk and left the police station for a drive to Campbelltown via James Locker's home in Lidcombe.

Chapter 76 A Medical Failure

As soon as he got home, James Locker reacted instinctively and took a triple dose of his medication due to the misconception that more is better. He soon realised that it was not a great idea as he saw the wandering corpse of Emily Luong coming towards him haunting him with an eerie distorted voice. She disappeared and appeared randomly, and there were fire and flames spread throughout the room. Time was moving extremely slowly, and James could see how his flesh slashed open and closed back and forth. He realised that he somehow had been poisoned and with a great effort he managed to get to the bathroom to throw up. By chance, his eyes met with his reflection in the bathroom mirror, and it was the worst horror James had faced thus far. He could see how the other face was smiling at him and talking a foreign tongue with a hissing voice. The last thing James Locker heard was a voice saying, *"YOU did this to yourself"* before he fell unconscious.

Chapter 77 An Interrupted Meeting

Adam Smith and Samantha Robinson arrived at the police station in Campbelltown. It was a lot more run down than the central parts of Sydney where Adam and Samantha usually resided. They stated their business to the receptionist and met with the local detective Alan Morse.

Alan Morse:

- Welcome to Campbelltown, I am Alan Morse. I hope the traffic was not too bad.

Adam Smith:

- No, it was alright. I am Adam Smith and with me is Samantha Robinson.

Alan Morse:

- Okay, this is peculiar; I thought the detective of your group, James Locker, would come?

Adam Smith:

- Yeah, that would make sense.

- But basically, it was a sensitive matter for him.

- You see your victim, Emily Luong has the same name as his ex-girlfriend, and he did not think he would be able to handle a case with someone close to him.

Alan Morse:

- Well, Emily is in a coma in the hospital, but this is a picture of her.

Adam Smith:

- Well, that's a relief as this is not James Locker's ex-girlfriend.
- So, tell us what you know about the case?

Alan Morse:

- Not very much. A local woman, Emily Luong, called in to report that a crazy drunken man who claimed to be Michael Fuller had threatened her at gunpoint. A traffic camera outside the building captured the following shots.

Samantha Robinson:

- Well, the video is unclear, but from the clothing, it looks like Michael Fuller. We do have location data from his mobile phone telling us he indeed was in Claymore at 1 AM and this explains what he was doing there.

- Can you upload the emergency call and traffic camera video to our evidence database?

Alan Morse:

- Yes, of course, anything else I can do to assist you?

Samantha Robinson:

- Yeah if you can do the on-site examination and talk to the neighbours that would be good, we are busy with the investigation of Michael's house since we arrested him last night, suspecting him of three murders. But yeah, I am not the one with the final say in this matter so James Locker will have to get back to you.

Suddenly, Samantha's mobile phone received a call from Gerry Livingstone.

Samantha Robinson:

 - Hey, Gerry! What's new?

Gerry Livingstone:

 - Well, I spoke to my pharmacologist colleague today.

 - James Locker must have a condition of schizophrenia considering that he is using Xenopropsyche. It's one the most potent substance on the market,

 - That's why his finding was extra critical as he found out that the pills you supplied him with are Xenoantipsyche, a class A psychedelic drug.

 - So, if your friend uses the drug believing that it will make him better, it's making him worse! it's worrisome news indeed.

Samantha Robinson:

 - Thank you, Gerry. I got to go!

Adam Smith:

 - Bad news?

Samantha Robinson:

 - Yes, we got to go to James' place straight away. I will explain in the car.

After having said this, they rushed out of the police station and left Alan Morse, and the rest of the staff at Campbelltown PD confused.

Chapter 78 The Killer Watches James Locker Fade Away

The Killer watched James Locker fading away on his bathroom floor. Or fading was not the right word as he was vomiting heavily, screaming for help and asking Emily Luong for forgiveness. It seemed like James had finally realised that he was the one who killed Emily Luong and that was a great relief as he was NOW ready to die. But how should the killing take place? The easiest way would be if James consumed enough of the Xenoantipsyche drugs, to die from a toxic overdose. But that was a highly unlikely scenario, as the Xenoantipsyche was a lot more dangerous to the mind than it was to the body. What other ways would there be? Well, there was always the option to kill him, as James Locker in his current condition would not be able to resist to it. But the killer knew that if he chose that path his plan to set Michael Fuller up for the murders would fail. James Locker killed by poison that Michael Fuller left in his house was an ingenious plan, and it also worked as the police would find several containers of Xenoantipsyche in Michael Fuller's home as well, containers planted there the night before.

The killer noticed that James was coming to his senses and noticed his presence in the room and reached out for him. The Killer hesitated for a while but then decided to take James's outstretched hand and hold it.

James Locker:

- Forgive me. I never meant to hurt her. I loved her I didn't want to hurt her

The Killer:

- I know that you loved her, but you killed her. You know why I am doing this to you, don't you?

James Locker:

- Yes, I do.

After having said that James fell unconscious and his body was cramping heavily. The Killer felt sorry for him, such a horrible way to die. But James had killed the woman in the world that had meant the most to him, and there was only one punishment worthy of such atrocity, DEATH!

The Killer realised that he would miss James once he was gone. For the last nine months, his primary purpose in life was to make James understand what he had done and to make him pay. Now the Killer was so close to that goal but what would come next?

While he would finally be free and could develop his relationship with Rebecca, his life would lose much of its purpose once James Locker was gone. It was interesting that he started thinking about this factor right at the end. If he had thought about it earlier, he would have chosen another path.

The Killer came back to his senses when he could hear police and ambulance sirens approaching. The police arriving was indeed unplanned for, but there was not much that could be done about that now. Realising he should NOT be there when the cops came, The Killer made a run for it and left the building unnoticed.

Chapter 79 At Auburn Hospital

A short while after the ambulance had delivered the unconscious James Locker to the toxicology department that was handling cases regarding drug overdoses Adam Smith and Samantha Robinson arrived there. They were greeted by doctor Jayachandran who took them aside to talk to them.

Dr Jayachandran:

- It's a good thing you called us, but his condition is still grave. It looks like a drug overdose or deliberate poisoning, but we must determine the cause of it to put in treatment. The problem is that I have never seen these symptoms before.

- And we need to identify the poison to commence with a treatment

Samantha Robinson:

- It's Xenoantipsyche

Dr Jayachandran:

- Are you sure? That's a bizarre drug to abuse and overdoses are unheard of.

Samantha Robinson:

- Yes, I am sure, just administer the treatment!

Dr Jayachandran:

- Well, the hospital cannot deliver unsafe treatments like this without consent from the patient or next of kin. It's a matter of legal liability. We need written permission to undertake risky procedures. Basing our treatment on what you think the patient might have taken is an unsafe way of determining treatment.

Adam Smith:

- What is the treatment for a Xenoantipsyche overdose?

Dr Jayachandran:

- That would be a shot of a compound called Flushout. But that substance can be hazardous if used to treat overdoses from Opioid substances, and we can't rule those out from the symptoms James is showing.

Adam Smith:

- I see, Doctor. Well, you just take your time getting the consents while Samantha and I are waiting outside.

They left the room, and once they got out of sight Adam whispered to Samantha:

- Look, I am not intending to let my best friend die while some stiff bureaucrat is waiting for consent

- Are you sure he has overdosed Xenoantipsyche?

Samantha Robinson:

- Yes, I am positive.

Adam Smith:

- Great, I am moving in. We need to find a shot of Flushout and give it to James. Those fucking consent forms can take hours to fill in, and I am not letting him die during that time.

Samantha Robinson:

- Are you sure? You know if it fails you the court might charge you with murder.

Adam Smith:

- Yes, I am sure.

- Look, just keep the uptight son of a bitch distracted while I find the shot and give it to James. Flushout sounds like the name of a standard compound, so it should be available in the room

Samantha Robinson:

- How would I do that?

Adam Smith:

- Well, the way he looked at you, it would not take much effort from you to keep him distracted.

Samantha Robinson:

- Okay, let's go.

They decided to move in. Samantha unbuttoned the two top buttons of her blouse which was enough to show her great cleavage but not enough to make it too visible what her purpose was. She then started flirting with Doctor Jayachandran while Adam found a shot of Flushout and applied it on James who immediately came to life and started cascade vomiting and rambling strange, incomprehensible sentences.

Dr Jayachandran:

- Oh my god man, are you crazy? What have you done?

Adam Smith:

- I am saving my friend, while you the doctor who is supposed to protect people are too preoccupied with protecting yourself by filling out bullshit forms instead of even trying!

Dr Jayachandran

- You are crazy; let's hope for both our sakes that he will come out okay.

After this conversation, a few hours of nervous waiting took place. Finally, James came back to his senses and started talking.
James Locker:

- Adam, Samantha. What happened and where am I?

Adam Smith:

- Congratulations you just had the trip of your life!

Samantha Robinson:

- Michael Fuller poisoned you. But you'll be okay the doctor can tell you more.

Dr Jayachandran:

- You took a massive overdose of Xenoantipsyche, when you were meant to take Xenopropsyche. Physically you'll be fine, but we'll have to keep you for at least one week for observation to determine what mental damage it caused you.

James Locker:

- I see, well that's for the best.

After that James Locker went back into a delirious state once again. Adam and Samantha looked worried, but the doctor calmed them down.
Dr Jayachandran:

- Don't worry. At least his vitals are fine now. As for the mind, it will take time to recover. You should go home and get some rest now; you look exhausted.

They left the hospital and when they were in the car, Adam started talking:

- Hey Samantha, where should I drop you off? Or we are going straight to my place in Lidcombe to get to know each other better after all the heroism that I showed you today?

Samantha Robinson:

- Well, it's incredible that you are still thinking about sex after all the stress we been through today?!

Adam Smith:

- Well, that's who I am. You never see James Bond at the end of the movies whining over all the wounds he has received or feeling remorse over all the lives he ended? You see him banging a hot chick!

Samantha Robinson:

- True as that may be, I am still going to decline. I am already dating Thomas; I assumed you knew that?

Adam Smith:

- Seriously?! Are the two of you dating? I believed that he finally had come out of the closet or started seeing a hideous woman. Thomas is so full of surprises!

- But unfortunately, I must now withdraw my sex offer. Where should I take you?

Samantha Robinson:

- Yeah, that's sad; I can't imagine what experience I must be missing!

- Well, I live in the city so drop me off at the train station. You must be exhausted as well, so you better get some rest.

A bit later, Adam dropped Samantha off at the train station, and they both went to their own homes.

Chapter 80 Wayne Bruce Helps Thomas Anderson Decrypting Michael Fuller's Computer.

Thomas was sitting in the Fuller estate and tried decoding the information on Michael's computer. He was tired and frustrated as the task was overwhelming for him. Information Technology and Internet security were supposed to be his specialties, and yet Thomas felt inept to even compete as he could compete with Michael's skills. The news of James ending up in the hospital did not improve his focus, and he was considering giving up and call it a day. But the poisoning of James Locker served as a motivator to Thomas. Michael had almost killed his friend, and he would find enough evidence to secure a conviction.

Another issue was that Samantha had failed to set John Dean up for the sabotaging the investigation. Thomas was afraid that he would do everything in his might to undermine the investigation in case they couldn't prove John's sabotage.

Despite his dedication, Thomas had almost given up when he realised that he could use his wildcard Wayne Bruce who had received clearance for working on the case by Barry Itch. Thomas called him, and he appeared in a heartbeat since his mansion was located nearby Michael's house.

Wayne Brucc:

- Hi, Neo, I have seen you in better shape, how can I help you?

Thomas Anderson:

- Yeah, I have been here since 3 AM, so I am not feeling sharp.

Wayne Bruce:

- Well, that's 14 hours straight. One cannot complain about your dedication. If I ever start a new IT company, there will be a place for you in it!

Thomas Anderson:

- Thank you, Wayne! That's very generous of you. But let us focus on the task at hand.

- I need to access the files on this computer, but they have a biometric lock. I also need to find out who copied the data on this USB stick and handed it to Michael Fuller.

Wayne Bruce:

- You have this guy in custody, right? I would suggest that you give him a glass of water tomorrow and cover that glass in a plastic material that absorbs fingerprints. That's more convenient than getting a court order forcing the suspect to unlock the files.

- As for the USB stick verification, did you know that a lot of systems these days save an invisible code every time you make a copy of a file? This is an antipiracy/ anti-terrorist surveillance thing, but if you know how to find it, it's quite easy to crack.

Thomas Anderson:

- Thank you, Wayne. Can you do this for me?

Wayne Bruce:

- Sure, it will take a couple of hours. You can crash at my place for the time being.

Thomas Anderson:

- Thank you, Wayne, but I can't leave an outsider with a crucial piece of evidence without police supervision. I can sit next to you while you are working.

After saying that, Thomas left the computer and the USB memory stick in the hands of Wayne Bruce. He was unable to keep his focus up though and soon fell asleep leaving Wayne unsupervised with the material. A couple of hours later Wayne woke him up.

Thomas Anderson:

- Oh shit, did I fall asleep?
- How did it go?

Wayne Bruce:

- It went well, I managed to find the coding I was looking for, and it proves that the files were copied by the user JDEAN between 22nd of August 2013 and the 28th of August 2013.

Thomas Anderson:

- Great, please join me and go to the internal investigations' office straight away, it's time to get this snake out of our organisation!

Chapter 81 At the Internal investigations' office

Thomas Anderson and Wayne Bruce went to the internal investigations office which underfunded and located in a rundown and grey office building in Redfern. Considering the state of affairs at the internal investigations department, a police officer who broke against protocol was likely to get away with it since the agency auditing them was in terrible shape. Thomas was not distraught by this as he had used his position in the police and the inadequate control of police officers to solicit bribes. He met up with the responsible officer Steven McLean who greeted him at the office.

Steven Mclean:

- Hello, officer Anderson, I am Steven Mclean the officer in charge here, how can I help you?

Thomas Anderson:

- Hi, Steven. I am here to give you some additional evidence in the case against John Dean at CSMI. I am sure such proof will prove that John Dean sabotaged our investigation as well as leaked information about it to our suspected killer Michael Fuller.

Steven Mclean:

- Yes, I have heard about the arrest of Michael Fuller. It's in the headlines all over Australia considering his relative fame within the police and all.

- When it comes to John Dean, there is no case pending on him so sadly I can't add any evidence to a case file that does not exist.

Thomas Anderson:

- Oh, that is strange indeed. The detective of my team, James Locker, spoke to Barry Itch the director of CSMI about John Dean and he thought a case was being started up.

Steven Mclean:

- Well, apparently he was mistaken. Now if you excuse me, we are closing now.

After witnessing the unhelpful and disinterested behaviour shown by Steven Mclean, Wayne Bruce felt compelled to intervene:

- No, you are not. I am an Australian citizen, and I have the right to file a complaint. My complaint is against John Dean who is a scandal for the police force.

Steven Mclean:

- Well that's interesting, whoever you are, and you can call customer service to complain about this, but we are closing our office for today.

Wayne Bruce:

- Nah I think I will pass when it comes to calling customer service.

- You see I am Wayne Bruce the IT billionaire. As a billionaire, I have a lot of ties with the New South Wales government.

- So, I will discuss your behaviour, Mr Mclean, with Michael Lawson the minister of police, when I see him during the state fundraiser this weekend.

Steven Mclean had not seen this headache coming five minutes before closing time. He was unsure of whether the man opposite to him was the man he claimed to be or not, but it wasn't a risk Steven wanted to take. With a loud sigh, Steven Mclean agreed to help them start up a case file against John Dean. 30 minutes later he summarised the case against John Dean.

Steven Mclean:

  - Look, guys, I have set up the case file against John Dean. I don't know if it's enough to get him convicted, but I will call high Command and make sure he gets suspended immediately.

Thomas Anderson:

  - Sounds good to me. As long as the snake is out of my face, I am happy.

Wayne Bruce:

  - And I am glad as soon as you have made the actual call. You don't seem to be the most cooperative of men Mr Mclean.

With an even louder sigh, Steven Mclean made the necessary calls to suspend John Dean from duty. Happy with the outcome Thomas went straight home postponing the after-work drinks suggested by Wayne.

Chapter 82 Initial interrogation of Michael Fuller

I t was 9 AM on the 4th of September 2013, and it was time for the first real interrogation of Michael Fuller. A short talk had been held the day before informing Michael of his legal rights but due to the poisoning of James Locker and the suspension of John Dean the team had been unable to set up a proper interrogation the previous day. Present in the room were: Michael Fuller, Adam Smith, Thomas Anderson, and Samantha Robinson. Thomas Anderson started the questioning:

- Can the suspect state his full name, date of birth and passport number, please?

Michael Fuller:

- Michal Samuel Fuller, 22nd of February 1957, M0992136

Thomas Anderson:

- Are you aware of the accusations against you? You stand accused of the murders of Antonio DiMaestro, Miranda DiMaestro and Jessica Hall. Furthermore; you are charged with the attempted assassination of Emily Luong and James Locker.

Michael Fuller:

- Yes, I am aware of this my lawyer was informed about this last night.

Thomas Anderson:

- Great!

- Well, Michael, you know how this goes down, so please give us a general overview of your actions these last few weeks, and we will be adding questions to your story.

Michael considered his options. He knew that the evidence against him was substantial and that there were cases in the past, with people convicted with less evidence against them despite denying everything. Michael had discussed this with his lawyer the day before, and they planned to admit all the minor offences he had done and to defame the entire CSMI so that the credibility of the police would be in the spotlight for the trial to come. Michael and his lawyer had decided to save some of the best contradictions in the police material for the court so the police force could not cover up the cracks in their case against him.

Michael Fuller:

- Well, I suppose what is interesting is what happened on the 19th of August 2013 the day I quit the force because of health issues?

Adam Smith:

- Well, initial analysis indicates that the head of Antonio DiMaestro has been decomposing for more than a month, but sure go ahead.

Michael Fuller:

- Well anyway. The 19th of August I get called over to Barry Itch's office where he accused me of possessing stolen cocaine from the crime scene of the Lopez case which occurred on the 12th of July the month before. There was a bag on the video where Lopez got shot, and then the camera went down, and when we got there, the bag was not there.

- Anyway, Barry Itch did not want this to be a public scandal, so he hired two operatives from a shady security company to search my house for the bag. Sadly, I consented to this and signed the consent form he gave me. The two operatives found the pack with 3.5 kilos of cocaine in my house and I had the options to either resign immediately or facing charges for severe drug crimes. I chose to leave.

Thomas Anderson:

- So, you are accusing the director of CSMI to cover up serious crimes? Do you have any proof to support these accusations?

Michael Fuller:

- I do. You see the entire situation felt very shady from the start, so I turned on sound recording on my mobile phone when Barry Itch was looking away.

- I can show you if you want.

Thomas Anderson:

- Well, since it's against protocol to let the suspect have access to the evidence, we can't accept that; however, we will do a thorough search for the file on your phone.

- But back to the new subject of the stolen cocaine, why did you take it? To use it or to sell it?

Michael Fuller:

- I did not! Someone placed it in my home to set me up.

Thomas Anderson:

- Well, that's a fascinating thought. You are aware that Australia has the most expensive cocaine in the world, right?

- So, you are claiming that someone spent cocaine with a street value of $500,000 to set you up?

Michael Fuller:

- Yes, that is what I am claiming.

Samantha Robinson:

- Are you sure that it was real cocaine that was in that bag?

Michael Fuller:

- Well, Barry Itch used the compound on a standard drug test in front of my eyes, and it turned blue for cocaine.

Thomas Anderson:

- I see. What did he do with this cocaine afterwards? I can't recall any significant quantities of cocaine found by our department this month.

Michael Fuller:

- Well, he asked me to open the bag and flush all the cocaine down the toilet, and I did.

Samantha Robinson:

- Let's move on. Tell us your reasons for going to the DiMaestro estate intimidating Miranda DiMaestro and then murdering her.

Michael Fuller:

- Okay it might have been a foolish, drunken choice but my reasoning was like this:

- I had been looking for Antonio DiMaestro ever since the Lopez case a month before. I wanted to question him about his part in the murder. But I never got the chance since the case was transferred to the organised crime department after the suspected gunman Angelo Ramirez died in a gunfight with airport police.

- But I never gave up the DiMaestro trail even though it was not my case anymore.

- So, I guessed that he was the one who set me up to get rid of me

- I did not intimidate her, and I did not kill her.

Adam Smith:

- Come on Michael this is ridiculous. You are saying that you suspected the man, whose head we found in your house for trying to set you up? Even if he wanted to set you up, why would he spend 3.5 kilos when 100 grams would have been enough to attain the same goal?

Michael Fuller:

- Well, I never killed Antonio DiMaestro. Someone placed his head in my home while I was away. As for the amount I don't know why they used so much.

Samantha Robinson:

- Okay noted. So, what were you doing in the DiMaestro mansion if you did not kill Miranda? Were you drinking tea with her?

Michael Fuller:

- I have never set foot in the DiMaestro estate.

Adam Smith:

- Well, that's interesting, as we found your DNA at several places in the house.

Michael Fuller:

- Well, it must have been planted there by whoever killed her.

Thomas Anderson:

- Okay. As you might be aware of the security cameras at the DiMaestro mansion was hacked, so the actual murder was not filmed. However, we did manage to backtrack the hacking to the IP address of your computer. Any comment on that?

Michael Fuller:

- I would not consider myself computer literate enough to comment on that.

Thomas Anderson:

- Fair enough. How do you explain your presence in the area at the time of the murder? According to our positioning data, you were connected to the same mobile phone base station for hours, thus being at the crime scene or in the vicinity of the crime scene when the murder of Miranda DiMaestro took place.

Michael Fuller:

- I was sitting at the local RSL club just down the road.

Samantha Robinson:

- Well anyone who can verify that?

Michael Fuller:

- I was not there with anyone if that's what you are asking. But I did sign in at around 10 PM, and that should be on their records.

Samantha Robinson:

- When did you leave Mosman RSL?

Michael Fuller:

- Around midnight.

Adam Smith:

- Well, that's a horrible alibi, Michael. Your phone was connected to the Mosman base station until 1230AM and Miranda DiMaestro was murdered between 1215AM to 1230AM. So, you are saying that you were in the neighbourhood without an alibi at the time of the murder.

Michael Fuller:

- Well, I might have left the Mosman RSL a bit later then.

Thomas Anderson:

- I am sure we'll find out somehow.

Samantha Robinson:

- Moving on. On the 22nd of August, you withdrew $10,000 in cash from your bank account. What was the purpose of acquiring such large amounts of money?

Michael was considering the option to hand them John, but he decided not to. Partly because John Dean had been his friends for several years but also because it seemed highly unlikely that John was the man behind his situation. After all, why would John sacrifice cocaine worth $500,000 to set him up and then ask him for $10,000 to help him? Such behaviour would not make any sense.

Samantha Robinson:

- Let it be noted, that the suspect refused to answer the question.

- We have reasons to believe that you have been meeting up with John Dean on several occasions the last few weeks, what were the purposes of those meetings?

Michael Fuller:

- And I assume you have figured this the same way you have calculated everything else, through your flawless mobile phone location data, right?

Samantha Robinson:

- That is correct.

Michael Fuller:

- Well in the case with John Dean it's straightforward. We are friends, and there is nothing wrong with us hanging out even after I finished working here.

Samantha Robinson:

- Very well and I assume the fact that you withdrew $10,000 in cash and the fact that John somehow managed to miss you in surveillance tapes from the crime scenes are entirely unrelated?

Michael Fuller:

- Well, John has been under a lot of pressure recently with his daughter being sick and his marriage breaking down. He could have missed it out.

Samantha Robinson:

- And the USB stick with sensitive case material that we found in your house.

Michael Fuller:

- I got it from other sources.

Samantha Robinson:

- Right...

- So, tell me about the break-in at James's house where you painted him a message at his mirror with blood that turned out to be Antonio DiMaestro's?

Michael Fuller:

- I did not do that...

Samantha Robinson:

- So, you claim that you have not broken into James Locker's house recently?

Michael Fuller:

- Well I did break in at a later stage because I reckoned there was something fishy about the entire *"break-in at James Locker's house"* scenario

Thomas Anderson:

- We have you on video while breaking in at James' house. A hidden camera took this video. But I do have another theory on why you broke in that second time. You did it so you could replace James Locker's medicine Xenopropsyche with the substance Xenoantipsyche, which is a dangerous drug for people with weak minds.

- Were you aware of James Locker's mental health issues?

Michael Fuller:

- Yes of course, as his boss I was mindful of the fact that he had a breakdown after the breakup with his ex-girlfriend. But he received medication and from what I could tell he was doing fine.

Thomas Anderson:

- Were you also aware of his colour-blindness which would make it impossible for him to see the difference between his medication Xenopropsyche and the substance Xenoantipsyche which almost killed him?

Michael Fuller:

- Well, I am sure it is in his file, but it was not a detail I ever reflected over.

Thomas Anderson:

- Okay. In your house, we found a quantity of Xenoantipsyche, with your fingerprint on them, how do you explain that? Were you a user yourself?

Michael Fuller:

- No, I have never used that drug.

Adam Smith:

- Moving on, you went to Jessica Hall's place drunk and intimidated her, before you went back and killed her, a couple of hours later. Why did you do that?

Michael Fuller:

- I confronted her because I thought she knew about Antonio's whereabouts.
- I never killed her or hurt her in any way.

Adam Smith:

- Okay, but you were in the neighbourhood at the time of the murder?

Michael Fuller:

- Yes, I was at my favourite whiskey bar which is next to her apartment complex.

Adam Smith:

- Okay, do you have anyone that can confirm that you were there at the time of the murder?

Michael Fuller:

- Maybe my bankcard usage can, otherwise I don't think so.

Adam Smith:

- Well, your bank card usage would not be enough evidence to your favour though as you could have asked anyone to stay and buy drinks with your card and pin number.

Michael Fuller:

- Well, I suppose I could, but I did not, I bought drinks for myself.

Adam Smith:

- Whatever you say, Mr Fuller, whatever you say.

- You went to Jessica Hall's apartment a third time that night, or you stopped in the elevator and claimed to be going to a friend's place, who were you seeing?

Michael Fuller:

- Okay, I admit I was going to Jessica Hall's home again because I was irate and frustrated. I felt that she was lying to me and that she knew where Antonio DiMaestro was hiding.

Samantha Robinson:

- Well, I believe you went back to take the precious necklace you stole from the DiMaestro mansion when you killed Miranda Di-Maestro the week earlier. You got second thoughts because although it was a smart way of setting up Antonio DiMaestro for the murders, it was just too valuable to waste on such a venture.

Michael Fuller:

- I don't know what you are talking about? What necklace?

Samantha Robinson pulled out a picture from the case folder of the expensive jewellery that was left on top of Jessica Hall's dead body.
Samantha Robinson:

- This necklace.

- A costly necklace. I did some research on it, and it turned out a Sydney jeweller sold it to Antonio DiMaestro for $85,000 a few days before last Christmas.

Thomas Anderson:

- Moving on.

- A few days later you crashed your car into a tree in Olympic Park. What were you doing out there?

Michael Fuller:

- I was on my way back home, from my investigation of James Locker's house.

- As you all know I got a concussion and was hospitalised for a couple of days.

Adam Smith:

- Yes, we are aware of that because it was a few relaxed days. No hacking of our computers, no break-in at our colleagues' and no murders.

- But once you left the hospital, you became homicidal once again. This time your victim was Emily Luong. Why did you attack her, she has no connection to Antonio DiMaestro as far as we know?

Michael was considering his options before answering this question. As far he knew they had not presented any evidence that he was at Emily Luong's place so they might be shooting blindly at him, then again if he denied an apparent fact, he would ruin his credibility. He decided to move ahead and tell them.

Michael Fuller:

- Well, I got a call from a mysterious person who called himself Jordan Palmer. He claimed that James Locker was collaborating with Antonio DiMaestro to set me up, and this was the reason the police had been unable to locate Antonio DiMaestro.

- Furthermore, he told me that James Locker's ex-girlfriend Emily Luong had incriminating evidence against James Locker and that I had to see her that night otherwise James Locker would arrest me on the evidence he had forged.

Adam Smith:

- Okay now you have passed the border for delusional paranoia I reckon.

- So why did you shoot her? The woman you tried killing was not James Locker's ex-girlfriend Emily Luong. I know that, and you knew that as well, as you have met Emily Luong on several occasions.

Michael Fuller:

- Yes, I realised that it was not the right Emily Luong the moment she opened her door. So, I got baffled, and then I left.

Samantha Robinson:

- Well according to the emergency call, Emily called in to report that a drunken delusional man who called himself Michael Fuller were threatening her with a gun and claimed that there was a conspiracy within the police. When a squad car arrived 15 minutes later, they found her, shot in the head.

- Did you go back and shoot her?

Michael Fuller:

- No, I did not.

Adam Smith:

- Okay. When you were arrested for drunk driving a couple of hours later, you were found to carry a Desert Eagle pistol. Why did you wear this gun, and what happened with the .22 calibre silenced revolver that you used for the murders?

Michael Fuller:

- I did not kill anyone, so I don't know where that weapon is as it has never been in my possession.

- As for the Desert Eagle pistol, I took it in case I was walking into a trap as I did not want to be captured by some low-life mafia scums without the chance to defend myself.

Samantha Robinson:

- So, you admit that you considered the option to kill someone that night?

Michael Fuller:

- I admit that I brought a gun in case I needed to defend myself!

Adam Smith:

- Okay, Michael. I think this concludes our initial interrogation of you. We will follow up with more detailed questions later, but as for now, we are done.

- If this were an employment interview, this would be the stage where we told you that we would get back to you and then you would never hear from us again. Since it's not, you will see us a lot the weeks to come. The custody guards will pick you up shortly and bring you back to your seven square meter accommodation brought to you, by courtesy of New South Wales' taxpayers.

After Adam Smith had finished his line, he left the room together with Thomas Anderson and Samantha Robinson.

Chapter 83 Strategy Meeting After the Interrogation

A fter the interrogation of Michael Fuller, Samantha Robinson, Thomas Anderson, and Adam Smith went to a restaurant for lunch as well as to devise their strategy for the work to come. They still had to solve the issue with John Dean, and if Michael's accusations were correct, they had a problem with Barry Itch as well. Since they did not know the allegiances of the other members of the team, they decided it was better to keep their thoughts to themselves for the time being. Once they had finished their meals, Samantha Robinson started the talking.

- So, what are your thoughts about the case? Do you think Michael Fuller did it? There are some strange things about it, I reckon.

Adam Smith:

- Oh, I am confident the bastard did it. He seems delirious from all the drinking and loneliness. I mean look at the facts. He was at all the crime scenes at the time of the murders, and we found a lot of evidence at his place. I say he lost it and went on a killing spree. Maybe that's why he was so good in the first place because he had killers' mind?

Samantha Robinson:

- I agree, but what about his motives? He did not seem to have any?

Adam Smith:

- Well, I knew that a comprehensive murder investigation should state the killer's motives, physical evidence, and witnesses. But we don't live in a perfect world as it is in the textbooks, so I think we have more than enough to get him convicted. If not that's for the court to decide.

Thomas Anderson:

- Yeah, I agree with Adam on this one. One can never be 100 per cent in any case, and it's healthy to be sceptical before judging, but sometimes we must take a leap of faith. If it was only the evidence we found at his place, it could be a setup. But he was at all the murder scenes even though he has no reason being there.

- As for motive, I don't think most serial killers that I have read about had a reasonable, rational purpose; I think it's just an urge to kill that drives them. Often this urge is fuelled by an extreme paranoia like in Michael's case.

Samantha Robinson:

- Yeah, I know that what you are saying makes sense logically, but my gut feeling says there is something fishy in this case.

Adam Smith:

- Well if people's gut feelings were always right there would be no need for logic and reasoning, would it?

- Besides a lot of times my gut feeling tells me that a woman I am talking to wants to bang. And then again, a lot of the times when I get that feeling the only moist, I am getting is that from her drink shoved in my face!

Samantha Robinson:

- Well, thank you for sharing a compelling argument, Adam!

- Moving on, how do you think we should proceed with Barry and John?

Thomas Anderson:

- Well with Barry we are not even sure he has done anything or if Michael's story is just a product of his delusional paranoia. Nevertheless, I will make a thorough scan of his phone to see if I can find the file.

- As with John Dean, I reckon the best way would be to have my buddy Wayne Bruce talk to the Minister of the Police directly as we spoke with internal investigations yesterday, but they did not seem eager to help or do anything at all. John Dean is suspended for now, but my feeling was that the case would be cancelled in a few weeks and then we will have status quo, with the risk of having John Dean promoted to detective. But if we get one more piece of crucial evidence, I am sure we'll get this snake!

Samantha Robinson:

- I do have an idea about that. Don't banks put in marked notes in case of robberies or suspicious cash withdrawals?

- The withdrawal of $10 000 in cash that Michael did would indicate illegal business taking place So, there is a chance the bank put some marked notes among the ten grand Michael received. What if we were to ask the bank if they put in marked banknotes among Michael's $10 000? If we ask the minister directly for a search order against John's house and if we find the marked notes we have enough proof for a conviction.

Thomas Anderson:

- Great. You and I will do that, while Adam will check Michael's phone for the supposedly incriminating audio file against Barry Itch.

- Finally, Johnson, Baker, Chung, and Lee can do detailed interrogations with Michael. I don't think spending time interrogating him will give us anything of value, but we never know, and better keep those deadbeats busy as well!

Adam Smith:

- Agreed. Let's do this.
- Oh, and Thomas, save your energy for tonight.

Thomas Anderson:

- No worries, I am not as bizarrely over-sexual as you are.
- See you tomorrow!

After finishing talking, they split up to continue working on their leads.

Chapter 84 A Search Warrant

As it turned out, the bank had placed marked notes among the $10,000 that Michael Fuller withdrew from his account two weeks earlier. The marked banknotes were good news as this would make it easier to prove that John Dean indeed had betrayed the team through sabotaging the investigation and leaking information to Michael Fuller. As Thomas Anderson had predicted, it was a lot easier to get the internal investigations to work on the case after Wayne Bruce spoke to the New South Wales Minister for Police and Emergency service Michael Lawson. With the assistance of internal investigations, Thomas and Samantha received a search warrant and went to John's house. John greeted them at his door.

- What the fuck are you two doing here? You have already gotten me suspended what more do you want from me?

Thomas Anderson:

- We want you out of the team for good. You see internal investigations are highly unlikely to do anything their own. We don't want you back, so we are doing their jobs.

- But we are only one tiny bit of evidence from putting you behind bars, and then you are gone forever. And as you can see on the search warrant, we managed to persuade the minister himself to sign it.

- So, I suggest you hang out in the garden with Officer Chung while the rest of our team search your house for the evidence we need.

A couple of hours of searching began. Finally, Officer Baker managed to find a bag with money in it, in a hidden compartment in the garage. Samantha Robinson made a quick count of the cash and estimated it to be around $8000.

Samantha Robinson:

- Well John, look what we found, $8000 in cash in a hidden compartment in your garage. How do you explain this?

John Dean:

- Well, I fell behind on my mortgage payments so a friend of mine lent me the money so I could get ahead, it's all legit.

Samantha Robinson:

- A friend you say? Who just happens have $8000 lying around in cash? Because seriously if it for the mortgage it would be easier for your friend just to transfer you the money.

John Dean:

- Well, he just happened to have the money lying around. Besides, you guys are not working for the taxation office, so I have no obligation to let you know about my private finances.

Thomas Anderson:

- That is true; nevertheless, we are confiscating this money to examine whether they stem from illegal sources or not.

- But don't worry, we'll make it quick so you can come by tomorrow and pick them up if our research can't prove that any crime has occurred.

After having said the team left John's house to go back to the police station and try tracing the serial numbers of the confiscated banknotes.

Chapter 85 Adam Smith Confronts Barry Itch.

Adam Smith shone like the sun when he finally found the audio file on Michael Fuller's mobile phone which proved that the circumstances Michael had provided about his resignation were accurate. Adam was very confused that the same man that forced him into spending five unpaid Saturdays attending workplace equality seminars for using inappropriate language would cover up serious crimes conducted by Michael.

Adam was considering how he could use the audio file with the cocaine discussion between Barry and Michael, to do maximal damage to the BITCH. Adam had never been a fan of Michael whom he found arrogant and the pushy, but his real nemesis in the CSMI was without a doubt Barry Itch, its director.

This was due to a clash of personalities as Adam and Barry were each other's opposites. While Adam, was outspoken, impulsive, messy, hard to offend and ultra-macho in his approach to things Barry was careful with what he said, very controlled, extremely tidy, very easily offended and very much against the macho culture of the police.

Adam could not understand why someone who was against chauvinism would have joined the police force in the first place. The reason for Adam Smith to become a police officer was that he would get a lot of macho atmosphere at work as well as a uniform that could be used to pick up and impress a specific type of women. As long as Barry Itch was the director of CSMI, Adam realised that there would not be much of a macho attitude at his workplace and as the uniform was not as good for picking up women as he had hoped, he was quite disgruntled with his work situation.

Adam decided to make copies of the recording and use one of the copies to confront Barry directly and force him to resign his job. The standard protocol would be to go to internal investigations, which Adam found was a time-consuming and backstabbing way of dealing with things. He preferred confronting his enemies full on, and now that he finally had a weapon against the man who had refused him any pay rise and promotions in the last five years it was time to strike. He entered the office of Barry where the latter was finalising a report to his superiors.

Barry Itch:

- Hi, Adam, are you enjoying the Saturday sessions with my wife? You must excuse me, but I am quite busy, I am finishing this report for the High Commissioner.

Adam Smith:

- Well, I can see why you and Wanda are a match. If I were you, I would not worry too much about that report. I am a lot more critical to your life as it is right now.

Barry Itch:

- I highly doubt that you will ever be an important person in my life or for my career Adam. Frankly speaking, I believe there is a very slim chance that you will ever get past police assistant in your career

Adam Smith:

- Well, that may be, but I will still have a higher rank than you will tomorrow!

After saying that Adam played the audio file with the conversation between Michael and Barry the day Michael got busted with the stolen cocaine. While Barry listened to this audio file, he felt a mix of fear and anger. Concern for his career and anger towards Michael who must be the man behind the recording.

So, Michael sold him out, despite Barry's leniency towards him. To Barry, Michael was the worst kind of traitor, and he was now free of his doubts that Michael indeed was the killer. Too bad that scumbag would drag him down the abyss with him. Unless... Adam had come to his office with the evidence to confront him instead of running straight to internal investigation with the recording. Was it possible to cut a deal with him? Barry decided to give it a shot.

Barry Itch:

- Hey, Adam. I must say I am impressed. You have me in a steady grip now, and despite our past differences, you decided to come by my office which means you are looking for something.

- Can I interest you with a mutually beneficial deal?

Adam Smith:

- Hmm. Mutually beneficial deal? Are you trying to bribe me?
- I like that idea...
- Show me your offer!

Barry Itch:

- Well, there is a position as a detective available since James Locker was only appointed provisional detective and is now in the hospital, I can fast track your application.

Adam Smith:

- Hmm, Detective Smith. I like that, and I am sure the ladies will as well. But there is a problem with the scenario. Every detective must meet up with you for a daily briefing every day. I can't see how that would be endurable.

- But don't worry. I have another offer.

- The Adam Smith "charity" needs some fundraising. What would be better than if the director of CSMI sponsors this fund with $10,000 and then receives an MP3player with recordings on it? I mean for sure the price is a little steep, but the money is for a worthy cause.

Barry swallowed hard. After all, he had a well-paid job and getting rid of that recording would be a good investment. But he was worried about what Wanda would say, as she kept an eagle eye on everything and explaining a $10,000 deficit would be a difficult thing to do. Unless of course, he forged a receipt for a charity to let's say Female Rights in Uganda. If he sponsored such fund, his wife would be proud of him! Of course, there was the problem when it was time for the charity tax deduction in the yearly tax return, but the receipt might easily get lost sometime before then. Barry decided to accept Adam's proposal.

Barry Itch:

- Okay. I accept your offer; how do we do this business?

Adam Smith:

- Oh, that's quite simple. We go out and have lunch together; we worked together for five years, so it's time for us to hang out. You withdraw $10,000 and donate them to my "charity", and I will give you a complimentary MP3player.

Barry Itch:

- I see. Well let's go then

After that, they left for lunch and the monetary exchange.

Chapter 86 Adam Smith Rats Barry Itch Out

It was 5 PM on Thursday the 5th of September 2013, and Adam was happy with his day. He had managed to solicit a $10,000 bribe from his nemesis at work Barry Itch, and the best of it was that he would rat Barry out anyway! Adam had made several copies of the recording between Barry and Michael so giving one of them away was not a big deal.

Adam also learned from John Dean's mistake when it came to soliciting bribes in cash. Knowing that the banknotes he received from Barry could be traceable, he chose a straightforward course of action to remedy this issue. By going around to different bars and put a lot of notes in the poker machines, playing a few games and then asking the attendant to pay out the remainder. By doing this, he would have all the money in new notes as well as receipts on his winnings in case someone was asking him why he had thousands of dollars in cash at his place. Happy with his choice Adam walked into the internal investigations office at Redfern and filed a case against Barry Itch.

Chapter 87 Barry Itch Resigns

It was 7 PM, and Barry Itch had had a long and troublesome day at work. As If getting blackmailed for a hefty sum of money by the idiot Adam Smith was not bad enough, he was also criticised for the inadequate level on the report he handed in, to the chief of the police. This criticism was strictly speaking a direct consequence of the interruption Adam had caused on his work and Barry was determined to get his revenge on Adam as soon as possible. The chief of police also informed Barry that John was arrested for sabotaging the investigation and leaking case files to Michael which meant that the CSMI was in worse shape than ever despite all his efforts to improve the organisation. When Barry believed that the day could not get any worse, he received proof of the opposite when the New South Wales Minister for Policy and Emergency services Michael Lawson called him.

Michael Lawson:

- Hi, Barry. You have had a few terrible days down at CSMI, haven't you?

Barry Itch:

- Well, I must admit you are right, but I can assure you that I have the situation under control and that I don't expect anymore more issues.

Michael Lawson:

- No matter how much I would love to believe you, Barry, I just cannot. A couple of minutes ago internal investigations received a recording of a conversation between you and Michael.

- They found the content of this recording urgent enough to interrupt my speech in front of the New South Wales cabinet, and I understand why.

Barry Itch:

- But sir, that recording is taken out of it's context.

Michael Lawson:

- Well, Barry, I cannot see any context where it's okay that a director of a branch of the police is letting one of his detective's get away with a severe crime. Of course, the cover-up is even worse in this case as the man you covered for is now a suspect for three murders and two attempted murders.

- I am sorry Barry, but there is nothing I can do to help you, the internal investigations are not going to let this one pass, so it's probably our best interests you come to my office and sign your resignation.

Barry sighed heavily out of resignation. He should have seen Adam's deceit coming a long way, but he did not. Anyway, there was nothing to do with Adam now, because if he tried striking back telling the minister about how he bribed one of his policemen to keep his mouth shut, well it would just strike back at him. Barry knew that the recording was not enough to get him convicted in a court of law, but he also understood he would be forced to quit the job anyway. And by resigning now, he saved himself from public battering and could potentially get an excellent job for a private security company in the future.

Barry Itch:

- I accept your offer and will resign immediately.

Michael Lawson:

- Great, there will be a press conference tomorrow at 10 am at Governor Macquarie Tower. See you then

- I am sorry that thing's ended this way Barry, I know you have been working harder than any other director for the police, but sometimes hard work is just not enough.

Chapter 88 A New Leadership of Central Sydney Murder Investigations Department

I t was the week before the election and the New South Wales Minister for Police and Emergency services Michael Lawson was overlooking his strategy in cooperation with his chief strategist Melanie Stephenson. The scandal at Central Sydney Murder Investigations where the former star detective of CSMI team 1 Michael Fuller was facing charges for a series of assassinations and police inspector John Dean was facing charges for sabotaging the investigation had led to the resignation of Barry Itch, the director of CSMI. Due to these scandals, the confidence in the police was at a record low level, which was terrible news for the minister of the police one week before the election.

Michael Lawson:

- Hi, Melanie, good morning. Don't tell me how the polls are going; I don't want to know.

Melanie Stephenson:

- Well, you are becoming historic in a way, but I guess being remembered for being the elected minister who gets the least votes ever in re-election is not what you want to be.

- It's a shame because we did some significant changes to the police during your years in office, but the people will forget them due to this debacle.

Michael Lawson:

- Well, it's a shame, but who said anything about history being fair. Speaking of which, can you suggest any radical changes I can do to the police now that I am guaranteed to not win the election.

Melanie Stephenson:

- I do have some suggestions that would make you historical in a more positive way. You can be the first minister of police who appointed an aboriginal person to a director role within the police. Furthermore, you can nominate the youngest woman ever to be a police detective.

- Here are the files of Dwayne Uluru a prominent aboriginal detective whom I suggest promoting to the next director of CSMI and Samantha Robinson an up-and-coming female police assistant who I recommend will be the new detective of CSMI team 1

Michael Lawson had a quick look through the two files his chief strategist provided. From a competency point of view, he believed that there would be more suitable candidates to fill the positions but just promoting the most qualified candidates would not make him historical, so the suggestions certainly sounded like a great plan from a political point of view.

Michael Lawson:

- Well, Melanie, it's an interesting idea, but I have some questions. CSMI team five which has been led by Dwayne Uluru for the last four years has the worst statistics of all groups, why would I pick Dwayne Uluru? Furthermore, the files say that Samantha Robinson has only been with CSMI team 1 for seven months and are still ranked as a police assistant. Why would she be promoted straight up to detective?

Melanie Stephenson:

- Well, see it this way. You might get a lot of female and aboriginal voters if you support a woman and an indigenous Australian. If they do not work out in their new positions and you lose the election, then it's your successors' headache to fire them. After all, firing the first aboriginal director of a branch of the police. It would seem a bit racist and illegitimate to some groups.

Michael Lawson:

- What about James Locker, the current detective of CSMI team 1?

Melanie Stephenson:

- Well, he is only on a provisional contract for that role, and I am sure the public will understand that a person with proven mental issues is not suitable to lead a police squad.

Michael Lawson:

- You have convinced me. Let's go ahead with these suggested changes. Dwayne Uluru's first task while be to appoint his successor in team 5, as that question is not as politically relevant.

After deciding on these changes Michael Lawson and Melanie Stephenson contacted the high command of the New South Wales police to have the changes implemented. They soon found out that both Samantha Robinson and Dwayne Uluru happily accepted their promotions.

Chapter 89 Rebecca Bell seeks comfort from Samantha Robinson

It was the 10th of September 2013 and one week had passed since the arrest of Michael Fuller. During this time, his daughter Rebecca Bell had been living in denial and hoping that it all would be a mistake and that the court would release her dad from all charges, or at least all the severe ones.

Samantha Robinson's first decision as the newly appointed detective for team one of CSMI was to hand over the case to the district attorney. The finalised police report indicated that Samantha believed that they had enough evidence to get a conviction against Michael which destroyed Rebecca's hopes about everything turning out fine. Her first reaction when Samantha told her about the decision was to cry and call Samantha a traitor who had betrayed her and her dad. After the initial response she calmed down, and the following conversation took place between them.

Rebecca Bell:

- I am sorry for what I said before; this just came as such as shock for me. The idea that my dad would commit several murders is just so unreal to me, so I hoped it was just a nightmare that I could wake up from. Your decision to hand over the case to the district attorney proves that I am probably not going to wake up from it...

Samantha Robinson:

- Well, I know it's probably not any comfort for you, but it was a hard decision for me to make as well... I like your dad, and my gut feeling tells me that he is innocent.

- But I can't let my sympathies prevent me from doing my job, and my job is to present the court with the most likely suspect for a case and then it's up to them to decide whether he is guilty or not. If I was to determine who was guilty or not, I would be too biased and would not be able to my job.

Rebecca Bell:

- Yes, I know that I am soon finished with my police studies.
- But I would love to talk to him so I can understand why he did it.

Samantha Robinson:

- Well, he will have visitor restrictions until after the trial, but I know what you can do meanwhile, that he would appreciate.

Rebecca Bell:

- Oh, what is that?

Samantha Robinson:

- Well, he told me after I notified him that his case would be handed over to the DA that he hoped that you would go on the whiskey tour to Great Britain and Ireland with his tickets now that he can't go. He reckons that it would be an excellent way for you to get closer to each other although you are apart.

Rebecca Bell:

- Well, I don't know. I am not a great fan of whiskey; the taste is disgusting.

Samantha Robinson:

- Well, I don't think you need to be a fan of whiskey to enjoy this tour. You will see a lot of beautiful and exciting places accompanied by the yellow leaves of the British autumn.

- Besides, I think a holiday would do you good to get away from this sad situation. Who knows when you get back in three weeks you might have come to terms with everything?

Rebecca Bell:

- Yeah, I guess you are right.

- Um, would you like to go with me? It would be awesome to go on holiday with you since we never had a chance to do that back in the days when we were together.

Samantha Robinson:

- Well, I would love to, but I just got my promotion and can't leave now. Besides, I have a boyfriend now, so it would not be the same as if we had gone back then...

Rebecca Bell:

- I also have kind of a "partner, " but he is only making me feel worse. You see I know he's very busy for a couple of weeks, but still, he should be there for me in a situation like this!

Samantha Robinson

- Yeah, I agree with you. You should dump this bastard. Oh, this is making me so angry; I want to confront the asshole for doing this to you! What is JP short for so I can find him and yell at him?

Rebecca Bell:

- Oh, the same old Samantha, coming to my rescue. I always liked that part of you, you know.

- His preferred name is James Pierce, but his real family name is not Pierce.

- Hmm if I could only remember what his real family name is...

- Oh, now I remember it's Locker.

Samantha Robinson:

- James Locker!? That's the guy who was appointed provisional detective for my team after your father left the police force. He is in the hospital after being badly poisoned, allegedly by your dad. He is still recovering.

Rebecca Bell:

- Oh really? I didn't know what he does for work; he is quite mysterious.

Samantha Robinson:

- Okay, I see, well I have a picture of him on my phone... wait...
- Is this the guy you have been seeing?

Rebecca Bell:

- Yes, that's him!

- So, my dad poisoned him? That's terrible. We should go see him in the hospital!

Samantha Robinson:

- I don't think that's a good idea. You see the poison turned him into a mental wreck.

- Thomas and his friend Adam went to the psychiatric ward the other day, and he told them that he did not want to meet anyone until his mind was right. I think we better respect that...

Rebecca Bell:

- But what should I do then?

Samantha Robinson:

- Just go to Great Britain on the tour your dad gave you. The trip leaves on Friday morning and lasts for three weeks. By the time you'll get back, I am sure James Locker will feel better and would love to see you.

Rebecca Bell:

- Okay. I would love to be there for him, but I guess you are right. But tell him I miss him if you meet him!

Samantha Robinson:

- I sure will. Have a great trip, honey.

After Rebecca left, Samantha felt very confused. Why had James used another family name in his relationship with Rebecca? Why had he gone after a lot of women while he was in Asia if he had a potential girlfriend at home? Why hadn't he told anyone about Rebecca? Samantha realised that she did not know James well enough to answer these questions, so she called Thomas Anderson for answers.

Thomas Anderson:

- Hi, Sammy. How were things with Rebecca? She must have a hard time with her dad accused of several murders?

Samantha Robinson:

- Yeah, she was devastated at first and blamed me for betraying her father, but she came to her senses and realised I was only doing my job.

Thomas Anderson:

- Yeah and you are doing it well.

Samantha Robinson:

- I am happy you see things that way.

Thomas Anderson:

- No worries! Still up for dinner tonight?

Samantha Robinson:

- Yeah, I am. I just found out some bizarre things about James Locker, that I can't get off my mind. Maybe you can help me out and explain since you have known him for a while?!

Thomas Anderson:

- Yeah almost four years, and we have been close friends most of the time, so I am the right source for information.

Samantha Robinson:

- Well, I just found out that the guy Rebecca is dating JP, is James Locker, just that he used the name James Pierce instead. They have dated on and off for three months now. What do you know about this?

Thomas Anderson:

- I have heard James Locker use the name James Pierce sometimes when he is drunk. Apparently, it some ancestor to him. He goes crazy when he uses that name, sometimes in a positive way as in doing unexpected fun things and sometimes in a negative way as in borderline psychotic.

- I don't know why he kept it a secret. I guess he feels vulnerable and doesn't want to risk embarrassment. Or maybe Rebecca is not the one for him?

Samantha Robinson:

- But do you think he is good for Rebecca? Adam told me James fucked a lot of women in Asia?

Thomas Anderson:

- Well, that is true, but you said that the last time you had sex with Rebecca was about one month ago, and they were dating back then as well. I guess we should just let them figure out their relationship on their own.

- Chemistry wise, I think she is a good match for him, she reminds me a lot of his ex-girlfriend in looks and personality. The only difference is that they are different races, Emily was South East Asian while Rebecca is Nordic.

Samantha Robinson:

- Well, can you at least talk to him? Rebecca means the world to me, and I don't want her to be hurt.

Thomas Anderson:

- Sure. I'll tell him Rebecca is an awesome girl and he should focus on her.

- Is there anything else?

Samantha Robinson:

- No, that's all for now. See you tonight.

Thomas Anderson:

- Yeah, you too.

Chapter 90 James Locker Leaves the Mental Asylum

It was a sunny day on the 24th of September 2013 when James Locker was declared fully recovered and was able to leave the Blue Mountains mental ward where he was submitted three weeks earlier. Three weeks was an unusually long recovery time from a Xenoantipsyche overdose but considering James' history of mental illness his doctors preferred playing things safe. He was met up by Adam and Thomas.

Adam Smith:

- Look who is back from the dead! I am sure you were healthy as a horse after two days and were too busy banging crazy chicks to leave!

James Locker:

- Sorry to disappoint you Adam but if you ever get submitted here you won't get laid with any women, as the male and female wards are separated.

- Although any woman who wants to have sex with you must be crazy. So, you know more insane people than I do, even though I spent the last three weeks' in a mental hospital!

Thomas Anderson:

- Ha-ha, the old James is back. God, I have missed our chemistry.

James Locker:

- Yeah so have I, you are better than the demons from hell that
kept me company for the first week in here.

Adam Smith:

  - I am honoured to hear that.
  - Should we drive you home?

James Locker:

  - Nope, let's enjoy nature, I reckon it's time to enjoy it now that I
  am free. Besides, it's better for you if we have some wilderness fun
  here as well.

Adam Smith:

  - Sure, let's go.

For a couple of hours, they walked around in the mountainous paths of
the Blue Mountains. The smell of vaporised eucalyptus was lying thick over
the mountains this day which gave them their characteristic fragrance and
bluish fog. After a couple of hours of bushwalking, the sun was starting to set,
and they decided to drive back home. Before dropping James at his house,
Thomas remembered his promise to Samantha to talk to James about his relationship with Rebecca Bell.
Thomas Anderson:

  - Hey, James, I hope you are not blaming Rebecca for what happened to you because it's not her fault...

James Locker:

  - Rebecca?

Thomas Anderson:

- Yeah, I mean she can't help that Michael broke into your house and poisoned you, it would be mean if you held her responsible.

James Locker:

- Oh yeah, Michael's daughter. Yes, of course, I don't hold her responsible, why would she think I do?

Thomas Anderson:

- Great.

- And Rebecca wants you to know that she is sorry that she did not visit you at the hospital, as Samantha told her that you did not want visitors, and she felt obliged to respect your wishes after what happened.

James Locker:

- Oh, that's sweet of her. No, I am not angry about that, I did not want anyone to see me in that condition.

Thomas Anderson:

- And finally, Rebecca is sorry that she could not meet up with you today, but she did not know when you would leave the hospital, and she did not want to miss out on the British Isles tour. But she misses you and is longing to see you as soon as she gets back if you still want to meet her.

James Locker:

- Um okay...

- Yeah, sure I can meet her if that is important to her...

- I am getting quite tired now but thank you for today it was great hanging out with you two guys again.

After leaving the car, James went inside; made some tea and watched some television. It had been a beautiful day, and it felt great to finally be out of the mental institution so he could get on with life. But what the fuck had Thomas been talking about in the end? Why all this talk about Rebecca, Michael's daughter? Had he even met her? From the way Thomas spoke about her, it seemed like they were close, but James could not even recall ever meeting Rebecca.

After thinking about it for a while, he decided that it was a mystery that would be solved once Rebecca Bell got home. If she wanted to meet up and discuss what had happened, she would be a lot better at explaining things than Thomas Anderson just was. Feeling very tired suddenly James Locker decided to go for an early night's sleep.

Chapter 91 Darkness Unfolds

J ames Locker felt like he was falling. He hit the ground and woke up. He reflected that the concept of dying in a dream and waking up was one of the themes of the blockbuster *"Inception"* that he had watched recently. James felt more awake than he had felt for a long time. He watched his nightstand clock. With eerie red light, it showed 3.00AM. Déjà vu, he always woke up precisely at 3.00AM. It was not 3ish. It was always 3.00AM sharp. What significance did this exact time have to him? James could hear noises from the basement, but how could that be? The door to the basement had been locked all year, and he had not been down since... Yes, when was the last time he went down there?

James suddenly felt petrified. What if Michael was not the killer? He recalled someone being in the room with him the day he got poisoned. That blurry mysterious someone left only moments before a squad of police officers and paramedics entered his house and took him to the hospital.

James had a feeling that this man was the Killer, and now this mystery man was in his home, coming after him. James knew the logical choice would be to run, but he could not, he had to know who it was.

James realised that it was the same feeling that drove Michael down the abyss. Michael had no logical reason to visit all the murder victims, but his desire to never give up and keep looking for the answers was his downfall. Would James fall into the same trap or would he flee and run away? The mysterious killer had come to James' house for a reason, and James felt compelled to find out what that reason was. It was evidently not to kill him, as the Killer had several chances to do so already.

James was contemplating his options: He could either leave the building, calling the police or he could grab his gun and confront the eluding shadow of death that had haunted him for the last couple of months. If he called the police, the Killer would know, and he would escape once again. But if he confronted the man, he could finally get the answers. The answers to everything he had been asking himself throughout the years. James decided to take his gun and confront his menace once and for all.

James snuck down the staircase. For every step he took the weird noise from below grew louder and more impactful. With a few more steps to go James froze with fear. His mind wanted to go on, but his body just refused to follow. Focusing all his strength, he managed to go the last few steps and entered the basement. At first, he saw nothing strange, but then he flicked the light switch. He looked up and saw the mirror. In the reflection, he saw him.

James Locker:

  - You! I saw you when I was a poisoned a few weeks ago.

James Pierce:

  - Fool! I have always been with you. And you have seen me a lot of times although you deny it.

  - Tell me, James, how do you usually feel when you watch your reflection?

James Locker:

  - I feel very uncomfortable. I have never been able to put my finger on why.

James Pierce:

  - Well, I can tell you, James. When you see your reflection you see me, but you deny it, and your denial of your true nature is like a splinter in your mind driving you sleepless and insane!

James Locker:

  - But, but..... who are you?? And why are you doing this?!

James Pierce:

- 'Why': The question that drove you here but as you will soon be aware is the least relevant question.

James Locker:

- ...

James Pierce:

- Okay, I will make it easy for you fool; you are going to die anyway, so you might as well know the truth! I will tell you who I am, why I did all of this, and how I did it!

James Pierce:

- My name is James Pierce, and I am you. But a better you, a stronger you, a version of you that deserves to live while you deserve to die!

- I have been your guardian all your life.

- Do you remember all those episodes in your life where you remember one thing, but all your friends remembered an entirely different story?

James Locker:

- Yes! I have had a lot of those episodes in my life...
- What about them?

James Pierce:

- Well, during those episodes, I was in control. To deny my existence, your subconscious made up a lot of memories that never took place. Like in Asia, where you thought you were dating the same woman all the time, right?

James Locker:

- Yes... Was I not?

James Pierce:

- No, you were not. Your friends' description of dozens of women were more on the money. A quite impressive feat if I can say it my-self...

James Locker:

- But I don't understand... Why would I block memories of having sex with women on my holiday, I have never been against promis-cuous behaviour?

James Pierce:

- Well... because you almost killed those women and I had to in-tervene for nothing bad to happen... But, let's reverse the tape to Christmas time last year. Do you remember anything special hap-pening?

James Locker:

- Well, I proposed to Emily, and she said yes, it was the happiest time of my life.

James Pierce:

- Yes, it was a great time for me as well. You see as your protector, I finally felt relieved, and I let my guard down...

- Do you remember what happened on the 2nd of January this year?

James Locker:

- Well, that day is very blurry. But I remember having a fight with Emily, she left with my money, and I haven't seen her since.

James Pierce:

- Yes, wasn't this a highly unexpected chain of events? From happily engaged one week, to a big fight and never seeing each other one week later?

James Locker:

- Of course, it was. Why do you think I have been obsessing over it for the last nine months?

James Pierce:

- Great! Do you want to see the same reflection you saw in this mirror the 2nd of January 2013 03.00AM?

James Locker:

- Yes!

The reflection changed in front of James' eyes. His eyes were brimming with anger, and he could see the corpse of Emily Luong in the corner. After a few seconds, the reflection changed back to the present again.

James Pierce:

- Was that the truth that you hoped to find?

James Locker:

- Did I kill Emily? Why would I do that? I loved her more than anyone else in the world

James Pierce:

- Well, that was what I thought as well. I hoped that your love for Emily would finally beat your hidden dark side. I call him the beast...

James Locker:

- What? I don't follow you at all?

James Pierce:

- I don't know what happened. I let go for a week, and it was like a long dreamless sleep. But something unleashed the darkness within you and killed Emily in this basement on the 2nd of January at 3.00AM.

- But this is what I have managed to puzzle together of the event.

- Emily was working as a receptionist at Antonio DiMaestro's business. One day you found a costly necklace given to her by him.

- Suspecting infidelity from Emily, your jealousy grew uncontrollably, and you killed her in rage.

James Locker:

- But I am not a very jealous person...

James Pierce:

- That's because I am in control, pulling strings in the background.

- Anyway, that night after disposing of Emily's body I made up my mind.

- I decided that I should aim to break free. I gave you freedom, and that's how you repaid me. You were not worthy of my protection anymore.

- So I stole your money and stored them in your basement, the place I knew your subconscious would never let you visit.

James Locker:

- But this was nine months ago. This mess started recently. Why wait?

James Pierce:

- A valid question which leads us to the question of why.

- You see when I first started out my life as a "free" man I realised that I did not have any reason to live.

- I thought for all those years that I could not experience feelings. If I were unable to feel anything, it seemed reasonable to be your guardian instead of breaking free to live my own life.

- But then it happened, like an angel from above, she appeared in my life. I am talking about Rebecca. You know her vaguely as Michael Fuller's daughter. But to me, she is perfection. My one true love. She is my Emily Luong, and we are meant to be together.

James Locker:

- That explains a lot! I remember when I saw her picture at Michael's house and reflected over how beautiful and familiar, she looked. I was also confused when Thomas spoke about her yesterday!

James Pierce:

- Exactly. But you have experienced this feeling a lot of time in your life, haven't you? When someone talks about something that makes no sense to you. That's why you played along, wasn't it?

James Locker:

- Yes, that was my reason, and indeed it has happened a lot in my life, I thought it was a normal feeling.

James Pierce:

- Well, at least you know better now.

- Anyway, when I met Rebecca, I made up my mind: That I would break free. I had to do this to have a functioning relationship with her as I am the one loving her while you are living in the past.

- But I am fearful of the monster that lives within you. So, I am doing this for Rebecca as I can't let you hurt her as you did to Emily.

James Locker:

- I don't understand. How do you plan to break free? And what has the last month's event to do with this?

James Pierce:

- I was planning to break free by showing you what kind of person you are...

- A murderous psychotic son of a bitch...

- And as we have our first real conversation in your life, I must say that I have finally managed to break down your shell of denial.

- Like an epiphany, the solution came to me...

- I realised that I could reveal your true self to you, by killing the people you secretly dreamt about murdering and then have you chase me, or to be more precise, chase your own shadow.

James Locker:

- So that's why it felt like a Déjà vu every time I arrived at a crime scene?

James Pierce:

- Yes, you are catching on just fine.

- The first one to die was Antonio DiMaestro. You and Antonio have met several times throughout the years as Emily worked for him.

- I promised him safe passage to smuggle cocaine into the country, and he willingly took me out on his yacht alone.

- While on the yacht I convinced him that Mauricio Lopez was planning to kill him to take control over his business. That way I managed to get a hitman sent after Mauricio who was the second objective on my list...

- After organising the hit on Mauricio, I shot Antonio. I cut off his head, gathered some of his blood in a blood bag, and took his keys, mobile phone, and the money he had brought for the drugs. I sent an encrypted message to the cartel he was supposed to do business stating that he was followed, and the deal was off.

- Then I sank the yacht and left on the ships motorised emergency vessel.

James Locker:

- But this is so strange? So, no-one filed a report about Antonio being missing or started looking for him?

James Pierce:

- Well, I did send out encrypted messages from Antonio's E-mail account. I don't think everyone bought it, but what would they do? Go to the police and file a missing person report about their boss, husband or sugar daddy who disappeared on his yacht while doing drug deals?

James Locker:

- Yeah, I guess that would not make any sense to anyone. But they could still have come after you?

James Pierce:

- Well, the mob is not an open organisation like the police. Most people only know a few individuals in the group and the rest is shrouded in obscurity. Secrecy is necessary for their line of business.

- The only one who knew about me except for Antonio was Mauricio Lopez, and he was about to get killed by Angelo Ramirez.

- I witnessed the murder over the CCTV, and then I sent the instructions on how Angelo Ramirez would receive his money. We never met, and he thought he was working for Antonio DiMaestro all the time.

- My next step was to hack the security system and steal the drugs. Knowing about Michael's obsession with work I knew that he sooner or later would know about Antonio DiMaestro and chase his shadow.

James Locker:

- But how did you know that our team would get this assignment?

James Pierce:

- I know how CSMI works, and I know how they distribute the cases.

- But I never planned for Angelo Ramirez to get killed, my plan was for him to get back safely to Colombia and then Michael would be obsessed with the case and Antonio.

- Unfortunately, I was interrupted when you decided to join our friends for a month in Asia.

- It was a very draining period, because I missed Rebecca a lot, and also because I had to remain vigilant and ready to react on your madness when you brought all those women back to your place.

- Anyway, I came back to Sydney, and I wasted no time in my next objective. To get rid of Michael.

James Locker:

- Why did you want to get rid of Michael?

James Pierce:

- Well, for two reasons. First, I respected him, and I feared him. If there is anyone in this city that would be able to uncover my plot it was Michael.

- Secondly, I wanted you to be more active in the search for me. With Michael out of the picture, you would be expected to take more responsibility for the case.

- So, I sprayed in some sleep-inducing gas into the house of Michael to ensure he would not wake up. Then I walked in carrying a gas mask and planted the cocaine with his fingerprints on it. I also planted a program that made it look like the hacking of the security cameras at Antonio's warehouse was Michael's doing.

I also took some fragments of his skin and some hairs to plant the evidence we already had in the case file.

James Locker:

- But, Michael Fuller was never arrested for stealing cocaine from a crime scene; he resigned due to health issues.

James Pierce:

- Yes. Who could see that one coming?

- It was a fascinating turn of events which only served to make things a lot more interesting.

- You see my original plan was to frame Antonio DiMaestro for the murders while you subconsciously understood that something was not right.

- But with Michael still in the picture, I changed my plan to frame Michael who in this scenario made a failed attempt at framing Antonio.

- It was easy framing Michael; his obsession was his downfall.

- I reckon most people would just let things go if they got away with having a lot of cocaine at home. But not Michael, he got obsessed, and he hunted the man who was behind the Lopez murder, Antonio DiMaestro.

- And without his job, which was what had held him together, he fell into the abyss which in Michael's case was his alcoholism.

- Fuelled by alcohol-driven paranoia, he was an easy target to frame.

James Locker:

- But how did you frame him, were you following him around everywhere?

James Pierce:

- No to be fair, it was a lot easier than that. You see we have his number on your phone right.

James Locker:

- Yes of course. I have been working under the man for ages.

James Pierce:

- Indeed, you have...

- So, I sent him a text message with a tracking virus from MY phone.

- I am sure you can imagine getting one of those texts when you are drunk. Takes ages to load and then there is no message. You would get frustrated, but most likely you would forget about it quickly.

James Locker:

- Yes...

James Pierce:

- Anyway, I now had a trace on his phone, I knew that he would go to the DiMaestro mansion to confront Miranda DiMaestro about Antonio sooner or later.

James Locker:

- Yes, so far, I am with you, and I would also anticipate such irrational behaviour from Michael. But that does not answer the question: why on earth did you/I want Miranda DiMaestro dead?

James Pierce:

- Why?!

- Am I supposed to tell you why?

- You were in love; I left you unaccompanied for one week. It ended with you killing Emily, the supposed love of your life.

- When looking for an answer, I found a notebook with some insane jealousy-driven delusional notes about Emily, Antonio, Miranda, and Jessica plotting against you. I assumed this was a list of people you wanted dead as you murdered Emily.

- I reckoned that killing the others while having you chase yourself would make you realise what a monster you were.

- As it turned out, my plan failed miserably.

- Despite killing every target on your list and leaving a blood-stained message on your bathroom mirror, you still refused to see the truth.

- So, I went to plan B, where I gradually got you addicted to the drug Xenoantipsyche by replacing your medicine with it...

- Then I planted the drug along with all the other evidence at Michael's place the same night I shot the other Emily Luong.

James Locker:

- But why did you do that?

James Pierce:

- Please, James, you must ask more specific questions.

- I planted the evidence at Michael's place to frame him and make you/me seem like an innocent victim.

- I shot the other Emily Luong to induce psychosis in you. Deep down, you knew that the Emily you loved could not be the victim, but you could not understand why you knew that and that knowledge drove you crazy.

- I knew that this experience would either make you realise what you did or make you take large quantities of "medication." You choose the latter, and that choice almost killed us, but at least it made you realise the truth

James Locker:

- But why didn't you murder the other Emily? Was that a message as well?

James Pierce:

- I am sure people will speculate about it, but to be honest, it was just a coincidence. My gun jammed after the first shot, and I could hear the police coming. Killing Emily wasn't important; I knew you would get the message anyway.

- So, James any final questions before we proceed?

James Locker:

- I don't know; I am so overwhelmed by all of this, I need time to think and reflect on what you just told me

James Pierce:

- Enough of that bullshit, I am sick of waiting for you to figure things out. I have been waiting for 32 years.

James Locker:

- Okay then... What do you want from me? Just tell me, and we'll take it from there.

James Pierce:

- I want you to acknowledge my existence! I want you to step back and be my guardian while I enjoy life with Rebecca. I have everything to live for while you have nothing!

James Locker:

- But you are a cold-blooded monster. There is no way I am letting you get away with everything you have done. I will stop you!

Suddenly, James felt an uncontrollable rage taking over his body. His pulse rose, and his vision became bloodstained. He raised his gun and aimed it at his reflection.

James Locker:

- I am going to kill you here and now. Any last words, you piece of shit!?

James Pierce:

- How do you think shooting a mirror with a gun would kill someone that is a manifestation of your subconscious?

Hearing these words of reason and logic James fell into tears. He would never be able to kill that monster that would take over his life until nothing good remained. James was crying and felt completely left out to the powers of the world. He could feel the hand of James Pierce on his shoulder. James Pierce spoke to him with a gentle voice to comfort him.

James Pierce:

- Don't worry James; everything will be fine, I will look after us both.

James made his decision. He looked deeply into his reflection and stared intensely into his enemy's eyes. He turned the gun towards his head and spoke:

James Locker:

   - I will end this right now! If the only way to kill you is to kill me, so be it!

James Pierce:

   - So, you are choosing to kill us both? But why? We make such a good team you and me.

James Locker:

   - I won't discuss this with you, the time for thinking has passed, it's time to act.

James pulled the trigger and fell dead to the ground...

James Pierce woke up from the shock a few minutes later. He was looking at the corpse of James Locker. The corpse had a bullet wound to the head and although James Pierce knew that the body of James Locker was only a manifestation of his subconscious it was still satisfying to see him lying there on the basement floor. James Pierce reflected that it was a satisfying feeling to die or in this case "die" Logically he was unhurt; an unloaded pistol was not doing any damage.

But due to the significant connection between the soul and the body James Pierce had felt dying for a couple of minutes because James Locker whom he shared the body with indeed died. Feeling relieved that things were finally over, James Pierce felt a tsunami of tiredness drenching his body. He went back to his bed where he had the best sleep he ever had. A great night's sleep.

The end

| Page

Don't miss out!

Visit the website below and you can sign up to receive emails whenever Martin Lundqvist publishes a new book. There's no charge and no obligation.

https://books2read.com/r/B-A-QIOG-YWYT

BOOKS 2 READ

Connecting independent readers to independent writers.

Also by Martin Lundqvist

Divine Space Gods
Divine Space Gods: Abraham's Follies
Divine Space Gods II: Revolution for Dummies

Sabina Saves the Future
Sabina's Quest to Open the Portal in the Sun Pyramid
Sabina's Expedition to Stop the Apocalypse
Sabina Saves the Future: Full Trilogy

The Divine Zetan Trilogy
The Divine Dissimulation
The Divine Dissimulation (Shortened Edition)
The Divine Sedition
The Divine Finalisation

Standalone
Matt's Amazing Week
James Locker The Duality of Fate
The Portal in the Pyramid
Money Laundering in the Laundromat
James Locker: The Duality of Fate (Second Edition)

About the Author

Martin's background

Martin is a Swedish male born in 1985

He has lived in Australia since 2012, and has been with his partner Elaine Hidayat since 2013.

Martin's writing history

Martin wrote wrote his first book, the psychological crime thriller James Locker: The Duality of Fate back in 2013.

After that Martin had a break from book writing for a couple of years.

In late 2016, Martin decided to take up book writing again and he finished his Science Fiction novel The Divine Dissimulation a year later.

In July 2018 Martin finished his third book, The Divine Sedition. which constitutes the second book in The Divine Zetan trilogy.

In 2018 Martin also wrote a short-story for children Matt's Amazing Week and a parody novella called Divine Space Gods: Abraham's Follies

In January 2019 Martin finished writing Divine Space Gods II: Revolution for Dummies

Martin's style

Martin is a multi-genre writer who likes to mix up his works. So far he has released works in the crime, science fiction, humor and children genre, and he intend to write more genres in the future to mix up his repertoire and improve his writing.

Read more at martinlundqvist.com.

www.ingramcontent.com/pod-product-compliance
Lightning Source LLC
Chambersburg PA
CBHW070056120726
47909CB00002B/403